PENGUIN CANADA

THE PUREST OF HUMAN PLEASURES

KENNETH RADU is the author of eleven books, including three story collections, four novels, three volumes of poetry, and one memoir. Of his prose works, *The Cost of Living* (1987) was shortlisted for the Governor General's Award. He has twice won the QSPELL Prize for Fiction, for *A Private Performance* (1990) and *Distant Relations* (1989), which was also shortlisted for the *Books in Canada* First Novel Award. He lives with his wife near Montreal.

ALSO BY KENNETH RADU

The Devil Is Clever: A Memoir of My Romanian Mother

Flesh and Blood

Letter to a Distant Father

A Private Performance

Home Fires

Romanian Suite

Strange and Familiar Places

Snow over Judaea

Cost of Living

Distant Relations

Treading Water

THE PUREST OF HUMAN PLEASURES

KENNETH RADU

PENGUIN
CANADA

PENGUIN CANADA

Published by the Penguin Group

Penguin Group (Canada), 10 Alcorn Avenue, Toronto, Ontario, Canada M4V 3B2
(a division of Pearson Penguin Canada Inc.)

Penguin Group (USA) Inc., 375 Hudson Street, New York, New York 10014, U.S.A.
Penguin Books Ltd, 80 Strand, London WC2R 0RL, England
Penguin Ireland, 25 St Stephen's Green, Dublin 2, Ireland (a division of Penguin Books Ltd)
Penguin Group (Australia), 250 Camberwell Road, Camberwell, Victoria 3124, Australia
(a division of Pearson Australia Group Pty Ltd)
Penguin Books India Pvt Ltd, 11 Community Centre, Panchsheel Park,
New Delhi – 110 017, India
Penguin Group (NZ), Cnr Airborne and Rosedale Roads, Albany, Auckland, New Zealand
(a division of Pearson New Zealand Ltd)
Penguin Books (South Africa) (Pty) Ltd, 24 Sturdee Avenue, Rosebank, Johannesburg 2196,
South Africa

Penguin Books Ltd, Registered Offices: 80 Strand, London WC2R 0RL, England

First published 2005

(WEB) 10 9 8 7 6 5 4 3 2 1

Copyright © Kenneth Radu, 2005

*Publisher's note: This book is a work of fiction. Names, characters, places and incidents
either are the product of the author's imagination or are used fictitiously, and any
resemblance to actual persons living or dead, events, or locales is entirely coincidental.*

Manufactured in Canada.

LIBRARY AND ARCHIVES CANADA CATALOGUING IN PUBLICATION

Radu, Kenneth
 The purest of human pleasures / Kenneth Radu.

ISBN 0-14-301629-6

I. Title.

PS8585.A29P87 2005   C813'.54   C2004-904934-8

Visit the Penguin Group (Canada) website at **www.penguin.ca**

PROLOGUE

. . .

Fie on't, ah fie! 'tis an unweeded garden
That grows to seed, things rank and gross in nature
Possess it merely.

—SHAKESPEARE, HAMLET

A FULL OCTOBER MOON is a poet's dream, a murderer's nightmare. The grounds bright, a man's shadow visible in the garden, his moving form apparent in the distance, how difficult to secure oneself from detection and apprehension. Difficult, not impossible. Police cars patrolling the winding road, sleek in blue and white, silent as sailboats streaming through a ribbon of moonlight on the lake. Up and down the road, pulling into driveways now and then, officers with holsters and clubs and flashlights get out of the cars to survey all they cannot see. Gardens are dead under the autumn moon, and what's still alive is dying back. The night is chilly, laden with hints of winter to come. Exposure in the light of the moon is not a problem if a man knows how to hide, but alarm systems give pause. So many sirens and sensors on the properties; a bat diving off a larch and dipping above the grounds for mosquitoes could set the bells ringing, the horns bellowing, the digitally created blasts screeching over the lawns. In this day and age, it's also wise to consider the possibility of invisible laser rays crisscrossing the grass. A step in the wrong direction and one is zapped and trapped by ruby rays. A garter snake slithering over the dewy grass can escape detection, perhaps. You'd have to crawl very low indeed. Has the world become a movie set after all? Do we have to be Arnold Schwarzenegger or Harrison Ford to survive? Where are the stand-ins and stuntmen to see us through the danger?

Time, time to move on, no more time available here. Lie low for a while, disappear, find a new town, slip into the crowd and get a job somewhere they won't ask too many questions, like the town before this one and the one before that, become one of the folks. Like, who really knows shit? And when the itch comes on again, scratch and scratch and scratch right through the fucking skin till I see blood. So bright it could be day. Harder to move, but what I did before I can do again. Cops on the road. Yesterday that gardener set off an alarm. Good thing, too. Able to rush right out of there, no one noticing. But the place is armed for war now. Opportunities scarce. No woman's gonna be caught dead picking her stupid roses these days. The thing is, gotta give over when the times get tough and do something else for a while. Goddamned moon, like I could use a cloudy night, see my shadow every time I move. Helicopters now and then and a police yacht with a searchlight like some humongous star, but still the lake's the best way out. Surprised they haven't mined it or lowered subs.

Knowledge is power. Knowing the lay of the land as well as your enemy provides advantages. Patience, too, waiting for the right time, the right moment, never acting in heat, always in the cold, cold moment. Success lies in suppression, not in passion. All this vigilance, this fortifying and relying on gadgetry, even armed private guards on some estates: and still, one passes through, one knows how to avoid and evade. The trees, the woods, the undergrowth, the lake and the waterfront, inlets and coves, dales and dells, gullies and ditches, pumphouses and sugar shacks, garages and woodsheds, guest houses and stables. Knowing what the people plan, vociferous in their anxiety, revealing their decisions and methods. Panic and secrecy are not companionable. Knowledge: knowing how one unguarded path can lead to another; even the dogs can't sniff you out in time.

Some people always assume immunity, always scoff over public concern, even quote parallels and history, saying it has ever been thus, righteously reminding us to consider a crisis on the other side of the world, nothing new, we're not exempt; confusing their pedantry with knowledge, their ignorance with courage. Their houses are not so well protected, their sense of safety deep as the iron in their souls. Some people are indifferent to history and terror, pushing their minor desires and piddling activities up to the level of cosmic significance. What they do negates whatever happens elsewhere. The limitless delusions of ego. Such houses are not impenetrable. Ingoldsby's house stands dark and squat like some giant brick box strapped with intertwining vines. The moonlight brushes them with a pearly sheen, and they're alive and breathing, ready to curl at the slightest touch and slither away in elegant shapes of S, the curved line the most beautiful line of all. The sweet seductions of the curve. My feet are covered with felt boot liners, which I shall burn tomorrow with the leaves. If discovered, the footprints will not identify me.

Even the back of Ingoldsby's house is layered with curved and twisted tangles leeching the lifeblood out of the stone. If stone can be said to possess life or blood. Not a light in a single window, only the reflected light of the moon casting a glow over the glass. A still-life painting, *nature morte*. The man must be sleeping. What's that noise? Stand still in the shadow of the tree, imperturbable as the trunk, hearing unfallen leaves rustled in the moonlight by the whispering wind. Wait for the noise to pass, the hum of the well-tuned police car engine and soft rumble of slow-moving tires on the paved road, headlights slipping through the branches. A copse of trees behind his house, and behind that a low-rising escarpment covered with wild strawberries and crown vetch, at the base the stony beach, dead fish rotting, their many fine bones exposed to the night air. The skeletal head of a rock gull, its eye sockets ground smooth by the tides.

Lying low, crawling, shirt damp to the skin, sliding down the embankment to the private beaches, finding the skiff moored in the reeds. Flat on the skiff, sculling with the hands close to shore. Take my time, take my time, take my time. Always possible to get away. Done it before, doing it now, will do it again. Last night set some fucking dogs howling. Lights flashed on like a bloody prison yard. Got away, though, didn't I? What a fellow does once, he can do again.

A dead woman's house next door. The new owners have yet to move in. No one has thought to install alarm systems there. Beyond harm, the dead have no fears, do not waken to terror. Presumably. Two houses side by side in the same condition of vulnerability: one evacuated by death, the other soon to be. How easy to pass from one property to the other without fear of exposure, without fear of unmuzzled dogs snarling for the throat, without fear of laser rays or sensor lights or banshee bells arousing the dead. The dead do not waken. The dead do not instill fear. The living terrify. Unarmed, I search for means. Like the Lord, the land will provide. Look in the right places and discover the means to obliterate.

Is he sleeping? Does he sleep alone or with a nubile girl? Does he dream of painting, his genius refreshed by wellsprings from the deep, deep unconscious? Does he awake with an erection throbbing to express itself? A eunuch, he called me. Words are indelible. All these killings—how can one sleep soundly anymore? A part of the brain remains awake, alert, willing the body to spring up at the slightest sound, ever vigilant. How can the compassionate and the innocent truly rest? My nights have been turned upside down and there is no rest, no rest at all.

His garden shed unlocked, and inside a rusty lawn mower, hardly convenient for the purpose. A newer power mower. Pruning shears large enough to trim hedges; one of the rusty blades, if adroitly handled, could cut through the protective layers of flesh and fat and sink into the heart. A trowel, a watering can, bungee cords, terra-cotta pots—gardening bric-a-brac all—and, my eyes do not deceive, a red plastic gasoline container with a yellow spout. The moonlight so clear that colours are distinguishable. Well now, we all possess the means of our own destruction. This is not a remarkable observation, a simple reiteration of banal fact. The container is almost full.

The cracked cement steps lead to the back door, itself half hidden with snaky vines one would like a machete to hack through. No machete, sad to say, in the garden shed. Ingoldsby has neglected his family home. The frame around the door is rotten. How easy to screw off the hinges. Break the glass. The unlocked door, now ajar, does not surprise me. He has no fear of a murderer in our midst, no desire to guard the castle from terror. Indifferent to the fate of furnishings and plate, Ingoldsby leaves the door unlocked from habit. He enters, closes the door, or not. He retires for the night, unconcerned about security and intruders. Ingoldsby has not followed the direction of his neighbours, who have installed the most sophisticated coded locks opened by numbers and cards. No alarm system sticker pasted on the window. As old as the house itself, the original lock has probably given way under years of the jiggling of a key. Not even a deadbolt inside.

Despite a rash of burglaries before the murders, Ingoldsby has not modernized the security of his house. Does he truly believe himself exempt from theft, not to mention other, worse, malefactions? Perhaps he's not afraid of life and its unpleasant surprises. So many of the houses have bars on the windows. Here, just leaded panes. Such is the nature of monumental ego, blinded by its own perceptions. I hesitate. The fact that the door is open suggests expectation, that someone is waiting inside. No, that is the fancy of the moment. Ingoldsby has no suspicions.

The water is fucking cold on my hands and arms. One good reason not to scratch in the winter. Bitches don't putter about their gardens so much in the winter anyway. Try paddling on ice. Least I'm wearing extra socks. So damned cold the water, freeze my fingers off. Not far. Know a cove, slip into it like a water moccasin. From there I can reach the highway. Not so sure about the dogs, but I can make it. Anyone sees me now, look like a log floating in the moonlight. Just a dead log floating away. Who sees shit anyway?

Patience the handmaiden of great enterprise, I cross the threshold slowly, making as little noise as possible, no more than the sound of a mouse skittering along a baseboard at night, and I hear a click and a snap, not loud enough to alert the conscious, never mind wake the sleeping. Step inside the back hall. How many years has it been since I've been inside? If memory serves, the kitchen is to the left, a pantry and laundry room to the right. The hall leads to the front entrance and a spacious parlour occupying the front half of the house with its high windows and wooden shutters inside, and a formal dining room off which there's a sitting room with fireplace. Bookshelves from floor to ceiling on two walls. His parents, I know, used it as their library.

Am I wrong? The question is luxurious in its irrelevance. Morality lies in good actions in the name of a higher ideal, not in prescripts or conventions or rhetoric. Unlike Hamlet, I have long ago given up pondering the ineffable. I do what must be done. Something must be done. I have defined the action and now proceed to do it. This lies within my power. What lies outside my power I do not attempt. Act locally. The moon streaks in narrow diagonals through the back windows and I see patterns on the floor. Good, solid oak floors. A painting of the night. In the parlour, I remember an Aubusson carpet, no doubt stained and threadbare now.

PART ONE

...

God Almighty first planted a Garden. And indeed it is the purest of human pleasures. It is the greatest refreshment to the spirits of man, without which buildings and palaces are but gross handiworks, and a man shall ever come to see that when ages grow to civility and elegancy, men come to build stately sooner than to garden finely, as if gardening were the greater perfection.

—FRANCIS BACON, *OF GARDENS*

1

· · ·

LORETTA FERROUX CONGRATULATED HERSELF on doing a good job of digging the compost and sheep manure into the new garden bed. The east side of her property received a few hours of sun very early in the morning and remained in dappled shade for the rest of the day, an ideal place for a shade garden. The roots of the new astilbe, hosta, the arching fronds and delicate white flowers of Solomon's seal, Jacob's ladders, ferns, lungworts, and bleeding hearts (the white, not the maroon or red, for she agreed with Morris Bunter, her gardener, that *Dicentra spectabilis alba* would provide a lovely contrast in the shadows) had all arrived by post from her favourite nursery. Although Morris offered his and his daughter's assistance, she was looking forward to spending the weekend arranging and planting them according to her design. Well, more or less her design, although she did admit, only to herself, that Morris possessed a brilliant eye for that sort of thing, and she was following his advice. But, and the but was big, she had significantly improved on it.

About Kate Bunter, Loretta wasn't so sure—not quite the steady, dedicated worker among the lilies of the field she would have wished. What nineteen-year-old was? And she had heard about that nasty business at the university involving her neighbour Donald Ingoldsby. How on earth could her daughter, Annick, be attracted to such a loathsome creature? Love was blind, they often said. Loretta believed that love deflated intelligence more than it impaired vision. Kate was not the sort of person to accuse without cause and substantial evidence. Loretta believed Professor Ingoldsby more than capable of such disreputable behaviour. Kate must surely have more on her mind than planting cultivars in groups of three, five, or seven.

At various times during the growing season, the sunnier, hotter parts of the grounds displayed lilies, coneflowers, campanulas, sedums, poppies, daisies, beebalm, and irises in their new bed. Kate had at least managed to transplant them efficiently. Morris, somewhat too insistent on his own view of things, was quite wrong, as far as she could tell. He had advised that July or August was preferable to early May for transplanting irises, after flowering, not before, but she disagreed. Nothing like a garden to arouse the tyranny in a wealthy woman's soul, she had overheard Morris remark to his daughter, as if he shared the same forgivable tendency. The May transplanting would do no harm. After ten years of consistent and concentrated study of gardening books, manuals and magazines, membership in a local gardening club, and exhilarating, often muscle-straining work, Loretta liked to think she knew as much about gardening as the next man. Morris Bunter's chatter about touch, instinct, patience, and, in his more dreamy moods over the rhododendron bushes, the paradox of poisonous plants, was more than she could tolerate.

It would take a mighty dose of their poison to kill a person, he had said last week, talking about poisonous plants, dismissing her reluctance to grow datura or aconite because of their noxious qualities.

"Sure, if you took the trouble to swallow a cupful of datura seeds or rubbed aconite all over your arms."

In his many years as a gardener, Morris had never experienced so much as a rash or eruption on his own skin, except once when his fingers inadvertently grasped a stinging nettle and swelled into fat, throbbing tubes. For decades, he had been planting datura or aconite, angel trumpets or monkshood, as they were more commonly known, without incident. Never mind a client sprawled dead among juniper bushes after ingesting, say, digitalis or artemisia. She herself preferred the more poetic names of foxglove and wormwood, and she had sloughed off Morris's unwelcome suggestions. Relying on sense rather than instinct, she had banned aconite and belladonna. Her gardens had reached, if not their final state, for gardens grew and changed from one year to the next, a presentable vision of beauty. She need not be embarrassed to host a garden party among her phlox and soap-wort, or worry about guests breaking out in a rash.

Although still distressed by yesterday's phone call from her former husband, Sylvain, who wanted to renegotiate the divorce settlement on terms more financially beneficial for his business purposes, Loretta didn't let his abuse distract her from the plea-sures of digging and delving. When they had first bought the property, he liked the size and style of the Cape Cod residence and its situation on the lakeshore. The neighbourhood boasted equally impressive homes, some almost a hundred years old, a few older, but most renovated and well maintained, Ingoldsby's house being a notable exception. Some people who called themselves artists, she gathered, were more concerned with the nether sphere than with gutters. At first she had resisted the charms of the house because the neighbourhood was high risk. Despite security systems, guard dogs, and iron bars on windows, burglaries were more common. The ingenuity of malefactors knew no bounds. A middle-aged woman had been taken to hospital two months ago, she read in the newspaper, after being hit over the head with a brass table lamp by an intruder whom she had surprised rifling through the silver drawer of the dining room hutch.

Loretta fell in love, though, her eyes wide open and her intelligence intact, with the gardening potential of the grounds, just under an acre of excellent loam. The high thick rows of cedar bushes created both a screen between their properties and the road and an effective windbreak. Here, it was possible to raise delphiniums and foxtail lilies, filipendula and lupins without exposing them to strong, damaging winds. The kitchen boasted an Aga range and the master bedroom a bay window seat where she read in the afternoon. With a large portion of the down payment provided by her own money, she and her husband had acquired the property. At the time they did not know their neighbours, Ingoldsby on one side in his dilapidated mock Tudor home, and much farther away on the other side, given the acreage surrounding the home, an elderly couple in a grey stone Georgian residence to whom Loretta had never spoken, although she had seen them drive by a few times in their black Lincoln. Across the road stood a charming home with a mansard roof, renovated and occupied by an architect of Japanese descent who once crossed over to congratulate her in perfect French on saving her house from dereliction. Since then, she had seen but not spoken to him. What was his first name?

After moving from their flat overshadowed by Montreal's mountain, where she had loved to stroll in the fall, she had given dinners and cocktail parties for many years in the new house for her husband's business clients and friends, having resigned from her position as a high school French teacher. His prosperity was such that, Sylvain had said, she didn't need to work. She'd have more time for her gardens, her charities, business trips with him to New York, San Francisco, Vancouver, and elsewhere, and reading, which, next to gardening, was her greatest passion. She read Proust faithfully once a year over a period of several days. And she often sat in the window seat of her air-conditioned bedroom, with its peach walls overlooking a prospect of garden and lawn extending down to the shoreline, drinking limeade and enjoying novels by Patricia Highsmith, whose portrait of Ripley, the brilliant sociopath, she found both repellent and fascinating. Perhaps that was the source of Annick's ardour for Professor Ingoldsby: the mouse entranced and paralyzed by the cobra; Loretta didn't know, but she preferred her culprits and villains in print.

As for the promised trips to wonderful cities, Loretta went twice with Sylvain to Toronto. She passed most of the time in the Royal Ontario Museum, the Art Gallery of Ontario, and the library on Yonge Street above Bloor while he attended to business. He had also taken her to New York, which she had visited several times previously and found exciting but lacking the European charm and heart of Montreal. She attended one concert and two musicals on Broadway alone. Several years ago, during her only trip to Edmonton, she had returned early to their hotel suite from what was supposed to have been a full-day visit with two university friends who now resided in that city. She discovered Sylvain in bed with his executive assistant, a slender, quiet-voiced, and competent woman who wore Donna Karan suits as if she could really afford them. Loretta still remembered the angularity of Gloria's anorexic body. A skeleton stretching a sheath of skin, her hands on her pelvis, arms and bony knees jutted outward, elbows pointed, she balanced precariously on Sylvain's hairy, beach-ball stomach.

Her Edmonton friends, Loretta also realized, had lost interest in her as much as she in them. With a master's degree in anthropology and three summers of archaeological digging in the badlands of Montana, Elisabeth found a job as an assistant curator in the Royal Tyrell Museum, and bored Loretta senseless with her detailed description of dinosaur teeth. Once vivacious and flippant, she had grown methodical and humourless. Louise, once married to an Edmonton businessman temporarily located in

Montreal who had moved her out west with him, was now divorced, had become an interior decorator, and blathered religiously about the principles of Feng Shui. Barely fifty, she was also loudly singing the praises of cosmetic surgery, her shiny, wrinkle-free face as devoid of character as a death mask. Loretta could see that their polite interest in her own life barely concealed their indifference. If only they could have relaxed and talked "girl talk" the way they used to in their university dormitory. After a formal and stilted lunch in a Thai restaurant, Loretta backed out of their proposed afternoon jaunt, much to the relief she could see in Elisabeth's baggy eyes. She took a taxi to the hotel, hoping to shower and enjoy a quiet evening with her husband. Gloria, who accompanied Sylvain everywhere, was dining in a French restaurant she had discovered, which served a marvellous *coquille St-Jacques,* here, of all places, in Edmonton. And the waiters actually spoke French. *Étonnant!*

Flying back to Montreal earlier than scheduled on a separate plane, Loretta had filed for divorce the day after landing. Sylvain's protests had been muted and perfunctory, except over matters of money and property, which caused much unpleasantness. Money always did come between family members. Look at Annick. Demanding access to money over which she had no legal right at the moment, all in the name of love. Loretta looked over at Professor Ingoldsby's house and wondered why a man like that—he must be twice Annick's age—would be interested in her daughter. But then Sylvain lusted after Gloria—there it was. The "best before" date having expired on her youth and desirability, Loretta, too, had been replaced by younger flesh. She had sacrificed years of professional work and income to serve as his hostess and to some degree business partner. In fact, she had contributed a substantial sum of her own money in the early days to Sylvain's entrepreneurial ventures. In addition to half the house, to which she had a legitimate claim under the law, she received a sizeable portion of his capital and stock portfolio, more than he thought she deserved. Even after she'd bought his share of the house, he had not signed the papers with good grace. Pretending to more means than he enjoyed, Sylvain now resided in a renovated loft in Old Montreal, overlooking the port and within walking distance of the historic sailors' church.

Annick had not lived at home since she entered a private residential school at eight years of age. Although Sylvain had adored his daughter when she was very young, ultimately he didn't much care for parenting and sent Annick cheques and expensive gifts. Loretta, who tried to talk intelligently to her daughter on Christmas and other holidays, thought Annick irritatingly fey, when not sullen, and too preoccupied with one trend or another. Three Christmases ago, Annick of the spiked hair had given her mother the complete works of Deepak Chopra. Annick's hair, reddish bronze and green-tinged like oxidized copper, greased upright into wedges and spikes, cones and quills, reminded her mother of a stegosaurus spine. Thus far Loretta had not found a free hour to dedicate to Chopra's wisdom.

"It seems to me, Annick," Loretta had said during their last conversation, "that you make a virtue of idiocy, attributing cosmic significance to minor experiences of intuition and coincidence." She had been listening to her daughter effuse about the ineffable spiritual realities of pre-technological societies to which, with Donald Ingoldsby's guidance and encouragement, she had become attuned. The painter, it would appear, was also a holy man. If Loretta scowled, she hoped it looked like a suppressed sneeze.

"And where did this tuning occur?"

"Really, Mother, for an educated woman, you understand very little. There are many ways of perceiving the universe. You should try to keep an open mind. If you don't agree, at least spare me your mockery."

"Of course there are many ways of perceiving the universe, Annick. But there's a difference between an open mind and mindlessness, my dear."

Nor had Loretta released money from the trust fund established by her own parents, now dead, for their one and only grandchild. When Annick reached thirty or at her mother's death, should it take place after her twenty-fifth birthday, the initial capital investment of a million dollars with interest accrued over the years would be at her disposal. Her grandparents wanted Annick to establish herself without undue dependency on great expectations. For the time being, Loretta had the legal right as executor to dole out money from the accumulated interest as need and/or her sense of discretion determined. Now twenty-four, Annick wanted to help Ingoldsby purchase a house in Vermont, ideal for a proposed retreat, to be remodelled and redecorated at some considerable expense. If they didn't have the funds immediately to support a bid on the property, they risked losing it. Annick resented her mother's control over her future and told her so in no uncertain and obscene terms. When asked why Professor Ingoldsby, as a full-time teacher and artist of some renown, had neither capital nor, it would seem, credit at the banks, Annick sucked in her breath at the other end of the phone line, Loretta could hear, then exploded with nonsense about Loretta damaging her daughter's independence with her materialist obstructiveness. Loretta held the phone away from her ear.

Perhaps she had been a failure as a mother. Some women, she knew, mulled over maternal responsibilities as if they mattered in the end. Annick had always sulked or screamed as a child when she didn't get her way. Loretta remembered taking her daughter to La Ronde, the amusement park, and remaining on the ground holding Annick's candy floss or hot dog while the child was whirled up and down and around on one ridiculous ride or another. These days parents and counsellors attributed such fits of temper to food allergies or to attention deficit syndrome. Busy with her studies at university, helping her husband establish himself with money inherited from her parents, teaching recalcitrant, hormonally besotted teenagers, and not entirely delighted to have borne a child at thirty-one, Loretta now recognized that she had neglected Annick. Too late. *Tant pis!* Remorse served no purpose. Thank God for summer camps, private schools, and travel.

The beauty of astilbe, Loretta thought as she plunged into the earth with her trowel, aside from its feathery elegance, was the plant's resistance to insects and disease. An infestation of grasshoppers and leaf miners had damaged many of her flowers this year, gobbling up the columbine before her eyes. Neither companion planting nor clumps of garlic nor soap sprays had proven effective as deterrents. Agreeing with Morris on this point, she resisted the idea of dousing her plants with insecticides. If she had banished poisonous plants, their medicinal properties and beauty notwithstanding, she wasn't about to drench her gardens in noxious chemicals. She read all the alternative, organic gardening books and guides for advice, even considered ordering praying mantises, which displayed a voracious appetite for marauding insects. The elegant, spear-like leaves of her irises and lilies had been bitten and nibbled so much that they looked like ragged strips of lace. Her lupins and roses had been ravaged by aphids. No matter how often she drenched the pink roses with soap and tobacco-juice-based sprays, the minuscule green bugs returned a thousandfold. Ladybugs controlled the aphid population, she knew, but preying mantises were universal predators, failing to make distinctions between good and bad insects. Oh well, not to be disheartened, she always mused with a shrug, more flowers survived than not.

Not entirely pleased by it but wise enough to accept the inevitable, she acknowledged that principles of devastation operated in her own garden. Morris Bunter might well have meant as much when he said gardening taught patience. It was Kate's idea to plant feathery coreopsis among the irises in the new bed so when they finished blooming, the yellow flowers of the tickseed would continue well into September. Covered with delicate blossoms, the coreopsis had lacy leaves that allowed enough sun to reach the iris rhizomes: a perfect combination. Kate had seen pictures of the arrangement in one of her father's gardening magazines. Loretta did admit that Kate had done a good job of scraping away the rot of rhizomes. Annick's rage still echoing in her ears, she regretted, though, that Kate had overheard the argument yesterday morning.

"You understand nothing about what I feel, and you're jealous because I have a man who loves me and no man will look twice at you. What a bitch you are!"

Dear me, the heartlessness of children. Where had love and duty fled? No doubt Kate, gardening in the patio border and fluent in French, had heard everything.

"Does he know how much money you have in trust?"

"Oh, for Christ's sake, Mother, will you step out of that stupid melodrama you live in. He's not after my money. He has his own."

"From teaching? From his painting?"

"You just can't get it through your bourgeois head that not everybody loves money as much as you. Donald's a great painter. And he was never a poor man. There are other things in life besides your fucking money!"

"Indeed. Like your education. Just how much do you think it cost me to keep you in Europe for three years?"

"Take it out of my trust fund. I'm sure you've dipped into it before now."

"You may think what you like, Annick, but it won't change my mind. Not a penny more."

It had taken her a moment to register what Annick had snatched off the console table. Right in front of Kate, Annick had bolted out the patio doors with a blue-and-gold vase filled with daffodils and the last tulips of the season.

"Annick, don't you dare! Not my Lalique!"

The sun glinted off the greasy spikes and quills of Annick's hair. From the back of the garden, her head looked like Medusa's on fire. She wore a black leather skirt and a black blouse wrapped several times around her torso. Elevated on six-inch-high platform shoes, Annick raised the vase above her head and hurled it against the cement fountain rising above a bed of Russian sage and lavender a few feet away, not fully grown yet. Loretta failed to reach her daughter's arms in time and almost slipped on a rhizome that Kate, foolish girl, had carelessly left at the edge of the patio.

The tulips and daffodils flew out of the vase like a flock of canaries before it smashed against the rim of the fountain's bowl and shattered into a thousand shards, falling like a shower of diamonds on the lavender.

"You stupid, stupid girl!"

And there, the visibly astonished Kate, witnessing family squabbles. Daffodils and tulips and coloured glass lay scattered all over the fountain flower bed.

If only Sylvain had intelligently accustomed himself to the divorce, as she had, and gotten on with his life. His business was in trouble, Loretta knew, in dire straits as he put it, and required a large infusion of cash if he was to keep his head above water. Sylvain enjoyed a command of clichés in French and English. The bottom line was ruination, he had told her, if she didn't relent. Loretta refused to meet with him personally anymore. The last time, in the presence of their lawyers, he had thrown an ashtray at her head. Her plan allowed for the placement of five astilbes in a quincunx, surrounded by a semicircle of Jacob's ladder.

After digging the hole for the fourth plant, Loretta leaned back on her haunches, thinking she heard a familiar sound behind her, but she didn't investigate because she liked to concentrate on the task at hand. The day was perfect for gardening, the temperature moderate, the breeze slight and refreshing, the sky clear. When Annick was five or six, Loretta had tried to get her interested in gardening the backyard of the house they had rented before Sylvain's business required a move to a downtown apartment. Annick had whined about not being allowed to watch television. Sylvain had taken Annick to hockey games and circuses, bought her junk food and toys. She was Daddy's little girl only as long as she remained little and Daddy remained interested. Loretta was relieved when he suggested they send Annick to the very best schools in Europe so they could devote their time to his business.

Annick returned home at twenty a pretty, petulant polyglot who deliberately switched from English to French to Italian and back to French, quoting de Sade, as though she expected an intelligent woman to give credence to his numbing puerilities. After Annick emerged from her "pseudo-Parisian phase," as Loretta called it, she began her serial relationships with insufferable men. Often university teachers and/or artists, they talked a lot about dance (excluding ballet), film (excluding Hollywood movies), performance poetry, digital photography, Eastern philosophies (many had toured India and Tibet), Tai-chi, Tai Kwon Do and tofu, and for those with a more Western bent, the Celts and their mysteries. Annick began demanding access to her trust fund, reverting to temper tantrums when Loretta declined. Professor Donald Ingoldsby was her latest lover and mentor. He had also lived in an ashram in his "first youth," as Annick had quoted him to her mother. Loretta despised people who journeyed to India and returned spiritually the wiser, exuding sanctimonious pieties, the cosmic insights they gained from meditation little more than risible gibberish, to her way of thinking. She wondered if the professor confused a privileged, academic middle age with both divine exemption from morality and the abdication of intelligence. Annick, being blinded by "spiritualities" (Loretta scoffed at her daughter's use of the plural), seemed not to care.

Through the glass doors Loretta had seen Kate pick up the pail of rotten rhizomes and carry them to the trash behind the garden shed. That girl was in a position to learn more about family business this morning than she would have wished her to know. It was not a good idea to compost the rhizomes, Morris instructed, because it was difficult to determine if the rot had originated from mere inattention to a crowded, too shady location, or from an infestation of the infamous borer, or from a hitherto unsuspected disease. Viruses had the nasty habit of surviving and thriving where one least expected them. Donald Ingoldsby's house rose above the western fence of the garden where her father had prepared the new bed for the irises.

One of the joys of gardening lay in its morally uncomplicated and perennial return of beauty for consistent effort. Regardless of the difficulties of the day, emotional upsets, or family squabbles, and there were many of those lately, gardening led Loretta out of that sordid and maddening prison house of other people's demands into a quiet, intensely vibrant world of peace and creativity. Gardens possessed a breathtaking serenity, insect infestation notwithstanding, which put life in perspective, assuaged disappointments, and enlivened her weary heart.

Five days earlier Loretta had advised the financial officer of her charity that she would be going to the police with her well-founded suspicions that Geraldine McCready was purloining funds from the charity coffers and directing them into her own purse. Geraldine had denied the accusation. Faced with Loretta's evidence and unsmiling demeanour, she then confessed, actually crying. Loretta had offered the box of tissues on her desk. Geraldine promised that she would return the money as soon as possible, but her personal debt load and financial responsibilities were such—three children in university, her husband debilitated by Lou Gehrig's disease and not entirely covered by supplemental health insurance—that if only Loretta would understand, be patient, show a little compassion, no one else needed to know.

"But, Geraldine, as the financial officer you've violated the foundation's trust. I do know and must act accordingly!"

Fraud, duplicity, and misappropriation of funds had occurred; her moral obligation to the charity offered no alternative. Although she had granted Geraldine a week's reprieve, Loretta didn't expect an immediate resolution to the problem. Wishing to handle the matter as quietly and efficiently as possible, she wondered how to approach the police and stifle the inevitable scandal. She felt sorry for Geraldine's husband, who subsisted on a diet of vitamin-enriched liquids and costly prescription drugs.

Standing up, Loretta stepped back from the shade garden in her new yellow wooden clogs ordered from a gardening catalogue. She wanted to establish a sense of placement visually. Not all the written plans or drawings in the world really took the place of the eye when it came to arranging a garden. She acknowledged Morris Bunter's genius in that regard. He knew exactly where things should go and how much space they would take within five years. One developed an instinct for the right composition, as if a garden were a canvas waiting for a painter to apply a brush. Colour, form, and texture were important, although Morris shied away from talk about artistry and colour combinations. "Nature doesn't use oils and a brush," he had once said.

Finding gloves cumbersome, like so many gardeners, Loretta preferred direct contact with elemental dirt and manure. Often scratched, stained, and callused, her hands, of course, bore the brunt of her labours. Shaking hands with Gloria when Sylvain first introduced her, Loretta had remarked on the unblemished silkiness of Gloria's skin, a comment that made the woman blush. Loretta pushed up the brim of her straw hat and turned toward the sun to feel the warmth on her face. Her sweatsuit would be too hot for the work, and she would have to change into shorts and cotton shirt.

Sufficient time remained before lunch to deadhead the spent blooms of the early flowers before the heat intensified by noon. Of all the necessary tasks of gardening, deadheading perhaps gave her the most pleasure. With her pruning shears and her trug, she wandered from one bed to another, snipping off faded and wilting flowers like the defunct tulips but leaving the stems and leaves to encourage new life and vigour next year. The various fragrances of late spring enchanted. In the only time she ever visited Annick's apartment in the packed streets of the McGill ghetto, starved for green, the noise of the city a constant thrum, she had been over-whelmed by the scent of jasmine. Annick connected her spiritual well-being to aromatherapy. Jasmine candles burned in tubs of glass in every room. Loretta disliked jasmine, finding it like heliotrope, heavy and more conducive to headaches than medita-tion. But, she supposed, one woman's scent was another woman's poison. She preferred more subtle, less insistent perfumes and required of them only the pleasures of smell, not spiritual tuning. And, yes, the pleasures of memory, for Proust was right in that respect. Loretta's prolific bergamot always reminded her of the Earl Grey tea and lemon cake she had often enjoyed as a child with her own mother.

Later in the afternoon, after showering and scrubbing the dirt from under her fingernails, she would dress, drive to the charity office on rue St-Denis, and make a final decision about Geraldine. There were also library books to return, some groceries to buy, and invitations to write. She was hosting a luncheon for the executive board of her charity. Geraldine would not be invited. In the evening, after a light supper, she planned to watch David Suchet's prissy Inspector Poirot on *Mystery*, her favourite television show.

The breeze picked up the aroma of her Munstead lavender bushes, which she had planted around the fountain and coddled and protected against the winter for the past several years. So many gardeners she knew enjoyed little success with lavender in this region, a gardening zone in which they did not ordinarily survive more than a season or two. Heavy mulching after the first frost and before the first snowfall helped.

Brushing her fingers through the stems and leaves, Loretta smelled the lovely, curative scent of lavender. Thinking of imperceptible slivers of glass caught in the bushes, she pulled back a moment but slipped her fingers through the sprigs again. Perhaps there was something to aromatherapy, after all. Years ago, her mother had hung beribboned sachets of lavender in the closet and placed them between folds of silk stockings and her lingerie. At story time, before she went to sleep, Loretta snuggled against her mother, who always smelled like a generous bouquet of lavender leaves and blossoms, which Loretta now dried and hung in her own closets. Who could despise the world with such loveliness in it?

After the mayhem, Annick had run down the patio steps, halting and panting a moment in front of Kate, her face as white as a movie vampire's, her brown, deep-set eyes surrounded by purple mascara. Some of the spikes and wedges of Annick's hair bent at awkward angles as if they had snapped.

"My mother's an evil woman—you watch out for her," she heard benighted Annick say, hissing the words out in a mephitic spray of spit, although her daughter smelled sickly sweet of jasmine-based cologne. Screeching profanities, she ran along the garden as if goaded to madness by a cloud of infuriated wasps and kicked open the back wooden gate, which should have been bolted in the first place.

With her foot Loretta slid the rhizome off the patio.

"Would you please not make a mess?"

"I'll clean up, Mrs. Ferroux, and I'll sweep the patio."

"Good. That's what I want to hear."

Before Kate removed pieces and slivers, the lavender bushes glittered with glass. Loretta decided to proceed with the dead-heading before taking a break. Perhaps kneepads she had seen advertised in the supply catalogue would be a good idea. Not to mention the gorgeous, bearded irises to replace the rotten ones Kate had discarded. A bit expensive at several dollars a rhizome but well worth the price. The day was just too magnificent not to be outdoors in the gardens. If love were indeed the informing principle of the universe, as Annick in one of her spiritual harangues had pointed out, then it was real and manifest in her gardens.

Lifting the pruning shears from her gardener's belt, Loretta walked toward the side of the house, where several of her best rose bushes flourished. Her left foot sank into a depression in the lawn. Still insecure in the new clogs, she stumbled and fell forward near the rotten beech trunk where the heavy axe, which she had recently painted red to serve as a garden ornament, used to be lodged. The shears flew out of her grasp. She landed first on her right knee, then on her hip and shoulder.

"Damn!"

She rested her head on the grass, still damp from the dew. At first Loretta thought a cloud had covered the sun, although she hadn't noticed any in the sky. Then the shadow passed over her head. Joni Mitchell's song about clouds and recalling love's illusions came to mind, a song she hadn't heard for years. Shaken by the fall and raising herself on her knees, Loretta was relieved that nothing had broken. Although not old or stricken with osteoporosis, she was still afraid of suffering fractured bones and hips. She took a breath and made every effort to get a grip on herself.

A childish fancy, seeing shapes in clouds, a game even she had played as a child. Had she sprained her ankle? It hurt when she rested her weight on it and began to stand in her stocking feet. She had fallen out of both clogs. That sound? A cat—whose it was Loretta didn't know—had crept through the cedar bushes and was scratching in the freshly dug plot, using it as a litter box, the sound of its scraping paws so soft, like fingertips rasping a skein of silk.

Half standing, Loretta looked up. She imagined the irises she planned to order as blue as the sky. Unsteady, her vision blurry with stars and shifting shadows, she turned around, thinking that the cat was leaping after a bird among the hostas. Breathing quickly, she stood for a moment in the shade, trying to recall what she wanted to do next. Oh yes, the gardening trug in the shed. Kate Bunter must have put it back. First, find the shears. She spotted them a few feet away from where she had fallen. Bending to retrieve them, her back toward the shade garden, the cat's paws now rasping more loudly than she would have thought possible, Loretta noticed the rotten trunk of the beech tree. The axe was not lodged there. She didn't remember removing it. A swift and violent shadow passed in front of her eyes.

2

· · ·

MORRIS STACKED THE BAGS of sheep manure, cedar mulch, and peat moss in the back of his red pickup truck. He disliked working with peat moss, finding it an overrated substance. Sure, it helped to retain moisture if applied wet, but it often dried, formed a crust, and prevented water from penetrating the soil. Useful perhaps for helping to break up heavy clay. Too much of the gardening topsoil sold these days at the nurseries nonetheless contained more peat than he thought necessary. Well-rotted manure and homemade compost, as far as he was concerned, were the key ingredients for successful gardens. In his own yard, he had never used peat moss. Of course, it took time for organic waste like lettuce leaves, potato peels, and apple cores to decompose into useful soil. Garbage couldn't be rushed. True, one needed a lot of waste to produce relatively little compost, but just look at his lush perennials; they were worth the effort of digging manure into the soil. He had no difficulty filling his two compost bins with his own organic waste and that of his neighbours who didn't garden.

The last bag in the truck, Morris removed his baseball cap and scratched his scalp. After the rush of the May holiday weekend when thousands converged on the nurseries around town, his favourite nursery was not busy today; it seldom was on a Tuesday morning. Without being crowded, he meandered among rows of bedding plants, black plastic pots of rose bushes, flats of perennial seedlings, and stands of coniferous and deciduous saplings with their root balls tied up in burlap. But he did have work to do at three different gardens. The Honnikers wanted him to eliminate the mushroom rings on their front lawn. Indifferent to grass as a rule, although he recognized its utility, Morris knew how to deal with fungus in the soil. The Lims, who had recently arrived from Hong Kong where they had lived in a fifteenth-floor apartment and who now occupied one of the new, pseudo-palatial homes on the waterfront, asked him to design and "install" the garden, Mr. Lim's word, as if gardening was no more than outdoor plumbing or a precast module one inserted in place. They had originally planned to hire architectural landscapers rather than mere gardeners. Neighbours told them about Morris Bunter's work, which they could see for themselves in the community. His fee impressed them even more. Morris did not charge exorbitant rates—a fair wage for a fair day's work had always seemed appropriate and sufficient. For the larger landscape projects, like trees and artificial ponds and cobblestone pathways that circled the estates, he first advised other, more expert and costly hands, unless the client insisted that he undertake the project.

Of course, Mrs. Ferroux required his services today. He didn't like to keep her waiting, if only because she could sour the day with a word or look. Not that he minded her terribly, but he didn't need her voice booming over his head, telling him how to do his job. That was the wealthy for you. They assumed money conferred knowledge of and expertise in areas they knew nothing about. Hadn't he worked for them most of his life? With his hands in the muck and mire of rotting vegetable matter or shovelling shit into the soil, he had acquired some knowledge of human nature.

Kate had promised to come home and not hang around the university with her friends after the meeting. The business about

Ingoldsby was being settled. The university officials conferred, and the harassment committee heard witnesses to the point of numbing repetition: the same story, the same facts, over and over again. Kate herself had been questioned several times, harangued by the faculty representative speaking on Ingoldsby's behalf, until she calmly reminded him that she didn't have to listen to him, that she could very well take her case to outside authorities. Basing his entire argument on the supposition that Kate was wrong, perhaps criminally so, he suggested that countercharges of libel and slander could be launched. Kate retorted that he could do as he pleased, but she was going to the police. Wasn't she really vengeful and bitter over a low mark, spiteful by nature, and a bit of a tart, toying around with the libido of unsuspecting professors?

At that point, the academic dean called the faculty rep up short, warning that *he* had overstepped the bounds. Kate was not legally obligated to hear his insults, unwarranted and inappropriate—the dean's words. She was doing the university and, he reminded everyone present, even Professor Ingoldsby a courtesy by agreeing to attend the proceedings in the first place. After that particular meeting, the dean privately asked Kate please not to go public, to be patient—the administration was doing all it could to see that proper procedures were followed according to the terms of the contract in cases like this. They wanted to dismiss Ingoldsby, but they were constrained by the clauses and regulations as she was not. He even apologized, Kate told Morris, for the faculty representative's rudeness; she mustn't believe his attitude was shared by many professors.

Good girl, she had stood her ground, even threatening to walk out of the proceedings when the faculty rep got carried away with his own rhetoric. The particulars had not changed. Other students, strengthened by Kate's resolve, came forward and corroborated her story. And the unimpeachable eyewitness of what had transpired in his office. There was no doubt about Ingoldsby's guilt. Kate expected the sexual harassment committee to deal justly with her case. Even the faculty representative's bluster collapsed when the dean slapped his wrist. She wasn't afraid of a countersuit. It didn't matter if a lawyer attacked her character and credibility in a public courtroom—the story would be "out there." The facts were incontrovertible. Administration, always nervous and eager to distance itself from Ingoldsby, as were many faculty, begged that she give the deliberations time to take their course so they could avoid any loopholes through which Ingoldsby might slip. He assured Kate that justice would be done without the necessity of a public scandal that would shame the university, *her* university, as if she had a personal stake in its reputation. Kate recounted the proceedings to her father. Morris choked on the bean soup he had prepared for supper. Soak the white beans overnight, he had learned from his late wife, Maria: a ham bone boiled in the broth also enriched the flavour.

"He shouldn't have talked to you like that."

"Anyway, the dean criticized him for it and he backed off. All this seems so much trouble. I'm so tired of it."

"Trouble? You didn't cause any trouble at all. How many times have I told you Ingoldsby's actions are not your fault."

"Many times, Dad. Let's drop the subject. The soup's good."

What was a father to do? The impulse to throw a rock through Ingoldsby's window was easily suppressed, but last week, when he had seen the man leaving the house next door to Mrs. Ferroux, Morris approached and asked him what kind of man did the professor think he was? What kind of teacher? What gave him the right to insult and humiliate his students? He didn't threaten the art teacher, was very careful not to threaten. His purpose was to engage in a civilized conversation, a matter of curiosity, say, a point of information. Ingoldsby was a professor, an artist, and obviously possessed a range of knowledge and understanding ordinary folk could never hope to acquire. Ingoldsby's house, inherited from his parents, Morris had learned from Mrs. Ferroux, was covered with ivy. Charming, but ultimately destructive of the brickwork. There was very little in the way of gardens; the landscaping consisted of patched, weedy lawn, too many scraggly potentilla bushes and browning junipers pressing against the foundation. Mrs. Ferroux said it was scandalous how Ingoldsby maintained his property. Surely there was a bylaw or something against general seediness. She suspected, and later information confirmed, that Ingoldsby was short of money. Actually, a bylaw did exist against crabgrass and dandelions, but someone had to lodge a formal complaint. Not even Mrs. Ferroux troubled herself to go to the town hall over weeds.

With his recently sharpened edging spade, Morris had been refurbishing the edges of Mrs. Ferroux's garden that followed the curve of her flagstone pathway to the front door. She had once run rows of eye-searing marigolds on both sides of the stones until Morris persuaded her to thin the plants and intersperse the orange blooms with blue veronica. The effect was stunning and rescued the marigolds from their unfortunate reputation of being hope-lessly institutional and functional. Gardening was a matter of transforming the banal by imaginative arrangement into the exceptional and beautiful. Even Mrs. Ferroux was beginning to recognize that and was allowing him to go about his business in her garden beds. He saw the professor walking toward what looked like an authentic, now dented, Volkswagen, not the remodelled version, parked in the driveway. Tall and somewhat rounded in the shoulders with curly brown hair and a Vandyke beard, the professor wore, under a brown leather sports coat, an acid-yellow shirt, the colour of cushion spurge in the spring.

Why Morris assumed the teacher would wear a suit and tie, he didn't know, but the clothes surprised him. Of course, artists didn't dress like ordinary people, Morris remembered. If he dropped his spade now, brushed his hands against his own jeans, the knees stained with earth and grass, he could approach the man and politely introduce himself. Kate had pleaded with him not to go to the university and confront Ingoldsby. That had been his first impulse after hearing the story, Kate struggling to hold back the tears as she spoke. Unwilling to submit to Ingoldsby's offensive behaviour, she had gone right to the administration office, bypassing the chair of the department entirely, and laid the charges. Didn't even confer with her own father until after the event, did not even ask his advice.

"The bastard! I'll kill him," he had said.

"No, you won't, Dad. Don't even think of going to the university and speaking to him. Don't make me regret telling you in the first place. Promise me."

Which he had. But neither he nor the professor was on campus at this moment. Morris recognized an expedient way to break his promise when he saw it. Nervous over the proceedings before they even began, she hadn't eaten for three days until he took her to her favourite Chinese restaurant and told Kate how unhappy he was seeing her school life spoiled by this matter. She shouldn't give Ingoldsby the power—that was what she was doing, letting him harass her still if she continued this way. Well, she began to eat an egg roll, and Morris talked about their neighbours and her plans for attending university in another city, possibly country, to undertake a master's degree after earning her B.A. from the local university. Then Kate got up to fill her plate at the buffet with chow mein, sweet-and-sour chicken balls, shrimp-and-vegetable fried rice. Eat first, then worry on a full stomach, his wife used to say. As he watched Kate at the buffet, it nearly broke his heart then and there to see how much she looked and walked and sounded like his beloved

Maria, who had died from cancer several years earlier, although it still seemed like yesterday.

And Ingoldsby had dared to insult his daughter, to violate her trust! He had to speak to him, man to man, gentleman to gentleman. Teachers liked to be approached softly. He started walking toward the Volkswagen, his tongue becoming thick and fuzzy like lamb's ear, composing an introductory speech in his head, hoping to sound at least as intelligent as the professor. Morris wished he had spent more time over books the way Kate seemed so willing to do. Sometimes he imagined the Great Wall of China stretched right around the earth and divided people like him from people like teachers, scientists, and artists who understood the mysteries of the universe. Kate had at first admired Ingoldsby, his ability, she said, of teaching her to see colours, forms, relationships, and understand pictorial elements the way she hadn't been able to before taking his class. Wasn't a good teacher supposed to do that? Morris had nothing but respect for good teachers. Like good gardeners, they took barren or unproductive land and transformed it into paradise, in a manner of speaking, their minds attuned to higher things in life.

He had always been self-conscious about his incomplete education and gave more credit where none was warranted. In front of all the students in his class, Ingoldsby had called Kate "a cock teaser," after she knocked his arm off her shoulder. A word and a gesture, however offensive, did not constitute criminal behaviour. Ingoldsby's flirtatiousness with students had become part of university lore. Kate had been reluctant to go beyond the minor incident in the classroom, but under Morris's sympathetic insistence, she had. A daughter needed to see her father's concern when it mattered most.

"He felt me up," Kate whispered, her cheeks flushing a hot and purple-tinged pink like campion flowers. Having encouraged her,

Morris did not want to hear, so embarrassed by Kate's confession that he didn't know where to look. Kate continued.

"In his office. I went there, invited really, to discuss a drawing, so he said. He stood next to me—we were sort of leaning over his desk to look at my sketchbook—I smelled liquor on his breath—and his hand slipped between ..." She looked at Morris, whose face showed the signs of struggle between wanting to know more and not wanting to hear anything so personal about his daughter.

"I was wearing black tights with my short skirt—you know the one with pleats?" Morris nodded.

"Professor Ingoldsby slipped his hand between my legs and squeezed."

She paused. Her face lost its tan, became the colour of winter. Morris searched for a calm voice.

"And what did you do?" He heard his question, but the voice sounded ghostly, as if emerging from the throat of a dying man.

"I couldn't believe it. I remembered freezing a moment. He pressed harder just as another professor walked into his office without knocking. She saw everything. I straightened up and elbowed Ingoldsby with my left arm."

"Then what did he do?"

"He sort of chuckled, and explained to the professor that he was going over my drawings and went on about how my perspective was all wrong like he never touched me at all."

"What did the other guy do?"

"Woman, actually. We looked at each other, and I could see her blushing."

"Did she say anything?"

"I don't know. Maybe something about the door being partly open—I don't remember exactly. Anyway, I just couldn't stay in his office a moment longer. I wanted to go home and change my clothes. But the other professor saw everything and said so at the hearing."

Sometimes Morris didn't know what shocked him more: Ingoldsby, or his few but vocal defenders at the university who had rushed to his aid like muskox surrounding their threatened calves, as if Kate, his dear, sweet, trusting daughter who only wanted to learn, was at fault for Ingoldsby's violation of decency and ethics. Ingoldsby's cohorts insisted on his innocence, or, if not exactly innocence in the light of the evidence, they lined up extenuating circumstances that would have excused the devil himself. As teachers will, their discussions around his abuse, the meaning, the intent, the context, the provocation, the stress of his job, his political stance as a hedonist and Rabelaisian became more and more involved until the professor's moral culpability disappeared beneath a welter of verbiage and supersubtle sophistries that bore no relation to reality. No, Kate replied to his questions at one meal or another, the administration and most of the teachers did not support Ingoldsby or his friends, but every man had a right to a hearing. It was in the contract.

Cap in hand, his voice properly modulated, not aggressively staring the professor directly in the face, Morris had decided what he would say just as he stepped directly between Ingoldsby and his car. Both men stopped. Morris tried to smile, looked at the facade of Ingoldsby's ivy-covered home, and cleared his throat.

"Yes? Can I help you?"

Kate was right. A rich, mellifluous, slightly English-accented voice.

"I … I work for Mrs. Ferroux."

"Yes, you're her gardener. I don't require the services of a gardener. Please excuse me, I'm late as it is."

"I just want to say …" And he raised his eyes to stare at Ingoldsby. Why, the man wasn't any younger than he, the same web of wrinkles around the eyes. The professor was in a hurry to get somewhere, Morris could see as he tried to marshal his words, which scattered like flowering crab blossoms blown off the tree by a strong wind.

"Just because … what I mean is … you've no right … my daughter …"

"What are you talking about? I don't know you."

He stepped around Morris, who without thinking clutched a sleeve of the leather coat.

"What the hell do you think you're doing?" He grabbed Morris's wrist and pushed the arm away.

"I want to know why you think you can insult my daughter."

"Your daughter?"

"Kate … what gives you the right to say … do … the things you did to her? All because you're a teacher? Shame on you. I want to say that … yes … shame on you. A grown man ought to have more sense, especially a teacher."

He was warming to his subject. Not just because the blood was pumping into his head and his heart drummed so loudly that he heard it beat against his ribs. He raised an arm and Ingoldsby stepped back. Morris stepped forward. He had no weapon except his fists, which almost had a will of their own as the fingers tightened.

"You shouldn't be talking to me like that."

"No sir, I should not, and that's the problem. A man like you is making a man like me say these things. Is there something wrong with you? I wonder. Is there something really wrong that you think you can harass and fondle and say obscene things to my daughter and get away with it? It seems you're kind of sick—I mean, a sane and healthy man wouldn't assault his students, would he?"

"I don't need to listen to this. You take one more step toward me and I'll call the police."

Morris remembered relaxing his hands. He wasn't afraid of the police, because so far he had done nothing illegal, nor had he even threatened the man. Dumbfounded: that was the word he later found to express his amazement over the teacher's sense of grievance by the Volkswagen. Morris was dumbfounded. Willing to call the police at the very first sign of harassment, Ingoldsby had not refrained from harassing Kate and, from what Morris had heard, was even denying the charge, testimony notwithstanding, throughout the proceedings. All Morris said was shame on you and what gives you the right, and the teacher held up his hands in horror and prepared to call the police to protect him from what? A conversation on the sidewalk? Morris had never struck anybody in the face in his life. Although he wanted to, Morris hadn't punched out the professor. Anyway, Ingoldsby fussed and fidgeted with his keys before unlocking the car door, sliding behind the wheel, and driving away with a squeal of tires, exhaust spewing out of the tailpipe. Wherever he was going, he needed to get there fast. Should never have let him leave without making him realize there were limits to what a person could do or get away with.

The university committee, influenced by an administration anxious to reach the only possible decision, would render its verdict any moment now. Best not to think about Ingoldsby today. Gardens needed tending, and if he spent more time at the nursery he'd never complete the work today. Mrs. Ferroux wanted her gardens in top shape in time for her party. She wanted the new bed completed, without poisonous plants, thank you very much, the old beds weeded, edges between lawn and gardens sharply distinct, the cedars clipped and pruned. Morris figured two, maybe three hours tops, this morning, which left him enough time to check out the fungus at the Lims' and suggest a few gardening ideas for their property, shaped like a wedge of pie, the house standing at the apex and all the land spreading outward on both sides and behind.

Very little land in front of the house. No point grassing it over. He'd suggest stones, sedum, and Sambucus, creating an essentially maintenance-free landscaping scheme.

Checking his watch, Morris knew he would be there in fifteen minutes or less. By one o'clock, he would have finished his chores for Mrs. Ferroux, then would drive to the Lims' a mile away; the Honnikers lived only a block or two from them. One day he would open his own nursery, three greenhouses side by side, specializing in perennials for northern climates. So many amateur gardeners in North America had this romantic idea of the perfect English country garden of foxgloves and delphiniums. Fine, if you lived in England with its temperate climate and adequate rainfall. But the winters here could be killers of tender roots, the summers scorchers of leaves and wilters of blooms. Sure, exceptions abounded. He knew a garden where Tritoma flourished without being lifted and stored for the winter, and Mrs. Ferroux's lavender seemed to be doing very well indeed, just like the gardens in Hidcote, England, one of his favourites. He started the engine of his truck and sucked in his belly as he cinched the seat belt. Kate had suggested regular exercise, but, hell, he worked out enough outside without lifting weights for a fee in a club, surrounded by pudgy bankers and strutting bodybuilders. Almost fifty, he had long past given up any illusions about the male body beautiful. The growl in his stomach reminded Morris that he hadn't eaten a decent breakfast before rushing out this morning. Kate had made him a lunch of ham sandwiches and two boiled eggs, which—idiot—he had forgotten to bring with him. It looked like another trip to the doughnut shop again or Kentucky Fried Chicken takeout. Who had time to sit in a restaurant?

Pulling into Mrs. Ferroux's driveway, he just caught a glimpse of Professor Ingoldsby's house, looking burdened and withdrawn behind all that ivy sucking the strength out of its red brick. If it were his place, he'd pull it right off the facade and rip out the roots, repoint the bricks, change the windows to allow in more light—a rather dead-looking place, the windows small and mullioned. Ingoldsby had taken enough of his thoughts for the day. He grabbed the electric trimmer with its hundred-foot cord and walked to the backyard, deciding to prune the cedar hedges first, before finishing the new bed for the shade garden, which Mrs. Ferroux said she had already begun, having received the plants by mail a few days ago. She ordered all her plants through the catalogues because the varieties and species she wanted were seldom to be found at the local nurseries. The rich were often like that, Morris had learned. Inclined toward the exotic and foreign, climate zones notwithstanding. He must remind her about the bergenia and Jacob's ladder, excellent plants for the shade garden. There was an aluminum stepladder in the garden shed. When she heard him outside, Loretta Ferroux would no doubt stand on the patio and watch him for fifteen minutes or so, issuing instructions while he went about his business. With that voice of hers, raised almost to a shout because she assumed the ordinary workers of the world must be deaf, it was a wonder that the neighbours, admittedly some distance away except for Professor Ingoldsby's house, didn't hear and think a flock of raucous crows had settled in the trees.

He stopped at the top of the path where it ran into the bottom step of the patio and saw Mrs. Ferroux lying on her stomach, face smashed into astilbe in a circle of blood. He sat down to catch his breath and dropped the trimmer. Later he would think he had blacked out momentarily, for time seemed to have vanished into a black sack. Whether time raced ahead or it stopped on the spot altogether, he couldn't have said. He stared at the body, trying to reach a decision and to control his breathing. The police. Return to the truck and call the police on his cellphone. Tell them about

Mrs. Ferroux, the blood on her sweatsuit and the back of her head, the axe in the neck. Reason told him what to do. The yell Morris couldn't let out of his mouth flipped and veered inside his skull. His empty stomach turned and heaved. Call for help, call the police, call an ambulance—God, he couldn't believe the evidence before his eyes. As he tried to stand and return to his truck, Morris's body collapsed and slipped forward on the grass, where on all fours he retched repeatedly until his throat hurt.

3

. . .

AFTER DECADES OF CARTING COMPOST, traipsing through yards
and digging soil, Morris knew the lay of the land in this
community, every nook and cranny, every copse and ditch,
where the ground rose and where it declined, where the sun
shone all day and where it did not. Familiarity had bred attachment. Take the Bartle property: a house erected on a half acre of
open field, no trees except what the Bartles and the owners
before them had ineffectually planted. As usual, too many pines
(monstrous mugho at that), overgrown cedars, and weedy
Manitoba maples too close together and too near the house,
preventing their own proper development and the morning sun
from entering the east windows. Damp and mould replaced light
and air. Much of the terrain lay exposed to the harshness of
midsummer heat. Give us something we don't have to care for,
they had commissioned him several years ago. A mighty task that
Morris, as he drove by the Bartle house, was pleased to have
fulfilled. Not visible from the street, the hundred-foot-long curving
beds, shaped like open hands meeting at the tip of their fingers,
extended behind the house almost to the edge of their property.
Unlike some of his customers, the Bartles did not have an irri-
gation system, and did not wish to run hoses for such a long
distance from the outdoor taps, so the gardens would have to

rely on rainfall. Drought-tolerant perennials were the solution: plants that could survive a hot and dry spell.

Now Mrs. Ferroux's garden was smaller than the Bartles', more varied in shade and light, and more susceptible to a variety of treatments: like the lavender surrounding the fountain, the new iris bed, the hosta and astilbe for the shade garden. White blooms, he had advised, spots of brightness in the dark, a vivid contrast to the vermilion spreading around her head and seeping into the ground like liquid fertilizer. It had taken time to compose himself after phoning the police and retching on the lawn. Touch nothing, he had been warned, as if he even wanted to go near the body. His instinct had not been to extend a hand and feel, but to retract and recoil. The axe was designed to be a decorative touch in the stump, a kind of sculpture created out of ordinary, functional things. Waiting for the police, he tried to phone Kate while staring at Mrs. Ferroux's inelegantly splayed body, remembering that Kate herself had worked in these gardens and was scheduled to work here again tomorrow. How was it possible for her to return and dig and delve in a place where such a terrible violation had occurred? He wouldn't, he couldn't, let his daughter come back. The woman had obviously been murdered and, for all Morris knew, assaulted first, brutally violated, before the painted edge of an axe had split her skull. Who was to say it couldn't happen again on the same spot? Hadn't he read somewhere that murderers returned to the scene of the crime? His daughter spent time alone in the gardens.

Morris swallowed, hoping to calm his empty but overactive stomach and the heaving in his chest behind the wheel of the truck. The police had suggested someone else drive him home after their questions and preliminary investigations in Mrs. Ferroux's house. They told him to be available for further questioning. Was he all right? Did he need a lift? One of the officers had offered him a cigarette, but Morris had not smoked for ten years. The smell of tobacco now made him ill, more so over Mrs. Ferroux's body. Where was he before he discovered the body? Had he in fact touched anything? Seen anything? Anyone? Try to remember. Any little thing at all. He mentioned talking to Donald Ingoldsby a week ago but said nothing about the professor's hurried air and nervous eyes. When was that? What time? A week ago, he repeated. The police always assumed people looked at their watches and clocked their every movement. Morris didn't know what time he had actually spoken to Ingoldsby. Anyway, not today, not on the day of the murder. He had a general idea of what time it was when he left the nursery, that was all. No, he hadn't noticed anything suspicious.

Yarrows and thymes, sages and euphorbias, variegated sedums and woolly mulleins, artemisias and rudbeckias: these all flourished in the Bartles' drought-tolerant "prayer" beds, as Morris called them. Not too keen on single-colour schemes, he had chosen white and silvers, purples and yellows, clumps of pink and peach lilies, which, judiciously placed, acted as balances and coordinators of the entire scheme. So successful that many of the plantings now needed dividing. The Bartles were talking about opening up a new garden bed, talking about it as if they were planning to do the work themselves rather than hire Morris. Mrs. Ferroux did enjoy gardening, unlike so many of his clients who, if he had not been there to provide an alternative vision, would have hired professional landscaping companies. They arrived in their trucks, plunked down marigolds and geraniums, begonias and impatiens in geometric, heavily mulched patterns, pruned the cedars into ice cream cones or bowling balls. Neat and functional, without inspiration or originality, beauty clipped down to convenience.

That screeching bird trapped in his skull had exhausted itself and now lay panting on the bottom of his brain. Try as he might, Morris didn't know what to make of it. Things like that happened all the time—elsewhere. Biting his lower lip and frowning, which accentuated the deep creases in his forehead, Morris drove through a stop sign. Because he knew the neighbourhood so well, he realized he had done so after he crossed the intersection, momentarily horrified that he could have caused an accident, perhaps hit an unseen child. As in so many wealthy neighbourhoods, few people were seen outside, their spacious houses standing for the most part behind hundred-year-old chestnuts, oaks, and birches, except for the new section built on old farmland. Ravenous squirrels, no more than tree rats to Morris, made havoc of spring bulbs, foraging for and chomping on tulips with gluttonous abandon, chomping off rhododendron and magnolia buds, unless Morris took measures to prevent the marauding raids. With so many nut-bearing trees, controlling the squirrel population was impossible. The rodents ravaged bird feeders and gnawed their way into attics of some residences where they chewed wires, nested, and bred in the insulation. Only last month, Mrs. Ferroux had complained about the scurrying and scratching noises in her attic. Morris had jokingly replied that he wasn't an exterminator but a gardener.

"But don't you have to deal with pests?"

Yes, of the slithering and flying kind: slugs that could nibble holes into a hosta leaf virtually overnight, and grubs that consumed the roots of plants, as well as grasshoppers and thrips, Colorado beetles and hornworms; occasionally moles that tunnelled through garden beds and fed on corms and bulbs. He had no solution for clever creatures that infiltrated and undermined the hidden parts of a house, except accommodation and compromise. Accept damage and loss as part of the cost of living in this kind of neighbourhood with its ancient nut trees, part of an original forest before it became a preserve of the wealthy and their hired help, like Morris, paid to tend to their needs. So many cars parked in the driveways of these houses, with enough space for several Mercedes-Benzes, Volvos, Bentleys, a few Jags, Lincolns, and hefty SUVs. His rattling pickup, nine years old, refurbished engine three years old, scratched and gouged and oil-stained from all the years of transporting Rototillers and shovels, still functional despite rust holes, was not the kind of vehicle his clients drove. Interspersed among the luxury cars, smaller Japanese models, probably belonging to the sons or daughters or a maid who needed a means to get the groceries from specialty stores a mile or two away from the culs-de-sac and quiet streets of this community.

Loretta Ferroux drove a silver Audi that she parked in her three-car garage, one of the other two spots occupied by a Jeep that, Morris knew, originally belonged to her husband and now formed part of her share of the divorce settlement. Sylvain kept the SAAB. All the luxury cars in the world, though, didn't prevent a great swipe at the head, a crack in the skull, and a crash against the brain. Morris retched and almost swerved against a fire hydrant. He stopped the truck to rest his head on the back of his hand gripping the top of the steering wheel, and waited for the shaking and heaving to stop before he started again. Soundless, this crying, his eyes wet and red, but his sorrow was silent. Kate had often worked in the Ferroux garden—God, the horror of it! The police would want to talk to him again. Of course, being the first on the scene meant he was the first suspect, the murder having occurred, they surmised, that very morning, exact time of death to be determined. They were only doing their job.

He loved this neighbourhood, having lived for almost thirty years on the payments of the wealthy who relied on his gardening expertise. What better life: gracious homes, quiet and withdrawn like discreet, aristocratic women, stupendous trees that grew assured of their social status, their leaves changing into wonderful clouds of colour in the fall, providing mulch to overwinter his perennial beds. Morris regarded all the gardens as his property, really, having acquired vicarious ownership through the application of manure. He had come to depend on the steady peace and beauty of this neighbourhood, on the aura of indifference and immunity to the travails of the world. He wasn't really thinking about personal problems, though. Prone to alcoholism, drug addiction, adultery, and other deceptions, the people here were no better than anyone else. Morris allowed for the individual human foibles and peccadilloes of his clients. After all, such was the nature of the world; he was not a man to judge. In a larger sense, though, because he dug so deeply into the soil and saw the perennial rewards of his efforts, the neighbourhood imbued him with a sense of security, a concrete feeling of well-being. In this place, exempt from the monstrosities so prevalent in other parts of the world, people led rich, sometimes troubled, but mostly protected, lives. Guard dogs and barred windows, elaborate security systems and the occasional burglary notwithstanding, he worked safely here, as he transformed once unremarkable grounds, however large, into patches of paradise without worrying about his back.

Breathing deeply, he regained control of himself and reached for his cellphone under the dashboard. He tried to call Kate again, just to know if she was all right, though she disliked his keeping tabs on her, threatened to throw away her cellphone if he bothered her unnecessarily. What was a loving, concerned parent to do with a grown daughter, still dependent financially and, Morris hoped, emotionally on her father but too independent in other matters? She used to go out with different guys, all of whom mumbled and smoked and none of whom he liked, and didn't tell her father where they went and when they would return. Or they passed the evening in her room, behind a closed door, much to his disapproval, downloading music, Kate often explained, or chatting with friends via the internet. Complaining too much suggested lack of trust, treating her like a child, or "crowding her space," as Kate said. Morris didn't want to be like those stupid television fathers who often proclaimed that as long as his children lived in his house, they would follow his rules, as if paternal commands were somehow divinely sanctioned and inviolable. Of course, the kids stormed out of the house. Life was far too complicated to reduce it to a set of easily broken rules.

And, now, so horribly tenuous and short. Mrs. Ferroux's perennials in the shade garden would outlive her. He braked suddenly at an intersection, startled by the appearance of an old man, wearing a Tilley hat, crossing the road with a bag of groceries, celery stalks poking out of the top like a bonsai tree. He raised a fist in front of Morris's truck. Morris lowered his head, hoping the peak of his baseball cap would conceal his identity. He recognized the pedestrian, Mr. Ruskow, a retired university teacher and a small-framed man who used a sharp tongue to gain stature and who detested gardening. He never allowed so much as a tulip to appear on his land. Ruskow hired university students to cut his grass as short as possible, even during hot spells when it turned the colour of straw. But of course his own truck was a giveaway. Everyone knew Morris and his red truck, not to mention visible gardening supplies in the back.

Three blocks away was the shopping district, and Morris needed to get out of the truck, drink a coffee, try to reach Kate, and shake himself free of images of Mrs. Ferroux's shattered skull and bloody hair. The police would phone him again, knock on his door. He didn't like the idea of two or three cops on his porch steps, their squad car in public view in front of his house. Police, any authority figures, professors even, made him feel if not defective, at least deficient, guilty of ignorance or an unspecified crime or, worse, both, and they had found him out.

Nonsensical, but give a man a decree or gun and who's to say what ideas crowd his brain? What had he to fear? People at the nursery had seen him, the owners themselves with whom Morris was familiar, had talked to him, probably at the exact time the blade of the axe struck the skull. Kate could have been kneeling in the same spot as Loretta Ferroux. Jesus! Again, she didn't answer. Where the hell was she? Traffic thickening, pedestrians bounding across the street. Morris gripped the wheel with two hands and tried very hard to concentrate on avoiding disaster. He parked in front of a ladies' clothing store, specializing in cashmere sweaters, silk blouses, and lambskin gloves. Conscious of its popular boutiques and riverfront boardwalk, the town council had placed cedar box planters along the sidewalks, filling them, Morris noted approvingly, with thunbergia, which produced flowers of orangey gold petals surrounding rich brown centres on trailing or climbing vines.

Across the road was a waterfront café where he could sit for a while on a wire-legged chair, drink overpriced coffee, and gather his wits, which, this very morning, had scattered like pieces of broken glass. The terrace facing the boardwalk was too crowded, so he remained in the cool shadows of the interior, having ordered a large, simple coffee and a cheese Danish, although he knew his stomach would revolt. But he could take his time. Morris glanced behind him. Several people were chatting in French, drinking coffee and eating pastries.

A waitress dressed in a gingham apron wiped the counter. As he didn't smoke, pretending to eat was the next best thing while he tried to think. Where the hell was his daughter? He phoned again. No answer. What was Kate doing today? He recognized a couple of people who entered the café, but preferred not to exchange pleasantries. Of course, he knew exactly where she was. Kate had a meeting at the university, the final stage of the harassment committee's deliberation, the administration wanting to complete the proceedings before the beginning of the new semester, before Kate lost patience and went to the authorities off campus.

Checking his watch, Morris realized the meeting was now in progress. He would drive to the university, wait for her in the corridor outside the dean's office door, even though she had insisted he not get involved with the proceedings in any way. This was something she wanted to do without dragging her father in. He had practically begged her to allow him to attend.

She wouldn't be pleased to see him standing there. Why Kate didn't like to see him in the university, Morris didn't know, especially when he managed to locate her, knowing her schedule and classrooms, and offer to buy lunch or to give her the egg salad sandwiches and raisin oatmeal cookies he had made. As it seemed important to Kate, and given her decided tendency these past few years since the death of her mother to fall into "fits and snits," as he called them, Morris for the most part respected his daughter's wishes, even if it meant sometimes that he felt hollow and excluded. Kate was growing beyond the reach of his deep love, and nothing he could do would bring her back. Well, he had done enough mulling over his coffee and nibbling a Danish.

Paying his bill, he left the café and crossed the street, wondering how he could tell Kate about Mrs. Ferroux. She would tell him about the harassment proceedings and where matters stood. The administration wanted to wash its hands of this matter as quickly as possible, relieved that Kate agreed not to bring in the police and journalists. She was really doing them a favour by helping the university to rid itself of a chronic nuisance. Ingoldsby should be run off the campus, if not tarred and feathered first, which Morris regretted they didn't do anymore in civilized countries. Then Kate and he would drive home together in his truck, eat lunch, and offer support for each other on this brilliantly sunny, appalling day.

4

$\cdot\ \cdot\ \cdot$

THE ROOFS OF ITS BUILDINGS covered in overlapping burnt-umber terra-cotta tiles, the university spread on several acres along Riverside Road, opposite the river. The main entrance faced a public dock where the local population launched their small yachts and other watercraft in the spring and summer. Sometimes traffic blocked the road. Today, no one was backing a boat trailer down the ramp. In December this stretch of the river became a skating rink, temperature permitting, and froze to a depth of several inches by the beginning of January. Hundreds, if not thousands, of skaters, many driving from central Montreal, claimed it as an outdoor arena, often skating with flashlights and candles at night, fashioning evanescent patterns of light on the dark air. A certain section was cordoned off for ice fishing, and small, smoky cabins clustered together like a village. Morris used to play hockey on the frozen river when he was a boy and had taught his daughter how to skate before Maria died.

He passed through the gates and drove around the circular driveway leading to the administration building of the university. Four storeys high, concrete pillars rising on either side of its front entrance, its red brick chipped and browned over the years, its windows more grey with grime than clean and transparent, it followed the curve of the drive for several hundred feet.

Approaching the university always aroused a vague anxiety, as if a teacher was about to rush out and admonish Morris for failure to complete a homework assignment. Morris checked his face in the rearview mirror, hoping the wrinkles around his eyes and the white strands in his otherwise brown hair would give him immunity from pedagogical outrage. Licking a finger, he smoothed his eyebrows, which tended toward the shaggy. Kate had suggested he pluck them the way she did hers with tweezers, a procedure he'd rather not undergo. Driving slowly and watching out for students bounding between cars, he looked for a free visitor's parking space, but all six were occupied. There were other places to park behind the main edifice, or in front of the science building at the back of the campus, or behind the two residences, but he didn't feel like walking for ten minutes, so he drove around the driveway, which allowed parking for university staff and faculty on one side, until he saw a car pull out. Security guards, he hoped, wouldn't check this part of the campus and ticket the truck for a parking violation before he left.

Kate should realize that her father's concern equalled her independence, that his right to love and protect maybe even outweighed her desire for autonomy and attachment to any specific boyfriend. Under ordinary circumstances, he wouldn't have driven to the campus today, and he would have respected her wishes to stay out of the harassment proceedings entirely. That was all very well, although when he thought of Professor Ingoldsby, Morris also thought of decapitating grasshoppers, the marauders in the gardens that tried his patience the most. Devious little devils, munching on the leaves of his beautiful lilies and irises. He'd hold his breath, reach out with pruning shears in his hand, poise the open blades a whisper away from the thorax, then snap them shut, delighted by the miniature head flipping into the garden where its decay would enrich the soil. Out of rot, beauty.

As often as he cut one in half, another whizzed away, escaping before the blades clicked shut. His stomach churned with unease. The colour of Mrs. Ferroux's blood flooded his thoughts about Kate and her safety. It didn't matter that she was now safe—Mrs. Ferroux presumably had been safe in her garden—it was important that he tell Kate immediately and take her home so they could at least try to eat lunch together and wonder about the state of the world that bred such creatures as Mrs. Ferroux's murderer.

As for the landscaping in front of the administration building, Morris granted that it was neat and functional with its reliance on, God help him, carpet beds of red salvia and annual begonias in front of masses of pink and white petunias, behind which stood cedar bushes rising to the level of the first row of windows, rigorously clipped into giant balls, their needles more brown than green from winterkill. Clearly, the university lacked imagination and courage. Passing by clusters of summer school students smoking on the steps leading to the brassy front doors, despite the No Smoking signs plastered on the cement pillars, Morris remembered when he had bid on the gardening contract years ago. The administration, mistrusting a local gardener with a vision, who hired help as he needed it, chose a professional landscaping company in Montreal, which also paved private roads and undercut Morris's bid. Well, it was a university after all, so budgets and banality won over boldness and beauty.

Flanked by classrooms and offices, the main corridor, with high, brown brick walls and oak wainscotting, was dark. Morris squinted until his eyes became accustomed to the change of light. He himself had attended this small, venerable institution for a year at eighteen, taking a mishmash of courses until he found a part-time summer job in a nursery, taking care of seedlings in hothouses, pruning hybrid tea roses, transplanting perennials. He couldn't remember when he had enjoyed his summers more, so he stayed on for the fall, failing to register for the second year of the bachelor of science program. Laid off during the winter, he collected unemployment insurance. He read histories of gardening and magazines devoted to plants and landscaping. The following spring he was hired again by the same nursery, where he worked for seven years learning about trees and bushes, fertilizer and soil. He met Maria at the nursery over a flat of herbs, her specialty. She possessed an encyclopedic knowledge of the real and legendary, medicinal and noxious qualities of a wide variety of local and exotic plants. Her hair, he remembered, was black with purple highlights like the petals of the queen of night tulip, which he grew in his own garden in honour of her memory.

Kate's meeting began at ten and was supposed to end by noon. She demanded nothing less than Ingoldsby's dismissal, having studied the university's rules and regulations concerning harassment so thoroughly that she knew them better than Ingoldsby's faculty representative, who had sought to intimidate her. Anyway, her trump card was public proclamation and the police. Journalists in the hallways scooping up the dirt. What Ingoldsby had done was against the law, not simply a violation of the rules. The administration and most of the professors, his defenders notwithstanding, were eager to enforce university policies, apply its own strictures, and dismiss Ingoldsby, but he had a right to a hearing according to the terms of the contract.

Ingoldsby was a piece of work—Morris gave him that much. A middle-aged man who had travelled to India and Tibet, preyed on the romantic, sexual sensibilities of his half-enamoured female students who loved his voice, and mesmerized them when he spoke about painting and spiritual realities unbeknownst to Western, materialist-driven society, which he vociferously denounced in class. Living on their tax money, he mocked the values of his students' parents and humiliated any student who dared to challenge his insight and wisdom. Like a biblical prophet's, his rage was easily aroused. So Kate had said. She, too, had initially fallen under his spell and for a time locked herself in her room reading the *Tibetan Book of the Dead*. What did that have to do with oil painting? Morris had wondered. If you have to ask, Kate answered, you'll never understand, which was a useful way of avoiding an answer that made any sense. Some of the students were thrilled by Ingoldsby's reputation as a roué, who, rumour had it, invited girls to his office for more than academic purposes. When he patted her shoulder before the incident in his office, Kate had not minded, something the faculty rep had tried to build his defence on, almost accusing Kate of being a seductive whore trying to score high marks by encouraging the sexual interest of her professor. Morris found the registrar's office and approached the woman behind a counter piled high with academic calendars and brochures.

"The meeting is being held in the academic dean's office, room 203, directly above this office." She regarded Morris above her computer terminal, reading glasses perched on the tip of her nose. "But I'm afraid it's not open to the public."

"I'm not the public. I'm Kate Bunter's father."

He noticed the slight recoil in her upper body. Should he tell her of Mrs. Ferroux's murder? Would that distress her?

"I'm taking her to lunch. The meeting's over, you say, at twelve?"

"The dean has a luncheon appointment in the city at twelve-thirty. He's very punctual. Yes, the meeting will be over in fifteen minutes."

I found one of my clients, this morning, an axe having cleft her skull. I want to take my daughter home. She used to work in that same garden. Don't you see? It could have been Kate. Morris decided against speaking about Mrs. Ferroux. He didn't think the secretary would be terribly interested. After feigning shock and sympathizing, she'd return to her files and memos on the computer screen. The horror story happened elsewhere. He left the registrar's office and found his way to the stairs. In his day, boys took their hats off inside a building, certainly inside a school. Such was no longer the case. Every second male student, it seemed, wore a baseball cap in the hall and, from what Morris could see passing by the open doors, inside their classes. He had left his hat in the truck, hoping his hair wasn't too greasy from perspiration, heat, and its natural oils. Perhaps he should have rushed home, showered, and changed out of his jeans and sweatshirt into clean clothes, tried to look presentable and professional, less of a common labourer. Many of the teachers wore jeans but still looked down their noses at their social inferiors, who, in Morris's experience, seemed to be just about anyone who didn't teach in a university, however small. Oh, of course they said how do you do and spoke in a friendly manner, but he could just smell their condescension, so deeply ingrained that most of them were unaware that it took hold of their minds like the roots of goutweed that spread rampantly below the surface of the soil until they choked out other more desirable plants. You could always tell a university teacher, he joked with Kate, but not much.

If a man believed he was special, maybe he also believed he was exempt, his behaviour beyond accountability. How else to explain someone like Ingoldsby? Morris wondered. He opened the door to the stairwell just as a woman pushed by him and bounded up the steps. He couldn't be sure, but it looked like Annick, Mrs. Ferroux's daughter. The same spiky hair, orange like a day lily. Her long and white legs rising above platform shoes thick as hooves, she climbed the stairs, sure-footed as a mountain goat. Her mother. She knew about her mother and was … doing what, exactly, at the university? Ah, yes. Kate had told him about the argument she overheard yesterday. Ingoldsby had "a thing going" with Mrs. Ferroux's daughter. Ingoldsby and Annick Ferroux. Messing around with girls in class and girls outside of class. Annick wasn't more than twenty-five or -six. Morris had an appreciative eye as much as the next man, but he liked to think he operated within the range of normality and common sense. Youth with youth, fine. Young adults with young adults, fine. Older men and older women, perfect. That was the natural course of events; you didn't force relationships any more than you forced gardens; you couldn't expect a plant to develop properly in the wrong location and in the wrong soil.

Why was Annick in such a hurry? Had she stopped by her mother's house and discovered the police in her backyard, the yellow tape surrounding the garden, her mother's dead body? Surely the police had removed Mrs. Ferroux by now, after the coroner had examined the corpse on the scene and police photos had been taken. Annick's shoes clomped all the way up the stairs. Almost noon hour. The dean had an appointment downtown at twelve-thirty. It was a twenty-minute drive along the highway from the campus to Montreal's Hôtel de Ville. Pretty close timing. Hardly allowed for traffic or the unexpected. Suppose he was delayed by an accident or a murder? What would that do to his schedule? Morris took the steps two at a time, pleased that he wasn't breathless when he reached the landing. He found his way to the academic dean's office, outside of which a gathering of men and women milled about, speaking in low voices and, judging by their clothes and how they looked at him, presumably teachers. Behind three heads, Annick's wedges and spikes prodded the air. She was almost leaning against the closed door.

Many of the professors hemmed and shuffled, looking up and down and around or conferring in whispery, private conversations. He should tell the teachers what had happened this morning.

Together they could surround and capture Ingoldsby, hold him until the authorities arrived, so they could question him. Why should he, Morris, have been regarded as a possible suspect and not Ingoldsby? Morris sympathized with Annick, who had lost her mother; the young woman must have been in great pain, although he admired her composure in the midst of personal tragedy.

The teachers began staring at him, clearly wondering, Morris assumed, about his identity and purpose. Regretting his decision to come here, he began thinking Kate would be angry to see her father in a crowd of teachers, her father fetching her the way he used to every day during her kindergarten year. No matter what job he was doing, he took time off to meet his little girl as she trundled out of class with school bag dragging on the ground, coat unbuttoned, shoelaces untied, and her face bright and smiling when she saw Daddy. But now Kate had expressly forbidden him to trouble her at the university. Where had her strong mind and forthrightness come from? Didn't she want his emotional support? He had in fact phoned and asked the academic dean, who reminded him that students over eighteen did not need their parents' permission or presence for very much, as far as the university was concerned. It was entirely up to Kate, and the university would have to support her decision. Kate swore she'd remain silent in the witness chair if Morris so much as poked his nose in the door, not to mention never speak to him again.

"But why?"

"Because I say so and it's what I want."

At nineteen, she could be irrefutably logical, no more explanation required. The last thing she needed was her father pretending to be a knight in denim with soil beneath his fingernails rushing to her rescue. And he had promised to obey Kate's wishes in this matter. What did it matter if he told Kate the news of Mrs. Ferroux's death now or later? Had he panicked himself and assumed all hell had broken loose because his private domain, as he liked to think of the neighbourhood, had been savaged? The world obviously continued going about its business. Annick, of course, had a personal interest in the matter. The teachers had not.

The door to the academic dean's office opened. Out stepped a short man in a grey suit, sporting a yellow tie, his head bald and round as the globe cedars outside. He wore spectacles and carried a black leather attaché case. Was that the dean? Morris had never actually met the academic dean. Annick, stepping aside, tried to peer into the office.

"Mr. Ingoldsby will be out in a minute, if you would be so good as to let the people pass."

Morris caught the word *mister*. The dean had said *mister*, not *professor*. Annick obeyed, and two more men in suits, followed by three women, also suited, and two men wearing jeans and sport shirts, one of whom wore a beige linen sports coat, came out behind them. Where was Kate? Where was Ingoldsby? Surely they hadn't been left alone in the room together? The man couldn't be trusted alone with a pretty student. Why wasn't Annick shouting, Stop that man! Then Ingoldsby walked out in a mallow-pink shirt, the sleeves rolled up to the elbows, carrying his leather jacket. He spoke to no one as the crowd separated. Instead of shouting at Ingoldsby, Annick took hold of his hand and leaned into his shoulder. Morris noticed the great patches of sweat darkening the armpits of Ingoldsby's shirt.

Above their heads, names of honour students over the years had been inscribed on parchment flecked with gold and hung in black frames on the wall. Kate's name was on one of them. She had received straight A's last semester, but lately she had been losing interest in academic studies and her marks were slipping. If Annick was here, why hadn't she brought the police? Anyone with Ingoldsby's reputation deserved a good interrogation. Morris then considered the possibility that she had not yet learned of the murder, that he alone of all the people in the corridor was the only one who knew. Ingoldsby walked by Morris without looking at him. One or two teachers said something to the professor, patted his shoulders, and the man in the beige linen jacket accompanied Ingoldsby down the stairs. Morris wanted to pull him back up the stairs, collar the professor, and bang his head against the tiled floor. Firing was too good for him. At the very least, restrain him until the police arrived, a kind of citizen's arrest. Morris's energy and righteous fury, though, unaccountably dissipated at the moment of confrontation, and Ingoldsby disappeared down the stairwell. The other professors were dispersing; Ingoldsby's descent was followed by several supporters, trailing after him like devoted disciples. Stepping into the deserted office, Morris didn't see Kate.

"Dad! What the hell are you doing here?"

He turned and tried to smile in the face of Kate's dismay. By her tone, he realized the enormous error in judgment he had made. Morris smarted as if he had tangled himself, unclothed, in a patch of nettles. Every move stung. His daughter stood tall and, he would say, quivered—her body quivered in anger, as she raised and shook a finger at him.

"You promised me!"

She turned away and almost jumped down the stairs, taking the steps two and three at a time the way she used to as a child. Be careful, you'll trip and fall and hurt yourself. A parent's duty doesn't end simply because a few years have passed. There was no statute of limitations on love and solicitude; nine or nineteen, she was still his daughter. He thought it better not to speak. True, he had promised. But, Kate, sweetheart, wait … the way matters stand … Mrs. Ferroux, you see. Something terrible has happened.

I needed to see you. He did not speak the words, the sense of violating his daughter's trust so profound that Morris held his handkerchief to his face, not to cry but to wipe his brow and cover the expression, he was certain, of sorrow and uselessness.

5

. . .

HE DIDN'T KNOW if Kate would come home for lunch, or come home at all. The look on her face when she had seen him outside the dean's office earlier was all he needed to realize how disappointed and angry she must have felt, embarrassed, too, probably. Annick had scarcely acknowledged his presence, even though he had worked for Mrs. Ferroux almost from the day the family bought the property. Nor could she have known about the murder if she gladly took Ingoldsby's arm. Annick was no more aware of her mother's gardener than she was conscious of the carpet of periwinkle, the *Vinca minor,* covering the ground under the spirea bushes.

What was a father to do, now confused to the point of despair because Kate had disappeared with a fierce look. Checking his watch, hearing the noises of his empty stomach, worried about Kate, thinking about his afternoon work schedule, he tried not to remember Mrs. Ferroux's bloody head, which kept flashing in his mind like the sudden opening of a red poppy. Morris couldn't decide what to do. God, what to say to the daughter of a murdered woman? Ingoldsby should have been questioned as to his where-abouts—the man lived next door to Loretta Ferroux, for God's sake! And Ingoldsby had walked right past them as if immune to apprehension and justice. Where were the police? Questions flitted about in his head; answers sank into the bog of his confusion.

His purpose in going to the campus having failed, his legs refusing to follow the direction of his mind, Morris, no more informed now than he was earlier about the events of the day, found his way to the parking lot. Like a man lost in a forest of brambles and menacing trees without compass or hatchet, he took wrong turns in the university corridors, misread signs, bumped into students, seemed unable to hack his way through to a clearing. Eventually he recognized his truck. He sat behind the steering wheel for a few minutes, hands clasped between his knees, trying to restructure the day that had collapsed like unsupported spires of fox-tail lilies under the impact of wind. This had been a day like no other. It was absurd to pretend that everything was normal, that everything could continue in the same way it had before the murder. He remembered that Kate could have been gardening at the time, that it could have been her body he'd found—too horrible to imagine. Phoning his customers, only one of whom was home, Morris said a crisis had arisen—personal. He couldn't very well announce the matter of murder over the cellphone—they would learn soon enough—and he would have to reschedule the gardening chores.

Morris drove out of the campus and turned off Riverside Road before reaching the business section of the town. He lived on one of several blocks of small, compact houses built after the Second World War and during the fifties, an early subdivision designed to accommodate families of middling incomes, many of whom now worked in the industrial park a few miles away or provided repair and maintenance services for the waterfront estates and the newer subdivision of homes for the wealthy. Although small, his house had served his family well, especially after he built a deck at the back and a living-room solarium on the east side, almost doubling the floor space downstairs. Over the years, he had also installed a pine kitchen with ceramic floor tiles, added a private bath off Kate's bedroom upstairs, and opened the sloping ceiling by constructing a dormer with window seat when she was only ten years old. She had loved it. Even now, she read her school texts in the window seat, which looked over his gardens in the backyard.

His own skill and ingenuity, Maria's patience and financial acumen—how that woman could stretch a dollar—had enabled them to live economically and well on the income earned from gardening in the spring and summer and general handyman repairs for the wealthy in the winter. Morris prided himself on the fact that he had yet to collect unemployment insurance since he started his own business. Then again, perhaps luck, whatever that meant, had something to do with what he considered a more or less successful life to date. Other hardworking men and women, some in his neighbourhood, had lost jobs through no fault of their own, fallen sick, been hit by cars, lost money, lost their lives: all due to bad luck?

He tried phoning Kate who, he suspected, was refusing to answer her cellphone. Opening the refrigerator door, he grabbed an apple and a small hunk of havarti cheese, drank milk directly out of the carton, which he insisted Kate not do, noted that the breakfast dishes remained in the sink, and the stairwell rug needed vacuuming, then went out the back door to his gardens. Of all things, it was necessary for him to sit and take a deep breath here in the wonderful, private world he had fashioned, where murderers did not lurk in the shadows. Aside from the forsythia and French lilac bushes, the *Ginkgo biloba,* Russian olive trees, and a Japanese maple, there weren't many shadows to conceal a psychopath unless he managed to camouflage himself in the garden of high perennial grasses stretching a full hundred feet down one side of the yard. Ribbon and sea lyme grass, beautiful but insidious, sending out underground runners, invaded all parts of the garden where they weren't desired. Splendid to the eye, stranglers nonetheless. His variegated Japanese silver grass sounded like whispers and quiet song in the breeze, and the blue fescue deepened its blue in the sun. No, the place was too beautiful to hide a killer.

Standing on his raised deck, Morris surveyed his back lot with some satisfaction. As he took no pleasure in mowing a lawn, he had removed all the grass and laid out three long, rectangular garden beds, the vegetable patch stretching down the middle of the yard, and the two gardens along the fence on either side of the property. Between them, wide pathways of irregular stones interspersed with creeping thyme, phlox, and lysimachia led to the back bench and pergola covered with climbing roses. Behind them grew the Russian olives, which created a canopy of sun-splattered shade, partially concealing the compost heap and crowded garden shed. Rampant hop vines blanketed the shed. One of his mistakes. He had always admired the vigour and persistence of hops and once fancied brewing his own beer. Now, at least twice a season, he hacked the energetically invasive vines away from the door and window of the shed, where it was possible, he admitted, for a murderer to hide.

His yard was separated from his neighbours' by split-rail fences over which clambered golden and purple clematis vines, their roots shaded and cooled by the perennials in front, except for the fence on the other side now hidden by the grasses. The vines toppled over into his neighbours' terrain, but they didn't object to the labour-free blossoming on their property. It had taken several years for the garden to reach its richest depth, display varied textures and fragrances, and grow to carefully predetermined heights. The paradoxically seductive aspect about perennial gardens, though, was that they never truly achieved their final glory—not in the lifetime of a gardener, at any rate. Already Morris was thinking of transplanting, of adding new materials, of reshaping the beds along the fence so they curved, experimenting with more difficult plants, say, like meconopsis, the blue Himalayan poppy in the shaded section of the garden.

Walking down one of the pathways toward the back, he caught a whiff of the meadow rue that grew closest to the deck, its rosy clouds of blossoms catching the breeze. Catmint and mallows, painted daisies and dianthus, irises and campanulas in the one perennial bed carried his eye all the way to the back end of the yard where more meadow rue rose above the bench near the fence, underplanted with white and pink peony bushes, which, Morris could see, had outgrown their invisible supports. A few of the heavier blooms had fallen over like exhausted ballerinas in tutus on the pathway. Later in the summer a new flourish of plants and flowers would replace the June garden, later still, his favourite time of the year, the autumn garden of antique bronze, sunset orange, and intense red, the colour of blood.

Although it was still early in the season, he noticed the slender green shoots of onions and new growth on the tomato plants in the vegetable garden. Maria had regarded the vegetables as her private preserve. Morris tilled the soil, hoed between the rows, and cared for eggplants, which Maria always called *aubergines,* their French name, and okra, the latter indispensable for soups and stews. What he and Kate could not use, they gave to neighbours. He composted the rest. After Maria's death, he had reduced the vegetable patch by a third, reserving a section for his carefully laid-out garden of poisonous plants. The monk's garden of poisonous plants, a section in the Jardin Botannique de Montréal, had fascinated and inspired him to create one.

Designed as a circle in the centre of the vegetable rectangle, it was subdivided into eight triangles, the two sides of each triangle edged by narrow brick pathways that met in a smaller circle at the centre, where he had placed a stone sundial. The curving base of the triangles on the circle's perimeter consisted of mounds of cushion spurge and little shrubs of purple flowering hyssop. In the eight sections he grew aconite, nightshade, wormwood, and other plants. Because of their size, datura plants were restricted to a patch just below the compost heap at the back of the garden where they spread their white trumpet-shaped flowers angelically over decay.

Sitting on the bench, he bit into and choked on a Granny Smith apple, spitting it out, finding it difficult to swallow when Mrs. Ferroux's death lay on his mind like the mould that in a damp season discoloured the leaves of his garden phlox and beebalm. From this perspective at the back of the yard, the deck and his white frame house rising above it seemed in perfect proportion to his elongated garden beds. Maria at first had expressed doubt about his landscaping plans. A lover of red roses, she had wanted trellises of them, perhaps a pergola lifting clouds of roses under which she could sit on a hot summer's day. Aside from dianthus and Maltese cross, Morris preferred not to incorporate too much red in the relatively small space of his yard. Instead, he planted pink Thérèse Bugnet and white iceberg roses, and a yellow climber over one of the rail fences inter-woven with purple clematis. Maria, delighted by their delicate beauty, forgave him.

The day after her cremation he ripped out the weigela bush and planted red climbing roses, which now spread over the pergola at the end of his yard with a profusion of blossoms and perfume. Every year on the anniversary of her death, before going on his memorial visit to the botanical gardens, he sat on the pergola bench and remembered talking about roses with Maria. Remembering Maria among the bushes of the rose garden or the subtle loveliness of the monastery garden kept him from lingering too long on the last year of her life, when the cancer had spread, and she'd wasted away in pain before his very eyes.

If not incorporated judiciously like his Japanese blood grass, which bordered a portion of the perennial grass garden, red flowers and plants could dominate and overwhelm in unpleasing ways. Unless one understood the dynamics of the colour and possessed the gift of creating a red border as he had seen in England, red jostled and seared, disturbed the eye and unsettled harmony. Anything approximating the colour of Mrs. Ferroux's blood, for instance, would violate the best-laid plans. When the police planned to call or visit, Morris didn't know, although it wouldn't take them long to verify his story about the morning visit at the nursery. Apprehensive as if guilty by association, Morris reasoned that he had nothing to fear. But who wanted police pounding on their door? What about Ingoldsby? He wished Kate had not run off in such a fury, had at least answered his calls. What a cool character, that Ingoldsby. Wasn't he also a suspect? Given the man's reputation, was it such a stretch to think him capable of worse deeds? Morris allowed himself to imagine that a man like Ingoldsby could easily have axed Mrs. Ferroux. The havarti cheese softened in the tightening of his fist. Morris could not eat it.

The phone rang. Kate, at last. Why hadn't he brought the cordless phone outside with him? He ran up the path and the four stairs leading to the top of the deck and jerked open the glass sliding door so it almost jolted out of its grooves. The deck led to a sitting room, where he liked to spend winter evenings by the fireplace, enjoying the look of his winter garden and watching the nuthatches, purple finches, blue jays, juncos, and woodpeckers flit about the feeders for black sunflower and niger seeds, and peck at the sacks of suet dangled from the trees. He tripped over a leather footstool, but regained his balance before reaching the phone.

"Hello ... hello?"

"Mr. Bunter? May I speak to Mr. Bunter, please."

"You got him."

"This is Margaret Vickery. I'm phoning about my gardens. I believe you garden for Loretta Ferroux, who has recommended you highly. I wonder if you have the time to stop by my place this week to discuss what I have in mind."

Morris considered himself a polite man, but he was not capable of disguising his disappointment. Fortunately, Margaret Vickery couldn't see his face hazily reflected in the glass door. His mouth stretched wide and tight, his left hand pulling at his hair.

"Mr. Bunter? Are you there?"

"Ah, no, I'm not."

And he hung up, hoping the queasiness in his stomach would not build and rise to his throat. Highly recommended by Mrs. Ferroux. Highly recommended by a murdered woman. Just the other day, she had lived, spoken, and recommended his gardening expertise to a friend or neighbour—he didn't know which. The phone rang again. He did not move to answer. It rang several times, then stopped. Morris sat on the brown leather swivel chair that matched the footstool, his favourite seat in the winter when he enjoyed not just the garden and birds but a video or two on the television, or his gardening magazines, or falling asleep after a satisfying meal while Kate did her homework upstairs. Of all places in the world, the place he inhabited he loved best. Perhaps his deep understanding of roots and soil prevented any desire to travel extensively, nothing more than a brief visit or two over the years, like his month-long trip with Maria to tour the gardens of England the year before she died. His home, his garden, the breeze rustling among his perennial grasses, this neighbourhood, his larger community, including the gardens of the wealthy who had created a private world of ease and privilege: they all provided definition and satisfied his need to locate himself on firm ground.

Through the steady application of routine and skill, he had acquired purpose and a deep sense of security. However wonderful and memorable the experience in England, returning home had been more wonderful, coming back to his simple home surrounded by what he loved best to do, dig deep, transform, and remain. Morris did not envy the travelling or nomadic life. Nothing he had seen, heard, or read about elsewhere had tempted him to regret how he lived. Like perennials, he did not thrive under constant change.

Perhaps from another point of view, his life was too narrow, extending not much farther than the length of his lot, however paradisaical it seemed. Now retired, the Coles down the road travelled extensively every year, regaling the neighbourhood with their descriptions of inns and roads, restaurants and villages in Italy or Thailand, or whatever the country of the year happened to be. Morris, if present, listened politely, and the glaze over his eyes notwithstanding, tried not to let his indifference show. It didn't seem possible that Mrs. Ferroux, in the midst of her new perennial garden behind an imposing manor, should have been murdered. If Mrs. Ferroux, why not someone else? Why not Kate? The phone rang again. He picked up the receiver.

"Dad?"

Fortunately, she would not see the relief in his eyes and think him silly for needless worry.

"Kate … listen … please come home, Kate … please … I really need to see you, please."

"I just phoned to say I'm on my way. Not to worry."

His breathing sounded like the susurration of breeze-blown grasses. He held the receiver close to his ear, drawing assurance from her voice.

"Please, Kate, please come home."

6

· · ·

EVEN MR. RUSKOW ATTENDED the service. Morris was surprised to see him but not surprised by Ruskow's gruff response to his greeting on the steps, more a clearing of the throat as if the man were about to cough out a clot of phlegm than to say hello as he removed his hat before entering the church. Not a popular man, Ruskow had a sagging face that had pulled the left side of his mouth down into a permanent scowl. He did not invite familiarity. People said he had retired early from the university because of a minor stroke. Morris didn't know, but he had always given Ruskow respect—no more than the professor's due.

Erected on one of the three secondary streets that ran north of Old Town's main thoroughfare, surrounded on two sides by a three-hundred-year-old cemetery (the oldest grave being that of a fur trader), the red-and-blue stained glass windows framed with oak, the ornamental bell in the single tower polished once a year, caged by fine wire mesh to keep pigeons and bats from nesting and defecating in the belfry, the fieldstone church was the spiritual home of the Protestants in the community. A more imposing Catholic church, a replica of Notre Dame in Paris, soared above a grove of skyrocket junipers and feathery larch trees on another secondary street. Very difficult to grow anything under their branches, but Morris had succeeded in blanketing the ground with, appropriately, bishop's hat. The Protestant garden facing the street, for which Morris was not responsible, ran to rockery and unobtrusive plants. Adherents of other denominations drove to Montreal or other suburbs to attend their places of worship.

He thought it fitting to attend the memorial service in honour of Mrs. Ferroux, whose body, undergoing a delayed autopsy, had still not been released by the authorities. Apparently when her remains were returned to her family, Morris had learned, Annick Ferroux planned to have a very private cremation. She had appeared at the church alone, her body wrapped in bands and shawls of black gauze and chiffon, her legs encased in black vinyl boots reaching above her knees, bright as polished coal and creaking when she walked. Over her spiky hair Annick had pinned a transparent black scarf, tied under the chin, her face rigid as an icon. Her head bowed as she entered through the church doors, Annick did not acknowledge Morris, who, for reasons he could not explain, had assumed the position of unofficial welcoming committee at the top of the stairs. He had wanted to express his sympathy to Annick, having already sent her a card with a note. She took two steps at a time, and two spears of hair ripped and poked through the side of her scarf. Morris withdrew his arm, extended in half-hearted support of Annick, to prevent her collapsing from grief, but she seemed too sturdy and hurried to require assistance.

After everyone arrived, or not later than eleven, when the service began, he would enter and seat himself in the church. The interiors of holy places depressed Morris and made breathing difficult, their sanctity squatting on his chest to prevent the lungs from swelling with air. Because he didn't understand religious ritual, he had married Maria in a Unitarian church in the city, which looked more like a community centre or conference hall than sacrosanct premises. Maria's brother was a member, and Maria had fallen away from the Orthodox Church, though she still preferred a religious ceremony of sorts. She had read a child's Bible to Kate, but neither one of them had been concerned about their daughter's religious beliefs.

She wasn't buried in the cemetery behind this church. She wasn't really buried at all, Maria, whose voice seemed to speak in the breeze as it blew through his gardens. Morris was startled by the tears in his eyes. A porcelain urn contained her ashes: blue willow design like Maria's favourite set of dishes, too delicate to withstand the rigours of winter, easily cracked by a hailstone, now kept on her double dresser in their bedroom. What her wishes in the matter were he didn't know, as she hadn't specified, and overtaken by nursing and sorrow, he had failed to ask, but Morris didn't believe Maria wanted a religious service over her coffin.

After a day at the funeral home where friends and family paid their respects, a brief gathering at his house where they ate her cookies, baked in preparation for approaching death when her strength permitted and stored in the freezer, he drove to a crematorium on the other side of the city. Kate stayed home with his friends. He sat alone as the casket slid into a dark opening and disappeared behind the curtains. He still remembered the music. That much he had provided. Maria adored the singing of Maria Callas, after whom, it pleased her to say, she had been named—a harmless, often-repeated, white lie. She had in fact been named after her grandmother. Morris had chosen three arias, which played repeatedly until he left the non-denominational chapel, trying very hard, and almost succeeding, not to imagine flames consuming the wasted flesh of his beloved. Wiping his eyes to the strains of "Casta Diva," perhaps Maria's favourite Callas aria, Morris stood in the aisle for a moment, staring at the heavy, opaque curtains, half expecting them to open at the beginning of a play and out would step his wife, the scintillating star. He had walked into the sun and the deadly landscape of the crematorium-cemetery (the effect of excessive pruning of trees and bushes, grass trimmed too short, and too many tedious chrysanthemums in clumps). Behind him Callas's pained and overwhelming voice sang Gluck's *"J'ai perdu mon Eurydice."*

Before she died he had slipped into their bed, for Maria wanted to die at home, and held the white and wasted body of his beloved, her flesh so attenuated, her bones so brittle that he was terrified of pressing her too closely. He had wanted to hold her tight, as if the pressure and heat of his body could somehow ward off pain and death. She died with his lips on her cold blue mouth. Grief had not driven him crazy, despite the rage in his heart. The sense of loss deepened as the years went by, until it became a kind of ethereal garden of sorrow with grey perennials untouched by sun or rain, and he tended to the nameless, unfamiliar plants like a ghostly gardener digging in memory, regret, and constant worry over his now motherless child.

Just the wind picking up; Morris had enough wit not to believe in ghostly voices whispering among the trees.

"How are you, Morris? A sad occasion."

Mr. and Mrs. Honniker both shook his hand. Adele Honniker was crying.

"I can't seem to stop. Poor Loretta. She didn't deserve this. I ask you, Morris, who's safe anymore?"

Dressed in a brown silk suit with a brooch of green and red stones shaped like a hummingbird sucking the nectar of a dicentra blossom, which reminded Morris of his own bleeding-heart bush in the shadow of his front porch, Mrs. Honniker held a hand-kerchief under her nose. A fine-looking woman of fifty or so, with flesh on her bones, pleasing to his eye; if she hadn't already been married … well, there was no point travelling down that road at this time.

"Terrible, just terrible. How could such a thing happen here, of all places?"

Morris shared Mrs. Honniker's feelings and confusion. He had no answer. Mr. Honniker, Morris suspected, had undergone plastic surgery more than once to hoist up the bags under his eyes and to tighten his jowls. He put his arm around his wife's shoulder.

"Now, now, Adele. What you can't understand, you've just got to accept. Isn't that right, Morris?"

No, Morris didn't think it was right, but never one to debate the larger questions of life, Morris thought it inappropriate to enter into a disagreement on the top of the church steps. The organ inside began a loud drone, a sound he hated. Mrs. Honniker blew her nose. Steve Honniker, tall and bullish in a three-piece suit, always made pronouncements in such a way as not to expect rebuttals. Perhaps, like so many of Morris's wealthy clients, money had convinced Honniker of the irrefutability of his opinions. Mrs. Honniker had a point, though, as Morris surveyed the one or two houses he could actually see across the heavily treed street. Spacious and expensive, the homes carried decades of family life and certainty, inhabited by people who went about their business producing wealth that trickled down and benefited an ordinary guy like him; how, indeed, could such a thing happen here, of all places? They weren't living in an impoverished community or a politically unstable part of the world where, Morris thought, such things, however shocking, did not surprise.

An usher emerged from the darkness of the church and motioned everyone inside. The service was about to begin. The minister mounted his pulpit. Morris had discouraged Kate from attending, fearing to show his distress in her presence, although, after her initial exclamation, Kate had seemed unaffected by the murder. He wasn't fooled. She tried to hide many of her feelings from her father, pretending to be more impervious than she really was, and Kate did have that Ingoldsby business on her mind. Morris was relieved not to see Ingoldsby here. Surely he wouldn't have had the gall to appear at the memorial service.

Mrs. Ferroux had attended this church, sometimes returning home to see Morris in her garden on a Sunday morning. Although she disapproved generally of working on Sundays, she did not disapprove of Morris's working for her on a holy day in the spring when the gardens most needed his professional attention. Sitting alone in the pew farthest from the altar, Morris held his hands between his knees, dreading the possibility of having to sing a hymn, and waited for the good minister to begin. Above the heads of the hundred or so participants, Morris perceived the orange tips of Annick's hair pushing up her transparent black kerchief.

Reverend Logan had been the minister here for as long as Morris could remember. He was now an old man with a dowager's hump and uncut grey hair sprouting out of his nostrils. His wife, who wore broad-brimmed hats like the Queen Mother's shadowing her face, droned out the organ chords. Morris had seen her feet, now pumping the pedals: surprisingly small in black Chinese slippers, as small as it was possible for the unbound feet of a grown woman to be. Muffled and monotonous, alternately spoken in French and English, the minister's words scarcely reached the back of the church. Logan's bilingual rhetoric failed to reach the intensity of fire and brimstone, so Morris wasn't expecting to hear anything significant or stirring. Besides, he had worked in this neighbourhood long enough to know that the wealthy did not like their views shaken. Sermons should mollify and confirm their convictions, not disturb composure and rattle nerves.

Coughing at the church door, which had been left open to allow air to enter the holy precinct—Morris was already beginning to breathe deeply and sweat—made him turn. Geraldine McCready entered the church, walking behind her husband's automated wheelchair. Morris nodded. He had been working on the McCready property for a few years now, not as frequently since Angus McCready had fallen sick with expensively lingering Lou Gehrig's disease. They lived in a Southern-plantation-style home near the Catholic church in Old Town. Morris had heard via the community grapevine that the police had in fact questioned the McCreadys. Not surprising. Mrs. Ferroux and Geraldine McCready were on the same board of some charity, the name of which Morris could never remember. Loretta Ferroux always did "good works," pumping, so the story went, a lot of her family's personal fortune into humanitarian organizations, much to her daughter's and—this Morris knew very well—her former husband's dismay.

Mrs. McCready wheeled the chair past Morris, then stopped two pews in front of him, the motor of the wheelchair humming while Geraldine slid onto a bench next to the Honnikers, leaving Angus wrapped in a Peruvian poncho in the aisle. She had had her hair styled, wavy and rich black—not a grey strand to be seen, Morris noted—and was attired in a silk-and-linen suit. Despite her husband's costly medications and fees for several specialists, she flew to a Club Med in the Caribbean every February, and at least once to Europe every year, by herself, hiring private-duty nurses to care for her husband. Morris had learned from the live-in charwoman who looked after the household, a talkative Filipino woman, that eight of the McCready's sixteen rooms had been closed to save on expenses. Geraldine McCready had already informed him that she would be hiring students to cut her grass, requiring his services less frequently, although the gardens were going to seed from inconsistent care. She still owed him money for past services. Two Dobermans, usually kept inside, growled whenever anyone approached their house, before hurling themselves against the door in a frenzy of barking. More playful than menacing, they followed him around like toddlers when he worked on the grounds. Mrs. Honniker whispered loudly enough for Geraldine to hear. "Terrible business. How are you, dear? You're looking well. Shocking. How's Angus? Who'd have thought? Poor Loretta. What's the world coming to? Doesn't it make you worry?" Steve Honniker seemed to be asking his wife to shut up and listen to the minister. She brushed off the hand tugging on her arm.

"Now let us sing dear Loretta Ferroux's favourite hymn, "A Mighty Fortress Is Our God.""

After the completion of the organ's introductory chords, the assembly raised their self-conscious and muted voices. Holding the hymn book open at the appropriate page, Morris mouthed the words. Geraldine McCready's fine soprano rose above the other voices. She used to be a member of a choral group in Montreal and performed solos at their benefit concerts in St. Joseph's Oratory. Without glancing at the words in the hymn book, she sang from memory, her voice so clear and penetrating in the stuffy confines of the church that the rest of the congregation stopped singing to let Mrs. McCready carry the burden of song.

Morris was so taken aback by the appearance of Sylvain Ferroux that he almost dropped his hymnal. Also a suspect, so the rumour went. He wondered why Sylvain wasn't in custody. Didn't the police arrest anyone these days? Did everyone get away with murder? And why, if the police had interrogated Ingoldsby, hadn't they detained him? Although Sylvain Ferroux glanced at Morris, the expression on his bearded face did not indicate recognition of the gardener. He proceeded directly past Angus McCready in the aisle, not acknowledging him either, to the pew where Annick stood, presumably pretending to sing like the rest of the mourners. Morris could see his back, covered by a trench coat that he did not remove. The divorce had not been pleasant, occupying the gossips of the town for two or three years while Sylvain and Loretta fought over property and its divisions in the courts. Morris remembered the day Maria died—he had not realized such horror and grief possible, understanding for the first time what it meant to be driven mad. Did Sylvain feel remotely like that now? Did Annick? Could they have fought so publicly with Loretta Ferroux while she was alive and now feel sincere remorse over her death?

The singing stopped. A woman Morris did not recognize walked up to the pulpit, turned to the assembly, and began speaking in French about Loretta Ferroux, her tireless and self-sacrificing energy, her love of life, her humour. Long, halting, florid, and mendacious, the eulogy described a person Morris didn't know. What wonderful people we all became once we died, our crimes and misdemeanours washed away in a river of crocodile tears. Wasn't a member of the family supposed to praise the departed as well? After the woman returned to her seat, Mrs. Logan began pumping the organ again. Reverend Logan stepped forward in a hesitant, hunched kind of way to speak to Annick and Sylvain at the front of the church.

Morris shuffled out of the pew, deciding to leave before he had to speak to anyone. Neither Annick nor Sylvain required his condolences. Despite the row of stained glass windows, the morning light did not penetrate the interior of the church. Some kind of indirect lighting around the altar, covered in white cloth, and not the thick red candles burning on top of tall brass candlesticks, brightened the front of the church. A giant teak cross loomed above the altar. No Christ figure nailed to the crossbeam. Dark wainscotting around the walls, tapestries hanging between the windows, and wooden beams interlaced with tracery arching overhead diminished the possibility of light, except for the daylight streaming in through the church door. His breathing difficult as if the last gasp of air in the church had been sucked in by the congregation, he stepped between the rockeries outside the church, letting the fresh air fill his lungs. What he felt, he couldn't rightly say. It was hard not to think about Maria, lost forever, and Kate, who could be if he weren't diligent and alert. He was truly sorry and saddened by Loretta Ferroux's death and still uneasy about the murder, as if the ground beneath his feet had softened to the consistency of bog. He had to be careful where he stepped or he'd sink, no helping hand extended.

In the parking lot, crowded with Mercedes and Lincolns, he found his truck, got in, started the engine, loosened his tie, and waited until he began breathing naturally. Through the windshield, he saw the Honnikers hover around Annick at the church door. Sylvain emerged, still wearing his trench coat. The day was quite warm, too hot for a coat. The church had begun to swelter and smell from too many bodies crowded together in airless space. Morris could almost see the heat rising like steam off the top of their heads. Having taken off his navy blue blazer, which did not quite match his brown dress slacks, he cringed in sweaty discomfort under his white shirt, sticking to the back of his seat. The church was so uncomfortable, almost to the point of physical pain, that he wanted to rip off his clothes and plunge into the nearest private pool.

Why wasn't a church catering to wealthy parishioners air conditioned? Rich people insisted on their comforts. In fact, a kidney-shaped pool inlaid with green and gold mosaics depicting mermaids and Neptune writhing on the bottom lay gleaming on the Vanderzine estate behind the graveyard. Cars began driving away. Checking his watch again, he remembered the work schedule for the afternoon. Kate had promised to be home early.

Yet the memorial service had not really provided closure for the event, if that had been its purpose. An old man in a surplice mumbling a few incomprehensible words in the flickering of candlelight, a hymn sung, a eulogy spoken, an organ wheezing music did not really offer solace. He pulled out of the parking lot, careful not to run anyone down. He would have to drive by the Ferroux property to reach home. Sorry for Mrs. Ferroux and somewhat wilting like a perennial wrenched out of its accustomed locale and suffering from transplant shock, Morris wanted his small but satisfying world restored to the familiar, safe place it used to be the morning before the axe struck.

7

. . .

KATE DIDN'T SHARE her father's superstitions, her word for his reservations. When Annick Ferroux phoned to inquire if he would finish the work on the shade garden begun by her mother, Morris had declined, citing a heavy schedule, previous commitments.

"Perhaps your daughter would be free. I understand she also gardens. Did I not see her there, not long ago?"

Kate was scouring the iron skillet when the phone rang. Morris had burned the western omelette but she ate it anyway, washing it down with two glasses of orange juice.

"I don't think Kate is free, either."

"Free for what, Dad?"

He held his hand over the receiver.

"It's Annick Ferroux. She wants me to finish Mrs. Ferroux's shade garden. Apparently spade and pruning shears, the plant roots themselves, are in the exact spot where she left them, I mean, when she ..."

"It's okay to go there now? The police don't object?"

"Apparently."

"Tell her I'll do it."

"You don't want to go there, Kate."

"Why not?"

"Because."

Which sounded lame to Morris. He didn't want to go himself, but how peculiar and pathetic he would look in Kate's eyes if he explained why. It was wrong to dig in the soil where human blood had been spilled. Despite his lack of religious convictions, the ground thus became sacrosanct. Morris didn't realize he believed this until Annick Ferroux, now planning to put the house up for sale and wanting the grounds and gardens maintained in the best possible shape for as long as it took to find a buyer, phoned and offered him the weekly maintenance contract at a larger than usual fee. To delve into the soil soaked by Mrs. Ferroux's blood, for the sake of a few plants and the sale of a house, her bleeding body always in mind—inconceivable. It wasn't possible. Erect a statue—that he would help to do. The shade garden should become the unfortunate woman's resting place and memorial. Nothing else. Annick was not asking him, however, to build a monument to her murdered mother.

"I'll have to check my schedule, Miss Ferroux."

"No you don't, Dad, I said I'll do it. I can use the extra money and I have the time."

Kate stood behind him while she wiped the skillet dry.

"You can't," he whispered.

"Why can't I?"

"Well … well … what about Ingoldsby? He still lives next door."

That should end her persistence. Why place herself in a potentially hazardous position? Her presence could be construed as deliberately provocative if she worked under Ingoldsby's nose in Mrs. Ferroux's garden. No telling what the man was capable of. Surely the professor was a likely suspect, although Morris knew that he lacked any concrete information confirming as much. Ingoldsby had not even been taken into custody. Although he had spoken to Ingoldsby a week before the murder (a fact he did not mention to Kate), Morris conflated the two days, eliminating the separation of time, confirming guilt solely on the basis of wishful thinking. But that didn't mean Ingoldsby hadn't actually committed the act. It was only a matter of time before the police gathered the necessary evidence to arrest the man.

"Didn't you say I shouldn't let him affect my life, let him have any kind of power over me? Besides, all that business is over and done with."

A statement that only reminded Morris how naive the young could be for all their internet sophistication and righteous superiority. No business was really over and done with, especially not the business of destroying a man's career. Released from his duties as a professor—fired, really—Ingoldsby had signed a contract agreeing not to set foot on the campus or to communicate with Kate, in exchange for an early, very early, retirement, at a substantial portion of his salary. For her part, Kate agreed not to publicize the matter or seek legal redress. Morris thought the settlement unfair and too generous. Abuse a student and receive a permanent holiday at half salary. Castration had not been considered, he was sorry to say. Nothing prevented Ingoldsby from finding another job to increase his income. And the university administration, thanks to Kate's courage, got rid of an embarrassing nuisance. Like cats, some university teachers landed on their feet on ground where ordinary mortals perished. Morris did not believe for a moment that Ingoldsby gracefully accepted the consequences of his actions.

Kate was right in one way. The young often possessed the annoying ability to recover from injuries and calamities more quickly than the old. She was ready to move on and out of the university fracas. Morris was surprised that she didn't mind working in Mrs. Ferroux's garden, even after he had more than once described what he had witnessed. Nor did proximity to

Ingoldsby seem to be an issue. Going against his own best instincts and wanting to avoid a squabble, he relented.

"Kate is free to do it, Miss Ferroux. She'll be there tomorrow morning."

"Thanks, Dad. I really do need the extra cash."

"You won't mind digging in the soil where ..."

"You've got to get over things, Dad. Soil is soil. A plant is a plant. What's past is past."

Enough, already. His anxiety threatened to ruin the day, and her trite observations set his teeth on edge. A good gardener in a merely technical sense, regarding the activity more as a temporary job than a vocation, Kate still lacked the depth of perception and sense of time a real gardener needed, relying on the often quoted or the immediate to see her through the day. Well, perhaps therein lay the miracle of youth. Or a flaw in his character. Maria often said he was impatient with people who didn't share his views of life or gardening. She might have had a point, but life wasn't simple because Kate wanted it to be.

The next morning Morris drove his daughter to the Ferroux house, the sun unable to shine through the flat iron barrier of the sky. Windless and unnaturally hot, although not as hot as it promised to be later in the June afternoon, the thick atmosphere and dull light spread like mould on his spirits. The atmosphere sapped energy. More like the humid heft of August heat than June weather. If it brought rain, a prolonged, steady and gentle rainfall, not one whipped into a destructive frenzy by winds, the gardens would benefit. The green of the trees deepened against the dark morning sky, tinged with purple and reddish bronze like the leaves of bergenia in the late fall.

Down his street of bungalows and wartime houses, most of which had been covered in blue, creamy yellow, pink, or white aluminum siding, Morris drove four blocks south to the Riverside intersection—left to the university, right to the business section of town on the other end of which lay the older neighbourhood of wealthy, original families and the nouveaux riches. He switched on the radio to hear the news and traffic report. He rarely had occasion to take to the highway during the morning rush hour, and derived satisfaction from hearing about bumper-to-bumper lineups, delays on the bridges over the St. Lawrence, and bad weather in the winter making the drive very difficult. Many of the townspeople, those not employed by the new factories and warehouses in the industrial park to the north or in the business district of his community, worked in Montreal. Disdaining what they perceived of life in the suburbs, most of the university teachers lived in the city. A few like Ingoldsby resided either in the village or in their family homes in Old Town. Morris knew that Ingoldsby had inherited his property. Not even a professor could afford to buy the cheapest house in the Ferroux neighbourhood.

He looked at Kate, who was nodding her head and tapping her feet on the floorboard in rhythm with whatever music she was listening to through the headset, her Diskman on her lap. What a surprise, really, to be the father of an almost grown-up daughter, whose compact body and black hair reminded him so much of Maria. Kate had played soccer until last year, and swam regularly in the community pool, so the muscularity of her legs and shoulders was apparent. Her chin jutted out a bit, making her sometimes look aggressive and surly, even if she was really feeling uneasy or frightened or simply enjoying the pleasures of the moment. People read too much into faces, Maria used to say, and talked nonsense like astrologers, arrogance perceived in an eyebrow, passion in a nostril, or optimism in a flabby cheek. Maria had had no patience with fortune tellers in whatever guise. This, after Morris had once admired the flecks of burnished light in her brown eyes: eye drops, Maria had countered, to eliminate the redness caused by her allergy to tree pollen. If Kate, feeling confused and embarrassed, stuck her chin out in Ingoldsby's class, how had he interpreted that bit of body language?

Turning right, he could see the river on the other side of the boardwalk and park, which extended between the public boat launch and the senior citizens' residence. In summer, ancient, wrinkled men and women under hats and red-striped umbrellas, facing the river, slumped like sacks of laundry into the angles of white Muskoka chairs. As dark as the sky, the water looked solid, no light reflecting and sparkling off its surface. On his immediate right, he noticed the price of gas at the unfortunately located gas station, convenient but an eyesore, which had gone up a decade ago despite public outcry and petitions against it. Since then, the town's bylaws had been changed, preventing certain kinds of businesses and structures on the main thoroughfare; they did not, for example, have to tolerate the sleaze of strip joints or the stench of fast-food outlets. Neon signs did not flash *Danseuses nues* in his village. Of course, as the only gas station within a five-mile radius, it could charge a price usually higher than elsewhere, so the community paid for its exclusivity.

Traffic was light as people travelled east toward Montreal, and the stores had not yet opened. Mr. Ruskow was taking his morning constitutional, walking daily from one side of the town to the other before his breakfast. Morris waved, Ruskow tilted his head in return. He did not walk like a happy man, Morris thought. A delivery van idled in front of one of the restaurants, its parking lights flashing. Proceeding west along Riverside Road, or rue de la Rivière, the official French name, Morris passed the few restaurants, coffee shop, the touristy boutiques specializing in dried flowers, painted pots, exotic condiments, and hand-painted pasta bowls, Georges's hardware store, the post office, the pharmacy until the street curved to the north and passed between the public park on one side and the community pool on the other. Kate was a strong swimmer, winning silver and gold medals in the butterfly and backstroke competitions. Her fingers tapped her left knee and she began humming. Forgetting Maria's admonitions, he read strength of character in her shoulder muscles. Kate believed that she could look after herself, he was somewhat sorry to admit. When it came to the welfare of a beloved child, it was hard for a father to feel negligible. Morris refused to say *useless* as he shifted gears, but Kate's beliefs took second place to his anxiety.

About a half mile northwest of the community centre, Riverside Road veered to the left and entered what was locally known as Old Town, the preserve of ancient and new wealth and privileged families. The road then curved south toward the river and followed the banks until the water flowed into the Lake of the Whistling Woods, the Lac des Bois sifflants, although everyone simply called it Lac Bois. Morris glimpsed the motionless water of the river between the hefty stone facades, imposing iron gates, and obscuring bushes and trees of the lakeside estates. The stillness of the neighbourhood, its intense quiet, came from the imperturbability of well-being and sufficient money to buy anything, or buy out of anything. Except murder. A few Neighbourhood Watch posters in brilliant orange had been nailed to tree trunks. Morris was skeptical. Despite security systems, police surveillance (and their cars or vans had become more visible of late), Doberman, German shepherd, and Rottweiler guard dogs, and nosy neighbours, nothing really could prevent a psycho from committing mayhem. A neighbourhood so certain of its immunity inevitably became the ideal killing ground. If it weren't for Kate's insouciance and stubbornness, he had half a mind to turn around, forbid her to work here anymore.

He felt no fear for himself. The killer wasn't interested in male gardeners. Kate told him that Ingoldsby had flown to England almost immediately after the final deliberation and judgment of the harassment committee. If he had permission to leave the country, the police apparently had removed him from their list of suspects. Morris couldn't decide if that brought more comfort or more pain. His daughter at least wouldn't have to worry about Ingoldsby next door, possibly annoying her, if not worse (for he had not entirely accepted the police view that Ingoldsby was clear of suspicion). With the Ferroux house empty, though, Kate would in fact be alone for a few hours in the garden of a woman whose murderer remained at large. Would he return to the site of the crime, or had he already done so when yellow police tape criss-crossed the property? Why his daughter didn't see the sense in his concerns and opposition, Morris didn't understand, except she was as stubborn as … well, not as his wife—himself, really. "You're the stubborn one," Maria said more than once during their occasional arguments. What he wouldn't give to hear Maria's voice raised in protest over some minor disagreement. He really shouldn't cloud Kate's youthful optimism with his doubts. She'd stick out her chin and laugh, making him feel both old and silly. After all, Annick Ferroux was putting the house up for sale. Potential buyers would view the property, and someone would eventually move in and restore everything to normality.

He stopped on the road in front of the Ferroux house, surprised by the throbbing of veins in his temples and the moistness of his palms. The Ingoldsby house seemed to shrink behind its parasitic vines. The bushes need shearing, big time. He'd love to take a hacksaw and loppers to that landscape, imagining Ingoldsby unaccountably entangled in the branches and victim of a pruning blade. If the horror movies contained any truth at all, however, it sometimes happened that each piece of a butchered monster gave birth to more monstrosity, divisions guaranteeing procreation.

"What time are you picking me up, Dad?"

"Let's see. I have to talk with the Honnikers this morning and do some work there. I'll only be down the road a way. Say, eleven? Eleven o'clock, then. It's no more than a ten- or fifteen-minute walk from here, if you finish early and don't want to wait. You sure you don't mind?" He hoped his quiet desperation didn't show.

"Mind what?"

She had already opened the door and shifted her body to get out. Yes, of course his daughter would be just fine. Wishing for her well-being meant infallible protection, just as telling her to be careful whenever she went out guaranteed safety, as if his words possessed magical properties. If he failed to say them, horror would burst into their lives like a bomb exploding on a bus. Too old to control, too young to know any better, Kate now made her own decisions; what could he do? Kate didn't hear worry and regret in his voice. If she did, her father's fears did not influence her decisions.

Then she reached across the seat and kissed him on the cheek.

"Thanks, Dad. See you later."

One more glance at the Ingoldsby house, windows small and dark, designed to keep out the light, half covered anyway by the inexorable vines, and Morris assured himself no one was home. Of course Kate had to be safe. The worst that could happen today was a heavy downpour, possibly hailstones causing frightful damage. He thought of lupins beaten to the ground, and his vegetable seedlings bombarded and crushed. Unless the garden shed was locked, Kate would get soaked. There was no protective covering in the back of the Ferroux house, the patio open to the skies, although the garden shed provided shelter. He could always drive back in a matter of minutes to rescue his daughter from a deluge. A stocky girl in cut-off jeans and dirty running shoes, Kate sauntered up the driveway. When she disappeared behind the house, he pulled away as slowly as it was possible to go without stalling the engine, always checking over his right shoulder until he could no longer see the Ingoldsby property.

Her father fussed too much, sometimes getting on her nerves. Kate tried to laugh off Morris's concern as she dug into the soil of Mrs. Ferroux's shade garden. Having completed their intensive investigation of the scene of the crime a week ago, the police had removed the yellow tape, and presumably the murder weapon, but left the gardening tools, sack of manure, and the nursery plants where Mrs. Ferroux had last placed them. Since the murder, it had rained two or three times, so perhaps the roots had received enough moisture. Anyway, she had learned from her father that as long as some of the original root stock remained alive, new roots would develop in the ground and the plant would grow. The sky was heavy with grey humidity and windless expectation of a rainstorm to come later in the afternoon, but she would have completed her task before the storm broke. Her father would pick her up at eleven if she didn't walk to the Honniker place first.

If she didn't know that Ingoldsby was supposed to be in England at the moment, Kate would not have accepted the job. She certainly didn't want to let her father see her hesitation even for a moment when Annick Ferroux telephoned. Plugging her ears in the truck with the headset, listening to music, and staring straight ahead all the way here gave her the look of insouciance she wanted—a word she had learned last year and found very useful. Not that she was worried for the same reason as her father. Didn't he sometimes mix blood meal with the soil before planting? Blood meal, blood, dead animals, or a person: it was all the same thing as far as gardening was concerned, the roots sucking up nourishment from rot. Nothing that could hurt her, but tell that to her father, who believed he could understand people by their plants. Morris being so bitten with anxiety, she didn't want him to explode in a major fit over the Ingoldsby incident. The look of insouciance, brushing problems off like insects, not giving them any obvious attention, helped to calm her father down.

After placing the astilbe in Mrs. Ferroux's original quincunx arrangement, she looked for the garden hose or watering can. Astilbe were heavy feeders (she had dumped manure into each hole) and drinkers, thriving next to shady ponds. Attached to a faucet protruding from the west side of the shed, the hose when not in use was coiled on the side opposite the door. Mrs. Ferroux also owned a collection of watering cans, many of which had rusted over decades to the point of leakage, now kept on three shelves in the shed. At least two were serviceable because Kate had herself used one in early June when she last worked in this garden. The door was in fact locked, so the gardening tools and wheelbarrow would have to remain outside, but the hose was handy.

The noise Kate heard, a kind of sharp sliding of wood on wood like a window raised abruptly, made her point the hose over the fence toward Ingoldsby's house. It could well have been the first distant crack of thunder. Turning on the tap, she dragged the hose to the shade garden, water spraying the pathway. She reduced the pressure of the spray and filled the holes with water, letting it soak deeply into the soil, then added more water until the dried roots appeared to soften and change colour before her eyes. Kneeling, she pushed compost and soil into the hole, getting her hands mucky. Dad always said to wear gloves, but she found them a nuisance. Anyway, she had forgotten to bring a pair and didn't see any lying around Mrs. Ferroux's garden. Wet the ground around the base of the plant before covering it with mulch. Dad was forever telling her how to do things. Heavy drinkers, astilbe did not drown; they grew splendidly in wet terrain, only desiring some protection from the desiccating sun.

One thing for sure, although Kate loved flowers as much as her father, she didn't wish to become a professional gardener or landscape architect, as her father often hoped in his more fanciful moods when it came to her future and career. Travel first, work later. There remained the possibility of postgraduate study in a foreign country. Or work at various jobs to earn money to travel, then come back and decide what to do for the rest of her life. Perhaps go to England to see the Brontë house in Yorkshire. She liked *Jane Eyre* better than *Wuthering Heights*. Heathcliff struck her as both a boor and a bore. Kate didn't see the devilish attraction one whit. As if stung by a bee, she straightened her back and felt the hairs of her neck frizz. She looked at the house. Lovely, dead and silent stone. A few birds flitted in the trees. She brushed the back of her neck with her dirty left hand, stood up, and glanced above the Ferroux house where the sky had darkened to purplish black. The rain would fall sooner than later. Thunder or lightning hadn't made the sound: too quiet, containing the implications of sound, like the quietness that comes from the failed effort not to be heard. Not a chipmunk or squirrel or cat in the perennial garden or under the bushes, no car passing in front of the house, no horde of racing cyclists who sometimes whisked down the street. The sound was much closer, like slippered feet on dry grass, a stifled cough over the fence. Kate turned and dropped the trowel from her right hand.

Donald Ingoldsby had crossed his arms over the top of the cedar fence, his Vandyke resting like a bird's nest on his purple shirt sleeves.

"Well, well, look who it is."

Kate stepped back into the shade, sinking into the wet soil of the newly planted bed, the spot where blood had flowed from Mrs. Ferroux's head. Her legs trembled on the ground where the woman had been murdered. Her father didn't think it right to dig in the soil; she hadn't agreed, except now that Ingoldsby sneered over the fence, his shoulders and arms making movements toward her, she was beginning to understand her father's apprehension. She remembered how her body jolted when his hand had slipped between her legs. The same streak of shock jolted through her body now. Then to exact revenge because she had rejected his advances, he began verbally humiliating her in class. If words were knives, Ingoldsby's words in the classroom had cut and slashed until they drew blood. Oh no, he couldn't have left the matter alone, forgotten that he had acted the jackass in his office. Annoyed by her evident distaste over his sexual advance, he launched into a ten-minute spiel of withering verbal abuse because she had been daydreaming and failed to answer a question about an Ingres *Odalisque*. After she had walked right up to him in front of the class and proclaimed that he had no right to speak to her that way, why need she fear his words now? How black the sky over the professor's head, which looked as if it wanted to detach itself from his shoulders and fly right into her face with its hairy smile. No light in the sky at all, black with silence and unfallen storm. She could walk right out of there without so much as speaking to Ingoldsby. Stay away from him had been the general advice, something Kate had little difficulty following. Trying to raise a leg, she felt it pulled back to the ground, grabbed by the unseen hand of gravity. Ingoldsby wouldn't dare climb the fence. He wasn't supposed to speak to her under any circumstances. The contract so stipulated. The contract provided protection, the agreement between the university and Ingoldsby, although Kate hadn't been there when he signed in the presence of the academic dean, the faculty representative, and two other witnesses.

"Kate?"

Ingoldsby's head sank below the top of the fence. Morris called his daughter again. She heard her father say something about the storm. He was worried, so he'd come to fetch her. Then he was standing above the spot where Mrs. Ferroux had fallen, above Kate herself, fallen to her own knees, pretending to dig in the soil, but thankful she hadn't collapsed from fear and glad that her father had come back early to take her home.

It was better not to say anything about Ingoldsby. She didn't want Morris to think she had been frightened. No telling what he would do, and, after all, Ingoldsby vanished as quickly as he appeared. Try as she might, she couldn't conjure up that expression of insouciance. If she bent her head any lower to hide her worry, surely only passing and momentary, Kate imagined it would fall off like a head into the basket after decapitation. Ingoldsby had broken faith—the contract meant nothing. The desire to tell on him the way a child would run screaming to her mother conflicted with the need to stand—in this instance "kneel"—on her own ground. What would Momma have done?

"Are you finished here? You need a hand? I don't like being here. I don't understand how it doesn't bother you—I keep thinking of that poor woman."

"Let me just tidy up the mulch where I accidentally stepped."

"I'll put the hose back. It looks like the storm's going to break any minute now."

While he rewound the hose, Kate looked up at Ingoldsby's windows. The curtains of one parted, and the professor's shadowy arm waved to her behind the glass.

8
. . .

FOUR DAYS OF STEADY RAIN prevented Morris from tending to the gardens of his clients or hoeing in his vegetable patch. Environment Quebec had issued a severe weather warning. The river had risen, its dirty waters flooding the park and some of the basements along the waterfront. From the back window he could see the ornamental grasses, bent and straggly from the deluge but likely to recover and straighten up in the sun. The stiff blue fescue seemed most resistant to pressures from heaven. Earth and water intermingled so deeply that the foot sank, failing to find solid ground. The softball game had been cancelled, rescheduled for next Tuesday night. He played shortstop, sometimes pitcher, the team composed of men and women of the town who got together once a week, weather permitting, and divided themselves into two opposing teams. They played on a field behind a drug company in the industrial park, a five-minute drive from the nearest rib-and-steak house. Whichever team lost the game paid for barbecued ribs and beer. For two weeks after Mrs. Ferroux's death, Morris had not played and was sorry to miss the game this week because of the rain.

Content to stay home one day, Kate said something about going crazy on the fourth if she didn't go out. After talking for several hours on the telephone or chatting via the internet on her computer, she announced her intention of spending most of today with friends. He would have thought she had exhausted every conceivable topic of conversation. Sometimes he wished he hadn't installed the computer in her room. Absolutely indispensable for school, she insisted. It cost him more than his budget could handle at the time, and six months of payments remained. Kate had been thrilled when he presented her with a fully loaded hard drive and a seventeen-inch monitor, giving him a big thank-you embrace. She had in fact used it for academic purposes. Hang the expense— what made Kate smile and hug him was worth every penny. Now she spent more time downloading what she called alternative music than searching school-related websites. Her music was clanging trash cans and howling cats, if anyone asked his opinion, which she played too loud. More than once he had asked her to turn it down. Kate wasn't usually so thoughtless, but these past few days her voice sounded strained, as though her throat was inflamed and it pained her to talk when she troubled herself to speak at all. After the second day of ceaseless rain, she ate sand- wiches alone in her room, downloading more music. The third day Morris had been tempted to unplug the computer. No matter how smart the machine, he still controlled the juice. Some areas of Montreal suffered from power outages caused by branches twisted off the trees by furiously whirling and pelting wind.

"What are you planning to do?"

"Just hang around with Lizzie and Tarun, take in a movie, maybe drive to town."

"Drive?"

"Yes, Dad, drive, you know, like in a car?"

"Who's driving?"

"Tarun has a licence, I told you, and his own car."

He had at least met Tarun, who wore Doc Marten boots and drove a rusted safety hazard of a car with rattling fenders and explosive exhaust. Deferential and quiet-voiced, despite the boots that appeared oversized and too heavy for his skinny legs, with black wavy hair and skin like dark honey, he didn't often look Morris in the eye. What were his intentions toward Kate? She had been seeing too much of Tarun lately. Many boyfriends Morris could abide; one exclusive relationship worried him, made him think of things he preferred not to think about.

"But it's raining pretty hard."

"The car has a roof, Dad."

It was so cozy and safe inside their home with the lamps on, and he thought, if she had a mind to, they could play Scrabble. Kate was a whiz at Scrabble, now able to match or beat him without so much as consulting the official dictionary. He had played during many a winter night with Maria, who insisted on using French and Greek words. She had memorized all the peculiar two-letter words, as well as the English words for the Hebrew alphabet, which gave her a distinct advantage. And Nancy, who lived down the street with her two adolescent sons, promised to come over later in the afternoon and teach him something about Cajun cooking. She worked as a nurse's aid in a Montreal hospital while taking courses at night school toward a nursing degree.

Morris admired the fullness of her thighs. Her soft fleshiness reminded him of Maria. Impressed by Morris's gardens, she asked his advice about what to do with the scruffy, treeless yard behind her five-room house with the poor plumbing and rotting window frames. Her mate and father of the boys had deserted his family and disappeared altogether from their lives. She had cut and styled her long red hair, which used to hang down her back like a horse's tail. Quite a smart-looking woman now.

"I invited Nancy for supper. You like Nancy."

"Sure, she's all right, but I need to get out of the house."

He looked out the front window. Water sluiced down the street like fast-flowing streams. A speeding car could hydroplane and veer into a crash against a hydro pole. Trees bucked and lunged under the wind that drove the rain hard against the glass. Did Tarun drive too fast, ignore road conditions? Roads were slick, visibility poor, thunder and lightning possibly as a new front approached. Already Kate had dressed to go out, wearing capri pants, a glossy green, the hue of which he had never encountered in a garden, and a white-sequined tank top that fitted her a bit too snugly. She needed a sweater, a loose-fitting sweater. Although mild, the temperature would drop later in the evening to an unseasonable level. If she agreed to stay home, he'd switch on the electric heat to remove the dampness, or try to light a fire in the fireplace. Nancy would show them her recipe, using the red peppers and frozen shrimp he had bought, and they'd have a really nice supper together while the world went wild outside. If the electricity failed, cheerful company in candlelight would ease the tensions of confinement.

"I think you should stay home, Kate. The weather's pretty bad. A severe weather warning has been issued."

"Even if I wanted to, *which I don't*"—and the heightened tone in her voice indicated she wasn't about to change her mind—"I've already promised. Tarun's coming to pick me up."

"In his car?"

"No, Dad, we're taking his horse."

"Not a very safe car."

"Of course it's safe. How would you know anyway?"

Cars skidded on slick roads, but he refrained from speaking. She opened the refrigerator door and stood looking at the contents, bending once or twice to the lower shelf.

"There's never anything to eat around here."

Which wasn't true. Morris prided himself on a well-stocked pantry and a refrigerator filled with everything he needed to concoct a balanced meal. Seeking instant gratification and a bit too prone to snacking on fast foods, Kate had lost patience with shopping and cooking since her mother's death. What a treat it used to be for her to go shopping with Maria, driving to the Jean Talon market where her mother lingered long over stalls laden with fruits and vegetables, talking with the farmers and merchants, fingering the glistening, firm *aubergines* that she needed for her *moussaka*. Or she wandered supermarket aisles like an explorer, always returning home with a box of sugar-coated corn pops, her face smiling with satisfaction. If he didn't prepare the meals, he shuddered to think how and what Kate would eat. At least she washed the dishes, so he couldn't complain. Now, this Tarun fellow … What kind of guy was he, really? What lay beneath that air of courtesy? Could he be trusted? How skilled was he with a hydroplaning car?

"Tell me about Tarun."

"What's to tell? He's just a guy."

"That's what worries me."

"You worry too much, Dad."

"Is it a wonder when you think about what's happening in the world?"

"Yeah, well, it's not happening to me. So relax."

"Anyone else going with you?"

"I told you, Lizzie's coming."

Thunder rattled the windows, then the street glowed in quick, successive flashes of eerie white from explosions of sheet lightning. The lamp lights flickered. An island-wide power outage was inevitable. Why didn't Kate allow for nature's ferocity and adjust her plans accordingly?

"I really wish you wouldn't go out, Kate. You can see how bad the weather is. It's too dangerous."

"The danger only exists in your own mind, Dad. I mean, really!"

Well, no, the danger did not exist only in his mind. The storm existed outside it: the branches broken off the trees were tangible, the thunder and lightning audible and visible, streets disappeared under the deluge, basements flooded, riverbanks overflowed, no doubt cats and dogs drowned for all he knew, people, too, and the fact that he could no longer see past his front porch. All these were demonstrable proof that real and present danger existed outside his own imaginings. Fortunately, Nancy lived within a brief walking distance. He should call and ask if she would like him to meet and escort her to his house. He didn't want to be insistent or sound crazy or paranoid, but why invite misfortune when Kate could stay home and wait the storm out?

"I'd like you to call this Tarun guy and cancel. I'm sure he'll understand."

"Why do you call him 'this Tarun guy' like he's some kind of jerk? You don't really know what he's like at all."

"That's precisely my point, young lady."

Oh boy, whenever he said "young lady," Morris knew the conversation had reached the danger point. He was now talking down to a bad child who needed reprimanding. Kate reared up against the tone in his voice. She would bolt from the house if he pushed his paternal authority, whatever remained of it, too hard. There did come a time, though, when common sense fell before the onslaught of rasping nerves and scarcely repressed panic. He had been trying very hard not to fight, ignoring the music as best as he could, letting her monopolize the television, even forgiving Kate for quitting her part-time job at the department store in the mall. She didn't need to work that much; hell, it was summer, and she helped a lot with his gardening, for which he paid her a fair wage. But she could at least have discussed it with him before deciding to chuck the extra money earned at the department store. She was spending too much time with Tarun, who, for all the manners and soft-spoken voice, could be leading his daughter down the proverbial garden path. What kind of guy was he anyway that he'd risk his own girlfriend's life in weather like this? His parents, Morris knew, both doctors from India, participated in religious rites at their temple in Montreal, but their faith did not guarantee Tarun's character. Or his ability to drive in a storm.

"Well, I'm going out and that's that."

She leaped up the stairs and Morris bounded after, just in time to prevent the door from shutting. Kate sat in front of the vanity and attacked her hair with Maria's silver-backed brush, part of the expensive set he had given his wife one Christmas many years ago.

"Do you mind? This is my room."

"Your room? I pay the bills and this is my house."

God, there it was! He couldn't believe he had stooped to that stupid comment. When losing a battle—not a battle, they didn't really fight, but an argument, a disagreement—a father could always resort to a kind of financial blackmail, proprietorship. Morris hated sounding like so many other parents on the baseball team he heard complaining about their teenage children. Kate turned, and he stepped away from the threshold, startled by her fiercely determined eyes. Morris regretted every word the moment he spoke it, but damn it, he wasn't being at all unreasonable as he heard thunder and the lamp lights flickered again.

"Fine, you can have your fucking room when I move out."

She slammed the brush down on top of the hand mirror. Don't break it, Morris wanted to shout, it belonged to Maria. The mirror did not crack. Move out? Kate was planning to move out? And the language! Where had she learned to speak that way? Her boyfriend, no doubt. Her fucking boyfriend, his religious parents notwithstanding, probably used the word ten times in every incomplete sentence he uttered. What happened? How had he reached this point that his daughter wanted to move out in a fit of rage and swore in front of her father? What the hell had he done that was so terrible? Just rain. Four days of rain. But a severe weather warning and flooded streets and fallen branches dragging down hydro wires! Bad music and no gardening. Enough to drive anyone crazy. Nancy would set it right. She had a way of talking with young people. Her sons, not much younger than Kate, seemed to be happy, although they did precious little around the house to help their mother, as far as Morris could tell. Nancy never criticized her children. He gave the woman credit for tolerance.

"What the hell are you talking about? Moving out? I don't want you to move out."

"You don't want me to do anything."

"That's not true, Kate, and you know it. I only want what's best for you."

There he went again. Get a grip and try not to sound like a television dad. Too many parents said that when they really meant they wanted kids to do exactly what they were told without question: instant obedience. Morris heard the sound of his own voice. His throat tightened to prevent other, more harmful, words from escaping. Once in a whirlpool, it was difficult not to be sucked down and lost forever. Still, he was right. Deep in his bones, he knew more about the dangers of life, the risks of travelling in a storm, the ulterior motives of boys crazy with lust, their stupid driving habits. Why would Tarun be any different from any other hormone-driven prick? Morris knew what the boy really wanted. Was he a good driver? Did he carry a kirpan? No, Tarun wasn't Sikh, what a pity; if he was he wouldn't flash the knife. But there was such a thing as a switchblade. Take a breath. Kate was right. Relax before panic knocked him entirely off balance. Take a deep breath. Just pause, inhale, relax, try to correct imbalances and restore proper relations. Step off the threshold so Kate could pass without feeling he would physically bar the way.

"Are you going to let me pass or what?"

A car honked repeatedly outside.

"Kate, I'm worried. Take a moment to think about it. You must try to understand."

"Tarun's waiting for me, Dad."

"I can hear the horn. He has a problem walking to the door and ringing the bell?"

"What? So you can slam the door in his face?"

"Kate, I have no intention …"

His arm was braced against the door frame, blocking her exit, which wasn't his conscious intention. He wanted to reason with his daughter. She pushed it away. He couldn't let her leave in this state. Love, not anger, impelled him to grab her wrist, pulling her back. Kate howled, sounding like one of the alternative singers she downloaded from the internet. Distracted by the fierce and sudden flicker of the lights, followed instantly by a total blackout to the sound of a thundering explosion, Morris didn't see the other arm with silver bangles on the wrist. But he felt the smack of a hand right across the left side of his face and the bridge of his nose, the bangles smarting against his eyeball, causing tears to spurt out of the ducts, blurring his vision. For a moment he didn't recognize Kate, her face smeary and deformed in the reflected flash of lightning, her voice so enraged and beyond conciliation.

"Leave me the fuck alone!"

Morris backed against the wall for support, covering his face. He didn't want to see his daughter. If he looked, what would prevent him from striking back, from physically restraining her? Nor did he want Kate to see the bloodless dismay and disappointment on his face. She raced down the stairs and out of the house. The door resounded, the house shuddered. Tarun revved the engine, squealed out of neutral, the tires skidding on the watery pavement. The car sounded like a motorboat shooting away from the dock. Caressing his cheek, Morris slid all the way down the wall, his bones softening, his heart coming to a standstill. The landing was dark, but lightning brightened the living room momentarily. If the electricity failed, how would Nancy cook the supper? Maybe he should call and ask for a rain check. Pain licked at the back of his eye, and his cheek burned like an ungloved hand inadvertently grasping stinging nettles. Tears fell, although Morris didn't feel that he was actually crying. He sniffed, thinking blood was beginning to flow down his nostrils. She had struck hard. Kate was not weak. The rain pounded the roof like a barrage of steel pellets, overflowing the barrels he had placed at the bottom of two drain spouts.

Strange, how the house sometimes shook to the clap and rolling of thunder as if a train had rumbled right past the front yard. Every sigh and sound of the dwelling he knew like symptoms in his own body. Still pressing against the wall, he raised himself, unsure of his strength, winded by the effort. Undecided about Nancy, he thought a cold compress would help what he knew was going to be bruising and swelling. In the darkness, the storm provided intermittent moments of light as Morris felt his way toward his bedroom, leaning against the wall to keep himself upright.

He would call Nancy from the phone on his night table. In his bedroom, the curtains also drawn open, the funeral urn with its Chinese lady on a high-arched bridge between drooping willow trees, their glossy blue highlighted by the flashes of light shooting through the window, glowed like an opaque lamp. A woman meeting her forbidden lover? Maria had known the story behind the pattern. Just the pain, just the automatic reflex of the tear ducts, the inevitable physical response to a blow on the eye. If he had someone to talk through this terrible eruption—terrible, he could think of no other word, terrible, terrible; it amazed him to be caught in such a terrible time—then the pain would perhaps subside. There was Nancy at the other end of the phone line. She liked Kate but she didn't know her all that well, and he didn't want to complain about his daughter to a woman who had nothing but praise for her sons.

A compress against his eye, yes, but first he needed to sit on the edge of the bed and catch his breath. Holding the urn on his lap consoled him. It was surprisingly warm for porcelain. Broken, out of tune, the melody, more a hum than a song, crept out of his mouth like incoherent whispers: *j'ai perdu mon Eurydice*. He rocked back and forth, raising the urn to his chest, and moaned as lightning burst wide, thunder rumbled, and the dark shapes of his room became strange and deformed to his eyes. The tallboy where he hung his shirts seemed to buckle and lurch, the dresser to shift on its casters. Just give him a few minutes, then he would call Nancy and cancel the supper. Wonderful woman, she would understand. No power, no supper, although he would have enjoyed her company. Holding the urn, he blushed to think of another woman now, not with the memory of Maria in his hands. How warm the urn of ashes against his cold, cold heart.

PART TWO

• • •

If plants (like humans) are well fed and full of vitality, they withstand diseases. Disease or pests may show themselves, but they do not get the upper hand.

Even in the worst cabbage butterfly years, when caterpillars reduced plants to skeletons, only a few scattered holes showed amongst the compost-grown brassica. One theory is that the marauders eat a little, and are satisfied, while with devitalized plants, they go on eating, seeking for something that is not there, *till they have destroyed the whole.*

—MAYE E. BRUCE, *COMMON-SENSE COMPOST MAKING*

9

. . .

Preposterous to maintain a house this large, but it had been their dream home. Perhaps the white Doric pillars holding up the extensive roof of the front porch lacked originality, and if the design reminded Geraldine McCready of Scarlett O'Hara's estate in *Gone with the Wind,* she forgave the architect's derivative imagination the moment she entered the central hall. Her eye detected an absence, though. So familiar was she with the arrangement of furnishings and artifacts that Geraldine instantly noticed the hedgehog boot scraper had been removed from its usual place on the porch. Heavy cast-iron body surmounted with a back of thick brown bristles, it had appealed to her sense of the homey and whimsical at a country auction near St-Louis-de-Gonzague. Imelda may have swept the porch and taken the scraper to wash out the dried bits of mud sticking to the brush. She remembered that Imelda had requested the day off to sign papers at the immigration bureau downtown.

The worries of the hour evaporated when Geraldine crossed her threshold. Spaciousness was not to be despised. The interior space eased the dark and closeted anxieties of her life, as well as eliciting gasps of admiration and envy from friends and acquaintances. Not that her house was necessarily more distinctive or imposing than other homes of Old Town, but the interior soared with light and air, the space defined, but not confined, by cameo blue walls and antique cream ceilings, wide-open double doorways, and translucent crystals of the chandelier massed like an avalanche of quartz and diamonds halted and mounded in mid-slide. Inside the homes of so many of her friends, interior decorators had worked their textures and designs to deadening effect. Like a visitor in a museum observing artifacts behind glass, one always felt on the outside of things, not daring to disarrange the collection. Her heels clicking on the ceramic tile as she approached the brass tray of mail on the Sheraton table under the mirror, sunlight travelling down the sweep of the staircase from the floor-to-ceiling window on the landing, Geraldine flipped through the notices, bills, and subscriptions. Odd, the dogs usually scuttled, yelping, to the door.

Outside in the yard with Imelda, then, who must have been home after all. What would she do without Imelda? A home this size required so much attention and unremitting physical labour, and the expense! Imelda's salary alone, not to mention the cost of maintaining the grounds! She could no longer afford Morris Bunter's gardening expertise. She would have to let the gardens go to seed and weed, and just keep the grass cut according to the town's bylaws. University students obliged once a week for relatively few dollars. But the larger, more complex work of managing the perennial beds and trimming the flowering bushes properly— no, she could no longer pay Morris to tend them. She still owed him a few hundred dollars for his work in the spring.

The heating bill last winter—how had she managed to pay that? And the second mortgage on the house? Her savings had disappeared, and their line of credit at the bank pushed beyond reason, she did not want to open the statement from the bank, nor what seemed to be yet another letter from the accounts manager. And the tuition fees! She couldn't cut the boys loose yet, with one or two years left of university; they were doing so well because she and Angus had insisted they concentrate exclusively on their studies and not worry about financing their education. After Angus returned home and rested from yet another gruelling, day-long round of hospital consultations, examinations, and treatments, she would discuss their position and possible solutions. A good soak in a warm bath would do wonders for her nerves, but so little time could be devoted to self-indulgence these days.

Despite her social philanthropy, Loretta Ferroux had shown little sympathy and no charity at all. What had that woman ever understood of the love that surpasseth understanding, of irrevocably plighting her troth, of what it meant to adhere to the sacred vow of better or worse when she had so blithely, it seemed to Geraldine, cast Sylvain off for nothing worse than a sexual peccadillo. If Loretta had even for a moment believed it possible to stoop to the very depths of degradation to save her beloved, then how could she even have considered calling the police? Geraldine didn't know what she hated more: having purloined funds from the charity, or having pleaded with Loretta to forebear, to understand the exorbitant and ruinous cost of Angus's condition. Loretta's adamant face of righteous indignation and moral superiority had tempted Geraldine to drive a letter opener through the woman's eye. Head of an organization that raised a million dollars annually for the well-being of the indigent and unfortunate, Loretta had turned her heart and mind against a friend and colleague in despair. So much for her love of humanity.

Approaching Loretta for a loan would have made matters worse as far as Geraldine could see. She would have been obligated, a recipient of Loretta's grace and favour, indistinguishable in her eyes from the people who received food baskets. Temporary theft was preferable to personal favour. The money would have been repaid in due course; she had only "borrowed" it (with every intention of returning the sum when finances improved). That said, she deserved some reward after working hard and faithfully for Loretta over the years, unloveable bitch that she was. To call the police. What a nightmarish day after she left the office, driving up and down and around the mountain and through the streets of Westmount, just to get away from Loretta's intransigent code of conduct. Her husband chronically sick; many of his investments unprofitable and bankrupting; medication sucking money out of their accounts; the boys' future imperilled; the horror of sudden poverty rushing up to her windshield as she drove south on Decarie to reach the highway. It was a wonder she had returned home without crashing the Mercedes. Loretta had given her a few days' grace, like the Lord granting divine mercy, and expected grovelling gratitude for that picayune favour. Geraldine dropped all the bills on the tray. The statement from the bank fell to the floor. In the nature of things, some problems solved themselves when events changed circumstances. Why think of Loretta anymore?

"Imelda? I'm home."

Not that she was glad that the woman had died—well, that wasn't true—she had been horrified and deliriously relieved at the same time when informed of the murder. Perhaps thoughts of murder had occurred to her, but she hadn't been able to visualize how to achieve it. Accident, chance, good fortune, whatever it was called, had fallen her way. Loretta's tower of moral rectitude had collapsed, unable to protect her from the massive assault. The least she, Geraldine, could do was attend the memorial service, surprised to see both Sylvain and Annick there, neither one of whom cared for Loretta. Annick's hair! It was all very well to walk around the streets with spikes poking out of her scalp like stalagmites rising from a cave floor, but, honestly, in a church service in memory of her murdered mother, surely Annick could have reduced the impact of her hair to a more conventional level. The point of memorial or funeral services was not to draw attention to oneself but to honour and grieve for the departed, regardless of one's beliefs or feelings. Appearances mattered more than convictions.

Geraldine was pleased that she had appeared very well indeed. The forms of human vanity and self-regard never ceased to amaze. The less people had to say for themselves, the more gyrations and convolutions they used to draw attention to their own insignificance. In the end, Loretta Ferroux was no better than the next person, possibly worse because she had thought herself superior. Geraldine didn't wish to be ungracious or unfeeling, but for all her good works and powers, Loretta nonetheless had it coming. You could only act superior for so long before someone brought you down. She tried not to derive petty satisfaction from the atrocity, which, admittedly, had shaken and frightened the community. How small we all are deep down inside, Geraldine often thought, how grasping after our own needs and desires, desiring attention and praise, saintliness notwithstanding. To be honest, how was she different in that regard from anyone else? Her designer wardrobe attracted as much notice as Annick's absurd hair and vampire clothes. Well, rumination on these matters often led to a sense of futility, and she had business to attend to. As for her wardrobe, for the sake of economy she would wear last year's fashions.

"Imelda?"

Where was that woman? She needed an early lunch today before driving back to the hospital to pick up Angus. So hopeful and weary he looked, bundled in the wheelchair, his body unable to follow the commands of his mind, tapping the back of her hand, courage and optimism mingled, she knew, with thoughts of suicide. The disease had ravaged and debilitated his entire nervous system—impossible to hide from the inevitable anymore. Never overweight, he had lost fifty pounds, his green eyes preternaturally beautiful, like a poet's, glowing with malady and despair. Not in the kitchen, its double-door steel refrigerator gleaming from Imelda's constant polishing. A costly dream of culinary architecture, the gourmet kitchen with shiny copper pans hanging from a great wheel above the island gas range elicited gasps of envious wonder more than it stimulated the appetite. When preparing a meal, Imelda, a tiny woman in starched uniform, seemed lost among the appliances and dishware. If not in the kitchen, she could well be hanging laundry outside, preferring sunlight to the European-style dryer in the spacious, bright laundry room off the kitchen.

Elevated above the grounds, the brick terrace extended the entire width of the house, wide steps leading down to the various gardens and gathering places. Morris had done a superb job with the initial design and later maintenance. So difficult to let him go. Creeping soapwort and euphorbia flanked the flagstone steps, directing one to the water garden, installed at considerable cost, something Morris had advised against, ponds being so prone to stagnation and scum, flies and frogs, if not properly pumped and maintained. He agreed that water was a desirable element of a great garden, but many a watery project began with enthusiasm and ended with regret. Not to mention the pergola on the west side of the pond. She didn't want a pathetic little thing but a convincing pond with water lilies and Siberian irises and water forever clear and trickling. Soothing to the nerves, a relief from trials and tribulations, as she sat in the shade of the pergola. Her pool of meditation, the heap of eulalia grass shading one of its corners, it induced calm reflection, the water a relaxation of her nerves. Why, there was Morris's daughter in a charming straw hat. A good idea, given today's especially searing sun.

"Oh, hello, Kate. I didn't expect to see you here."

Shorter than Geraldine and two steps below in the garden, Kate looked up from under her hat and smiled. A rather pretty girl, Geraldine thought, despite her squarish frame. Working with damp plants, Kate wore rubberized gardening gloves, floral-patterned, which fitted snugly on her hands. She was carrying a trug. The two Dobermans, Trounce and Midge, utterly useless as guard dogs, their ferocious barking at the door more pretense than real, knowing they had been trained to act a part in which they did not believe, sat on their haunches directly behind Kate, their tongues lolling out.

"Dad asked me to clear out the old iris leaves by the pond. Less prone to disease if the irises are kept clean. He said you wouldn't mind. He's also wondering if the reeds and lilies are getting too thick on the edge. They could choke the other plants. Would you like them thinned?"

"I'm sure I don't know. Does your father advise it?"

She couldn't very well tell Kate that Morris was fired, or about to be, in a manner of speaking, although Geraldine tried not to think in such harsh terms. Morris wasn't to blame for anything. Yet the consoling normality of Kate's going about her gardening business—such a pity to lose touch with the loveliness of ordinary tasks, even if she did pay someone else to perform them. Angus's illness, Loretta's murder, debts and worry, the horrors of the day: what had they to do with this young girl who wore a straw hat with a yellow ribbon and carried a perfectly charming trug filled with garden debris?

"He says it would be a good idea."

But she had to end this business with gardens and gardeners. Money had vanished. Scarcely enough to pay Imelda's salary next month, never mind what she already owed Morris Bunter. All this quiet, unobtrusive beauty of her backyard, acquired at great expense, would ultimately starve from lack of love and attention. The pool would stagnate, weeds run rampant, and perennials attenuate from overcrowding and lack of division. Perhaps it would be best to rip everything out and cover it with a green desert of lawn. Grass, being so functional, was cheaper to maintain. The dereliction of the gardens, though, was not her primary concern. If she had avoided disgrace and imprisonment by Loretta's death, she had not evaded financial collapse. What job could she find to help defray costs? What would pay at least a thousand a week clear, the very minimum, according to her rough calculation, to keep her current house and home over their heads? Property taxes alone reaching twelve thousand. Of course, people lived on less, but never having scaled the pinnacle of success, they had little idea of how painful the descent. She had quit her work as an insurance-claims clerk after the birth of her first child, deciding to stay home to raise him and the two boys who followed.

Angus's engineering career and his investments met all their expenses, before the layoffs and the devastation of his stocks in a market crash. Then the appalling diagnosis. Bad news tumbled on their heads by the ton. Now that he required constant attention, a private-duty nurse out of the question, Geraldine couldn't grasp how an inadequately paying job would help her situation. Angus needed her and she needed to help him, to stay by his side through the worst of it, not leave him alone so she could file papers in a downtown office for a pittance. Working for a few hundred dollars a week did not piece together a broken heart. If she did take a holiday once in a while—a simple trip to Europe with a friend or two?—placing Angus in the care of his brother, who had precious little to do now that he had taken an early retirement from his law firm on a very handsome income indeed, who was to blame her? James could do a hell of a lot more for Angus, if he wanted, which apparently he did not. Brotherly love did not cover debts. She just had to get away from it all or be swept away by wave after unending wave of creditors and responsibilities.

"Have you seen Imelda, my housekeeper, by any chance?"

"Maybe a half-hour ago. She told me she was going downtown on business and to let you know she expected to return before five."

"Thank you. Are you finished here for the day?"

"Yes, ma'am, I was just on my way. Dad's meeting me in the front at eleven."

"It's eleven now. Perhaps I should speak to him."

She did not move, not letting Kate pass on the steps. Wise girl to garden in the morning on a day like this. The heat promised to intensify in midafternoon. All that rain a few days ago had not lowered the temperatures. Humidity was beginning to rise again; she could feel it in the dampness behind her ears and around her neck. So lovely to sit in the honeysuckle shade of the pergola, "just like my own," Morris Bunter had said when he'd built it a few summers ago, so perfectly angled and situated that, unseen, she could sit and enjoy an unobstructed view of the pool, the steps leading up to the terrace, the glassy back of her house with the sheer, white draperies reducing the heat and glare of the sun in the kitchen and breakfast nook. Well, more spacious than a nook. Several feet long and five wide, the pergola was flanked by French lilac bushes, blossoms so royally purple, not the bleached mauve of the common lilac, so redolent with perfume that it positively made her swoon. It was impossible to think of losing all this. Why hadn't Loretta, possessed of wealth and loving gardens as much as Geraldine, understood?

"Mrs. McCready?"

Startled out of reverie, she looked down at the girl, thinking the hat a bit on the ragged side. Before relaxing in the pergola, she should probably change out of her Alfred Sung suit into shorts. Who was there to see an aging woman's cellulite thighs and varicose veins?

"I'll be leaving now. My dad's probably waiting."

"Yes, of course. You did a good job, my dear. Give my regards to your father, would you?"

Careful not to crush the saponaria or euphorbia, Geraldine stepped aside to let Kate pass. She would speak to Morris at a later date, when she had acquired the means to pay what she already owed before asking him not to return. For a time. When the situation improved and finances permitted, she would rehire Morris to restore the gardens. Clever, skilful man. Secure in her low pumps on the cracked and uneven flagstone steps, Geraldine caught the sun's light on the surface of her pond, reflecting the various and shifting hues of green plants, the puffy white of the clouds, and the ineffable blue of the sky. Graced by trimmed arctic willows and eulalia, astilbe, irises, and, in the shady stretches of the border, arching white flowers of the luxuriant cimicifuga, also forbiddingly named bugbane or snakeroot, two clumps of which Morris planted four years ago, much to her hesitation then and absolute delight now, the pond, her meditation pool as she liked to regard it, beckoned her to admire and tarry.

Nothing could be so terrible that calm reflection by the easeful currents of the pond did not offer escape, possibly hope. The suit was hot. The shade of the pergola would cool her down, if she only sat and emptied her mind while watching the light and colours shift on the surface of the pool. She was thinking of adding goldfish to the pool, somehow encouraging frogs and other amphibious creatures to take up residence. Except there was no point in adding life when money disappeared. Angus liked the gardens as much as she, although they were not wheelchair accessible at the moment. Some kind of ramp would have to be installed, leading down from the terrace. Oh, the expense of making life convenient.

The dogs must be scuffling behind the bushes, nosing in the undergrowth and lower branches. Of course, it was past the time of flowering, which was the one fact of lilacs she disliked. After flowering, they were rather unremarkable, but for a week or two of heavenly beauty, one forgave everything else. Fearsome-looking creatures, the dogs wouldn't harm a flea, nor would she want them to. It had been Angus's idea to buy the dogs for her protection. He did not have absolute faith in the electronic surveillance and alarm system. They must be nine or ten years old now. Angus had assumed the dogs were savage by nature. Kindliness had undermined ferocity, it would appear. Well, the safety of fleas didn't concern her.

"Trounce! Midge! Come here, boys."

Sitting on the bench and staring up toward the house, Geraldine noticed the shadow but assumed a cloud was passing over the sun. She really should wear her glasses all the time now. Morris had arrived to pick up his daughter and was taking the time to speak to her. He was holding out the hedgehog boot scraper. Why he would have it, Geraldine didn't know, but now seemed as good a time as any to inform him that his services would no longer be required. Delaying bad news served no purpose. As he entered the shade of the pergola, coming directly out of the sun, his features seemed momentarily shadowy. She squinted.

"Hello, Morris. I'm afraid I have some bad news."

The man did not return her greeting. Trounce and Midge appeared and, rather surprisingly, began growling. They loved Morris. They began leaping and barking when he moved suddenly forward, and she instinctively raised an arm. Before Geraldine spoke, the cast-iron body of the hedgehog struck the side of her head, knocking her off the bench.

10

. . .

WHEN THERE WERE TOO MANY DEMANDS for his services, her father hired university students to help him tend to the gardens. He didn't want her working on the Ferroux land anymore. Sometimes Kate thought her father didn't want her working for him at all, assigning duties to the new guys before giving his own daughter work to do. Perhaps she shouldn't have quit the department store, but if she had to assist one more harried and rude shopper fiddle with bras, shoes, or sweaters, she'd just go crazy and stuff a Cross Your Heart bra down the customer's throat. Not that Dad had gone completely silent since … well, Kate didn't want to mull over that scene. They still circled around each other in the house, afraid of touching, saying little more than pass the salt or we're out of milk. Weighted with shame, her head would not lift to allow her to look Morris in the face. He spoke in fragmented sentences, incomplete phrases, as if he was some kind of visitor from another planet who didn't have a real tongue or understand how language worked. All in all, moving out of the house was the solution. Life would be easier for Dad if she wasn't underfoot anymore, easier for her to live as she pleased without asking permission or defending her choices.

For the past week, Morris and the students were planting new trees, although he often told his clients—this time it was Mr. Ruskow who actually hired Dad to do the work—that it was better to plant trees earlier rather than later in the season, giving the roots time to stretch and settle in the new soil before the freeze of December. But people usually preferred their own ignorance to his knowledge, he said, especially when it came to gardening. God forbid that a mere labourer like him should know more about something than a professor like Mr. Ruskow. That was teachers for you, she overheard Morris saying to his student workers, instant experts on every conceivable subject. She thought of speaking up for Professor Ruskow, remembering how helpful he had been, a teacher who did not merely pretend to understand her position and complaints while supporting Ingoldsby all along. Ingoldsby used to mock Ruskow, once called him "a scholarly ape" with an "arthritic imagination." He accused Ruskow of mimicking other people's ideas whenever a student made the mistake of quoting him in class. Why she hadn't told Morris about Ruskow's kindness, Kate didn't know, except that it was an experience she wanted to separate from her father's worries and keep to herself. Ruskow had argued his point about the trees by scoffing and puffing his thin chest out like a budgie; her father smiled when he described the professor. Morris preferred not to argue with clients, especially former teachers.

"Nonsense, my man, I know a thing or two about trees and climate. If you don't want the job, others do."

Well, Ruskow paid a goodly sum for the task of planting what he called "a wilderness" of birches in the back half of his acre lot. Their roots wrapped in burlap-covered balls, each tree stood six to ten feet tall and required at least two people to handle, not to mention the digging and preparation of the grounds. For the other, less onerous, gardening tasks, Morris let Kate do as much as she wanted, mumbling one- or two-word instructions. The wealthy did not tolerate delays. Teachers were impatient. Like an interviewee trying to impress her potential boss, Kate had promised dedication to and completion of the required work. Even if it meant clearing the rotten leaves from the extensive patch of lamb's ear and trimming the grass on the Ferroux estate.

"No, absolutely not," Morris insisted at breakfast, which she had prepared that morning. Dad loved cranberries rolled inside crepes, topped with dollops of sour cream. They were talking about the schedule of gardening chores and what needed to be done. Maybe the crepes flipped out of the pan a little ragged and crisp around the edges, but he ate them anyway, kind enough not to notice, and thanked her for the breakfast in a tone that suggested Kate was more a waitress than his daughter—surprise that he didn't leave a tip—but she had cooked and he had eaten, which meant something.

"I can do the work."

"I don't want you on the Ferroux place, and you know why."

She noticed that Morris seemed to have recovered his language ability for the moment.

"Oh, you mean Professor Ingoldsby. That's over. Anyway, for all I know he's probably in Tibet or Sumatra now. It's summer. He travels a lot. I'm not afraid, Dad. I need the money and Annick Ferroux wants the grounds kept as clean as possible until the house sells."

Only part of which was true. She needed the money. Annick Ferroux wanted the grounds kept trim, the gardens weed-free. Despite the dismissive wave of her hand, Kate sensed a tremor of anxiety behind her air of indifference, just a little thing like a slug on a hosta leaf. The last time Kate had seen him, Ingoldsby had in fact violated the terms of the settlement by speaking to her. She retreated without responding, hating herself afterwards for letting Ingoldsby worry her, although she had decided against reporting the incident to the university authorities. Each complaint entailed further hassle. More discussions, recriminations, and frayed nerves.

Words, words, words. What harm in words? The argument of his defenders: what harm had his words done her? As if words could not draw blood. More than words that he should not have spoken to a student in the first place, she had replied, his hand, his reach, her body—*his hand—in his office, for Chrissake! I'm not making it up, I have a witness!* Still, nothing untoward really had happened in the garden, aside from his physical presence. She could withstand words—this time, she would not retreat. Nor did she want Morris to see her concern. He was too prone to thinking of her as a child in need of protection. The thing with slugs—she could hear Morris's lesson in her head—you don't see them in the day, but overnight they wreak havoc on hosta leaves, nibbling incessantly. You had to pay attention to the shadows and underside of garden life. Destructive infestation awaited the unwary.

"Do what you like, then. You always do. Same pay scale as before."

He licked the sour cream off the spoon and pushed himself away from the table. Not a graceful agreement, Kate admitted, a kind of gratuitous insult thrown in. Dad was still unhappy over their quarrel. But he had dropped her off this morning on the way to Ruskow's, where the university students would meet him, driving their own car. When was the proper moment to say she was sorry? Daddy's annoyed today, her mother used to say—just wait and let time take its course. Be patient. In the truck he had said little except to offer advice on deadheading, weeding, spotting telltale signs of disease or noxious insects.

"Thanks, Dad."

"Got your cellphone handy? I'll call to pick you up." Nor did he look at her before driving off.

Ingoldsby's front yard had turned brown and weedy, the half-dead englemannii vines snaking all over the house. Kate glanced at it, afraid that staring would somehow cause Ingoldsby to materialize. Annick had had the window frames and front porch of her mother's house painted. The *À Vendre*/For Sale sign dangled on chains and swung in the wind. By appointment, it read. Kate didn't know if people were viewing the house today.

Although the forecasters predicted another heat wave in a day or two, the weather had turned cool for this time in August, the sun bright and glassy in the sky, its warmth blocked by an arctic wind from the north. Although it was still too early for the first frost, Kate regretted not wearing a sweatshirt over her sleeveless cotton top and leggings under her cutoff jean shorts. At least the gardening today would keep her on the eastern side of the property, opposite the western fence over which Ingoldsby's head had appeared, the yard being so wide that he'd have to shout to be heard. Even then a strong breeze could lift his abuse up and away over the tops of the trees. Excessive rains had half drowned the lamb's ears, which thrived in dry rather than soggy soil. An extensive row of fifteen yards, behind which grew Wargrave pink cranesbill, another heat- and drought-tolerant plant, the lamb's ears showed signs of wilt and rot on their bottom leaves. Highly invasive if not controlled, they were kept from smothering the cranesbill by a green plastic ridge that her father had buried alongside their roots, so they flourished in a narrow strip all along the edge of the bed. With silvery grey leaves that were soft to the touch, the plant surprised by being remarkably sturdy, able to survive the coldest winters in the region. To break the tedium of rows of cranesbill and lamb's ears, Dad had placed clumps of white and purple liatris at intervals, as well as a couple of boulders, to give the bed some structural height and visual variation. Removing her brown leather gardening belt with its loops and pouches designed to hold her gardening tools—a steel-pronged weeder, two shears for trimming and deadheading, one narrow and one wide trowel, a fork, a ball of green twine, kneepads, her gloves, a chocolate bar, and an orange. She began grasping the damaged leaves of the lamb's ears, most of which pulled off easily.

After shuffling along the border on her knees for fifteen minutes, Kate raised herself and looked behind her back. More annoyed than startled, she saw Ingoldsby's head resting on the western fence again, his mouth open to speak, but the wind carried his voice out of hearing. She did not stand, ready to retreat. She sat on her haunches, reached for her tool belt, and snatched out the weeder, a sturdy tool, capable of digging deeply into the soil and prodding out the toughest root like tansy or loosestrife. The prongs a bit rusty—clean the soil off and wipe your tools dry, Dad always said, but she couldn't be bothered most of the time—it would serve as a weapon if need arose. Kate wasn't entirely sure what need would arise; she hoped none would, as she gripped the wooden handle of the weeding prong so tightly that her fingers ached. The important thing was not to demonstrate fear, not to show that he could bother her anymore.

Then the head disappeared. She waited a few moments. The wind picked up, a frosty sweep down from the Arctic Circle, although the actual temperature of the day registered fifteen degrees Celsius, well below normal for this time of the year. If she remembered correctly, a red sweater hung from a nail in the gardening shed at the back of the property. Perhaps it had belonged to Mrs. Ferroux, but Kate wasn't about to let superstitions about the dead and their clothes trouble her today. She shivered on the grass, the dampness of the soil rising up through the blades and seeping through her shorts. Clutching a handful of brown leaves, she continued working. The liatris had dried and would also need to be cut down. Annick had told her father she wanted the compost heap behind the shed removed, so please don't add to it. Use the orange plastic bags in the shed and haul gardening refuse to the town dump or take it home and add to his own compost, if he preferred. Even the new owners, Kate had heard Morris say over the phone, would appreciate the virtues of well-aged compost continuously breaking down into exceptional fertilizer. Rot had its purpose. No, the compost didn't attract rodents—he had never so much as seen a rat, never mind raccoons. But he expected little understanding from Annick Ferroux, who had shown no appreciation for the gardens on her mother's property. Time to rake the dead leaves. Grabbing the belt, Kate stood and secured it around her waist, the weeding prong sliding neatly into an elongated pouch shaped like a quiver for arrows.

The shed was built of two-by-fours covered with green shingles, one window next to the door letting in light, floor-to-ceiling shelves on two walls with pickling jars and coffee tins of packets filled with seeds Mrs. Ferroux had gathered in the late fall over the years and forgotten about. Rakes, pitchforks, hoes, and edging tools hung from coat hooks on the third wall. Two power mowers crowded the centre of the cracked cement floor. A barrel of metal parts and odds and ends stood in one corner, a bench on curled iron legs under the window, upon which sat three terra-cotta pots of dried chrysanthemums, flaky to the touch. Under the bench Kate saw a box of plastic bags and pulled one out. The light of the open door darkened. She turned. Professor Ingoldsby, dressed in paint-daubed chinos, running shoes, and a shirt pale green like the rind of a honeydew melon, raised an arm above his head, pressing against the frame of the door, the other hand holding a long-handled sledgehammer. The air being somewhat musty and dark in the shed, the sunlight behind his head, Kate couldn't make out the expression on his face. He just stood in the doorway, staring.

The sledgehammer shifted forward as if he were beginning to raise it. Her mouth went dry. She remained standing by the window, less than a yard from Professor Ingoldsby, grim, unmoving, watching the sledgehammer sway like a pendulum in a grandfather clock.

"You got me fired from the university. It's all your fault, bitch."

Mrs. Ferroux had been struck over the head. The police, everyone knew, had questioned Ingoldsby, but no charges had been laid. Which didn't mean he wasn't the killer, Morris said. A sledgehammer over the head, well, that would just about do it, Kate thought, as words emerged from the back of her throat, almost pulled back into the sludge of fear and tension. Yes, she was afraid.

"You shouldn't be here."

She was surprised by the calm tone of her own voice, scarcely betraying the urge to leap and claw his face off with the gardening fork. Her cellphone. If she moved to use it, he'd have time to act, to stop her. The sight of the phone, the suggestion that she wanted to call for help or to report him might cause Ingoldsby to react. Keep still—any untoward movement could be interpreted as a provocation.

He said nothing. The hammer swung by his thigh. Kate didn't think he was drunk. Standing so close, she'd be able to smell the liquor. More than once, he had been forcibly removed from town taverns for rowdy behaviour. She had smelled liquor on his breath in his office; no one needed to remind her of Ingoldsby's drinking habits. His eyes followed the direction of her hand toward the weeding tool.

Not booze; she smelled a sour odour, a weird cologne Ingoldsby must have splashed on himself, the chemicals of his body reacting badly to the ingredients of the cologne, like milk curdled from sitting for hours in the hot sun. He didn't look freshly showered. Dirty, not the dirt of her father who came home with garden soil beneath his fingernails and green stains on his skin, smelling of loam and lingering fragrances of flowers against which his body had brushed—a good kind of dirty smell—the smell of the earth and of growing things—not the nose-wrinkling sourness emanating from Professor Ingoldsby. Really, Kate thought, he seemed physically weaker than she was, although taller. If need be, her soccer-toughened legs could place a well-aimed kick.

If not her legs or the gardening fork, then the sharp pointed blades of the shears. Looking around, Kate gauged how she could move to avoid the swing of the sledgehammer without tripping over the lawn mowers. One slash at his face would give her enough time to escape. He'd have to stop and howl. Even wild animals noticed injury and licked their wounds.

"Donald, is that you? What are you doing there?"

The sledgehammer stopped swinging. Eyes bloodshot and pleading like a rabbit's caught in a snare, he cleared his throat, then shouted, his voice sounding dredged up and damp.

"Ah … Annick … just returning the sledgehammer I borrowed a few months ago—your mother's—and I thought you'd be in the house or yard somewhere."

Then he whispered, "You're lucky."

Sometimes the body moved with a will of its own, perhaps impelled by reflex and turmoil. Kate didn't know if she was more terrified than enraged, more relieved than furious, but she decided on the spot that she wasn't going to let Ingoldsby keep on taunting her. She wasn't a student in his class anymore. In the garden, he wasn't surrounded by adoring friends who made excuses for him. Here, he had no authority or power.

She stepped forward, pointing the open blades of the shears as Professor Ingoldsby backed out, dropping the sledgehammer just outside the door. Kate relaxed her grip on the shears and touched the cellphone in her gardener's belt. She needed to get outside, escape the close, musty atmosphere of the shed. Annick stared at her standing in the shed behind Ingoldsby.

"Oh, right, returning it just now, when *she* just happened to be here."

Kate did not like to be on the receiving end of Annick's rigorously pointed, black-nailed finger and the vomiting of the pronoun *she* like a vile substance expelled from the stomach. Annick's ankle-length black dress and the tight silver coils around her neck, heavy strokes of kohl eyeliner and the black lips on a white-creamed and powdered face reminded Kate of Anjelica Huston as Morticia in the movie *The Addams Family*. Except for the orange spikes of hair. Morticia's dead black hair hung long and loose down to her waist. Dad would have a major fit if she ever returned home with her hair crafted by a lunatic sculptor and arranged in unnatural colours and shapes, stiffened by mousse or gel. A lot of the girls and some of the guys at the university sported hairdos that looked as if the head had been spun in a whirlpool of dyes, then structured and dried, stiffened by mousse or grease, into parent-annoying forms. Thank God for a vampire when you needed one. Kate began breathing in the fresh morning air.

"Don't you know what's happened? Anyway, it doesn't look good, in the shed with Kate and a sledgehammer. You want more trouble with the university? I think you should leave right now, Donald. People may get the wrong idea of your being here."

Ingoldsby stepped back toward the door of the shed as Annick stepped forward, although Kate would have said that she floated. It didn't seem that Annick moved her feet, covered in a complicated twisting of black straps, at all but floated like a mirage toward Ingoldsby.

"More bad news. Geraldine McCready's been murdered, found dead in her pergola yesterday afternoon by the housekeeper. Haven't you heard?"

"What's that got to do with me?"

The sledgehammer dropped to the ground. How easily Annick had disarmed the man. Kate slumped against the door frame to keep herself from falling. Yesterday she had been gardening near that same pergola. The professor hadn't confronted her in Geraldine McCready's garden. He turned to look at her, his face now the colour of his shirt. A man approaching the end of middle age, he had at one time enjoyed a reputation for good looks. Not just a gifted painter but really hot. This man had held the sledge-hammer. When? Yesterday in the McCready garden? And today, most certainly today. He had been alone with her in the shed. Did he have anything to do with the recent murders? She mustn't let Morris's suspicions and innuendoes cloud her thinking. She reached for her cellphone. It was safe to call now, safe to call her father.

"I think you're finished here, Kate. You can go now."

She heard the words, understood, but her body did not respond. Ingoldsby scuttled away. Kate also heard the swish of Annick's dress against her thighs. Only after the professor and Annick had both disappeared did the nerves run riot and fear burst out and she began shaking on the threshold of the gardening shed. Phone Dad. Phone Dad. Come get me. Please. The tiny numbers of the cellphone almost invisible, her fingers kept slipping and punching the wrong keys.

11

• • •

RUSKOW STOMPED AROUND his young birch trees, wearing spiked aerator sandals designed to loosen the compacted soil of the lawn. He had to admit that Morris Bunter and his crew planted the trees so well that their slender white trunks looked secure and thriving, the ground-level sod replaced. A few neighbours expected him for lunch today. They wanted to discuss neighbourhood security. How could he refuse? McCready would also participate, poor man, wheelchair bound with a debilitating disease in the care of a private-duty nurse, his own wife a murder victim. Small, but tough and wiry as a young man, Ruskow had served in the Canadian army, had witnessed atrocity of one kind or another during peacekeeping missions. Properly disciplined and trained, soldiers knew their duty, how to react, how to defend. Always elsewhere, the enemy and purpose clearly defined. Nothing like this slinking about gardens and police cars patrolling his neighbourhood at night and Neighbourhood Watch signs, everyone on the lookout for the unknown: a devious, nebulous kind of war. Local committees convened almost every day now in various houses where frightened friends and neighbours rambled on and on like undisciplined students about what to do, *how could this be happening here,* how to save our women, what arms to carry. And the bluster and bravado masked paralysis.

Fortunately, he had never married, the opportunity not having presented itself. Women did not find him appealing. In his youth he lacked seductive charms; in old age he lacked charm altogether. He did, however, live in a renovated Georgian home, purchased decades ago when real estate values had plummeted for a time. Unlike Ingoldsby, he had never enjoyed the cushion and privilege of a wealthy family. He had worked at many jobs to pay his way through university, assisted occasionally by scholarships and his parents who lived frugally in Nova Scotia. He had inherited unexpected and very useful life insurance money from his parents, killed in a plane crash, God bless them, the very year the university hired him to teach art history. Specializing in Byzantine and Islamic art, he could turn his mind to any period of history when paint had been applied to wet walls or dry canvas.

For hours he had watched Morris and the men dig up the grounds and secure the saplings, supervised, really, for he didn't trust a worker to complete a task without the overseeing eye, like a teacher surveying his students while they wrote an examination. Students had to be told again and again, and once more, how to do something. When they appeared knowledgeable, a rigorous test revealed deficiencies of skill and understanding. He had spent most of his adult life teaching and correcting, would not have had it otherwise, and was not about to suppress his gifts simply because he had retired. Even to this day, scarcely a year after he had formally left the university, the administration sought his advice. Take that nasty piece of business involving Ingoldsby. The man should have been chucked out ages ago for indecent behaviour, but the administration was always too weak-willed or reluctant to act until forced to do so.

Ingoldsby gave the teaching profession a bad name. And Ruskow didn't want to think about the disgraceful attitude of a few professors who excused Ingoldsby's fundamental and appalling violation of basic trust between teacher and student in the name of solidarity, academic freedom, and contractual rights. The times mercifully had changed. Ingoldsby and his friends, though, had not, and still acted like troglodytes. Applauding Kate's persistence and moral outrage, searching for compromise to avoid scandal, he himself had suggested that the administration suspend Ingoldsby on full pay for the duration of the year, then on partial salary until he reached pensionable age. Money bought compliance. Ingoldsby, not gracefully, agreed.

Her sense of integrity and the rightness of her cause withstood the faculty representative's impugning of her character and the validity of her case, trying hard as he might to negate the eye-witness's testimony. He had privately spoken to Kate, advising her what could be done and how to go about it. Distrusting teachers, even those on her side (who could blame her?), Kate had agreed to listen to him in the dean's office in the presence of two other sympathetic teachers, both women. Chemistry, if he remembered rightly, and English: yes, they taught in the science and English departments, equally scandalized by Ingoldsby's crossing the ethical line.

"The administration has not traditionally been the best defender of student rights," he had said, pouring Kate a cup of tea. "The last thing it wants is public attention and scandal. You'll get talk and more talk and the taking of things under advisement and cowardly procrastination."

There was no doubt about Ingoldsby's guilt. Ruskow knew it even before learning the facts of this particular incident. A little more than a year earlier, before he retired and toward the end of his five-year term as chairperson of the arts department, he had tried to have Ingoldsby suspended for inappropriate conduct in his classes. Much of it had been sexually provocative, verging on the indecent, especially during his life-drawing sessions involving nude models, some of it drunkenness on university premises, some of it verbal obscenity hurled like poisonous darts against his own person. More than once Ingoldsby had assaulted fellow teachers while inebriated or befuddled by Lord knows what drug of the day. His friends, amounting to a small but influential cohort of defenders, gathered around.

The administration used to seek refuge behind student reluctance to lay charges, relying on the incidents to pass like short-lived cases of food poisoning. Speak to the student. Persuade her to drop the charge and get on with her studies, perhaps transfer to another class. Convince her that Ingoldsby meant no real harm. No one wanted to pursue the matter to its logical conclusion. Such arguments no longer availed. The times had changed for the better. Society was not so forgiving. Seeking justification, Ingoldsby's friends had rushed to his defence, using the oft-repeated argument that the man was a genius. Prone to certain patterns of eccentric behaviour, he was also a teacher with inviolable rights and tenure. Ruskow always believed that rights and tenure implied responsibility, that genius in the arts was an aesthetic judgment, not a moral exemption. Called into his office to answer the charges, Ingoldsby had at first laughed them off. Ruskow had been prepared for that, knowing full well that Ingoldsby made jokes at his expense. He had heard the abuse that to this day still rankled. When he announced that he planned to proceed with the matter to its logical conclusion, the painter had mounted a very offensive horse indeed.

"You've just been waiting for your chance to get rid of me, haven't you, Ruskow? Because you haven't enough creative spark to come up with one single original idea of your own, no more talent and imagination than an ape swinging in the trees. Just drives you crazy to see me having fun, to know the kids love me and laugh at you. Improper conduct, my ass—you're so green and putrid with jealousy that your mind's a dirty fish tank. You've got as much love of art and passion in your blood as a banana-sucking monkey. Chairman of the department, shit! A chimp could do what you do. Enjoy what fucking little power you have while it lasts, you pen-pushing eunuch. I spit on it!"

Ingoldsby had leaned on the desk while he spewed his venom. Ruskow remembered sitting behind his desk, unresponsive to Ingoldsby's rant, not even raising an eyebrow over the plethora of offensive metaphors, or when the artist claimed persecution by philistines and puritans. He focused on Ingoldsby's long-sleeved shirt: burnt umber, a colour he remembered from Italian paintings. If he flinched under the opprobrium, Ruskow didn't let it show. He glanced at the quartz paperweight on his desk, a useful weapon. Never, never let the fury show. Self-discipline, cold blood, and steady nerves in times of crisis served their purpose. He had been well trained as a soldier before he entered university, even if his body now lacked stamina.

The great mistake Ingoldsby made, as so many men like him did, was to assume himself infallible and impregnable by virtue of talent and gusto. So adamantly self-involved, the painter couldn't even begin to imagine, to fathom the depth of rage and hatred freezing Ruskow to his chair. Outside his office window he enjoyed a view of the playing field. Students were tossing a Frisbee, their natural spontaneity and camaraderie forever excluding him. He had never been one for games. Stiff in social gatherings, he retreated into pedantry or silence, neither endearing. When sober, Ingoldsby delighted with wit, ribald humour, and physical attractiveness. White clouds mounded in a blue sky like a Winslow Homer painting. Some ideas, so clear and inevitable, waited for the magical moment to reveal themselves, a kind of epiphany. Incredible, really, Ingoldsby's utter lack of appreciation for a person's character. If he had slashed with a scimitar, he could not have cut more deeply. The Frisbee, elegant in its arc of flight, a wingless bird, seemed to pause momentarily in midair, flashing in the sun, before wafting downward. For years, he had been mocked by the genius. One day, Ruskow decided then and there, he would utterly destroy Ingoldsby. It was only the mild stroke, causing him to collapse the next day in the professor's lounge and forcing him into an early retirement, that prevented him from completing the task he had set for himself. Ruskow would wait

When the time came, Ingoldsby's vanity and bravado would deflate and shrivel like his overactive prick in cold water. Revenge, as the man once said, was a dish best served cold. Drunkenness, snorting coke in class, fondling the live models (those who would allow it), insulting students who did not applaud his Dionysian exuberance, molesting Kate, and each time, friends defending and excusing him, the indisputable truth of the accusations so apparent that a child could have won the case against Ingoldsby in court. Of course, every man had a right to legal counsel and the best defence. Ruskow wondered, though, if defending a disreputable, transparently guilty man by pretending innocence or extenuating circumstances or exceptional gifts did not itself undermine justice. Legal rights so often led to ethical suicide. But it was ever thus. The rationalizations of teachers who admired or "understood" Ingoldsby's genius had sickened him, the historical pusillanimity of the administration disgusted, and his own failure to prosecute shamed. Indisposition removed him as chairperson, it did not exculpate.

Kate Bunter, brave girl, drinking her tea and following his advice, threatened to go to the law, to take the case off the campus and right into the public courts. The faculty representative, still blustering, failed to break her resolve, retreated. To this day, Ruskow liked to think he had shown Kate the way, had shown that most teachers disapproved of Ingoldsby, that many believed in and supported her case. Through Kate, he had exacted some sweet morsel of revenge as a taste of future, greater satisfaction. Ingoldsby, still refusing to admit to wrongdoing and apologize, accepted what came to be called "a fair and reasonable compromise," and "a happy conclusion to an unfortunate chain of circumstances."

Compromise, indeed. Pounding over the matted grass, Ruskow could still feel the anger and disgust over the Ingoldsby affair, not dissipated since last winter when Kate had laid the charge. He did admit more was involved than another case of harassment, however lamentable in itself. Years earlier, when the time came for the university to promote lecturers, Ingoldsby had spoken at the board meetings against his promotion. The board listened. Through the academic grapevine, an immaculate source of truth, he learned that Ingoldsby thought him insufficiently experienced, the few publications more banal than brilliant—let him acquire some more years under his belt. This from a man several years his junior, granted tenure exceptionally early on the grounds of genius. Ruskow waited years for an assistant professorship and tenure while Ingoldsby carried on like a latter-day hippie on a commune. As for the painter's trips to India and Tibet, returning spiritually attuned ... Ruskow stomped all the harder in his aerator sandals.

The man should have been publicly castrated. Why did some teachers, especially in the arts, believe their profession conferred infallibility? That creativity superseded morality, that pedagogy transcended accountability? No doubt about it, in defending Ingoldsby, arguing against his dismissal, they were really defending themselves, defending the public performance of their private fantasies or deformations of character. For years he had colluded himself, in a manner of speaking, letting silence be mistaken for approval or indifference. Even as chairman of the department, he had not carried through with his desire to rid the university of

Ingoldsby. Desire failed before difficulties. And the administration itself, so concerned with raising money and preventing scandal, mumbled and muffled its way through various incidents in the past when the social climate made it easier for Ingoldsby to act the part of clown and satyr.

His reputation for severity in class being what it was, Ruskow didn't think students really liked him very much, or not many students did. Ingoldsby used to make jokes about pokers shoved you know where, despising Ruskow's purely academic credentials. Ingoldsby painted large canvases in spectacular colours of spirals and funnels and convoluted, wormlike shapes, broken by brilliant eruptions of blue and gold, many influenced by shapes and contours of erotic sculptures on Indian temples, depicting, apparently, "the hypocritical and tortured workings of the civilized, therefore repressed, Western, therefore materialistic, psyche." So stated an advertisement for a vernissage at the Musée des Beaux-Arts in Montreal. Fashionable absurdities aside, Ruskow admired the execution and sense of colour of the experimental landscapes.

And the portraits! Ingoldsby's true gift. Psychologically penetrating. Breathtaking. A second Rembrandt, if he were given to hyperbole. Ingoldsby possessed an enviable skill with the brush. Beneath the gallery's stereotypical interpretation of Western life, the authentic ability and originality of Ingoldsby's canvases stared him in the face. If pressed, Ruskow would define the paintings as a collective self-portrait. Why did the man waste his time teaching and harassing students when he could live the life of immoral artist and sexual renegade so easily off campus? And whenever did the pernicious idea take root that art excused vile behaviour? Madman or satyr, van Gogh or Picasso, now so inextricably linked in the popular notions of artistic genius and character that some minor and would-be artists affected major derangement. What an affront to the great artists who conducted their lives on higher principles.

Why would anyone countenance such an absurd notion even for a moment? Unless it reflected some hidden corruption like the heartworm that had insidiously weakened and destroyed Samson, his beloved golden retriever. A splendid dog, dead at eight years.

Unlike the great Ingoldsby, he himself was not a creator, although he had tried. He did not sculpt, paint, or photograph. No unpublished novel lay hidden in the bottom drawer of his desk. Putting down the brush and pen, he had long ago recognized his own deficiency. He taught the history of art. Outside of the creative process, he nonetheless admired and cherished and fought for its essential necessity on the curriculum of any university worthy of the name. Of course, like so many theorists and critics, he understood little of creative origins or inspiration, academic treatises notwithstanding; they merely cited the visible consequences of mysterious process. It was a smug and usually envious teacher who regarded himself as more knowledgeable about creativity than the artist. Jealousy, often disguised as criticism, assumed monstrous proportions in the most displaced and discreet forms. Oh, beware the green-eyed monster. It doth mock the meat it feeds on.

Ingoldsby, prankster and devotee of Rabelaisian high spirits that he was, enthralled those students he did not despise and abuse. It didn't matter if a teacher was loved, Ruskow believed. That was a modern indulgence, amounting almost to a superstition. He did not look to *Sesame Street* for information or role models. Not every pedagogue, thank God, was a Mr. Chips, filled with absurdly sentimental notions about students and teaching. It mattered that his attitudes and demeanour remained examples of correct behaviour and that he followed the lesson plan rigorously to prevent any untoward spontaneity in class. Humour was the death of concentration. Ruskow disapproved of idle jest in class. No one, he was pleased to say, laughed during his lectures on Islamic or Byzantine art. Like a priest, a teacher must suppress sexual fancies and urges—and who did not have them around young and lovely post-pubescent students? If he did not ignore those impulses, he betrayed his avocation. Unless, of course, one was fortunate enough to be surrounded by colleagues who circled to protect their own against marauding wolves. Very few colleagues had circled Ruskow. His retirement party was a bland wine-and-soft-cheese affair. Not a song sung, not a tear dropped.

So Morris Bunter was Kate Bunter's father. He had known that all along, but it was the kind of fact that slipped out of consciousness. She was a forthright girl whom he remembered sitting in the dean's office during one of the consultations regarding Ingoldsby. She had thanked him for the advice and the tea. No, she had never lied during the entire process, her words and story remaining consistent and credible from beginning to end. That he could see. Ingoldsby lied and denied, and presented a pretty poor spectacle of manhood. Shame on him and shame on us all for coddling Ingoldsby all those years and ignoring his behaviour, never having the courage to challenge him, to demand decency and retribution, to fight for his dismissal, always bowing before self-serving theories of academic freedom and the rights of teachers to conduct their classes as they see fit, the invocation of genius as some kind of unbreakable, Mosaic law. Decency, apparently, following the logic of that argument, was a code of conduct for less exalted, sexually repressed souls. Like the Russian mule, he had heard Ingoldsby's slur on his character and name. Reprimand Ingoldsby for the celebration of Eros, one of the painter's supporters had said at the hearing, and you might as well chain him to a rock and let a shrike eat out his liver. Ruskow had corrected the mythological allusion, more annoyed by the teacher's muddled thinking than his faulty ornithology.

Shame on Ingoldsby for demeaning our profession in the public eye. The townspeople knew stories about the painter-teacher. The man was a clown and a reprobate. Living off the taxpayer, entrusted with the intellectual care of the impressionable young in a public institution, confusing academic freedom with self-indulgence, he had betrayed the public trust. Stomping on the grass, the ground as soft as he imagined Ingoldsby's torso would be, Ruskow often regretted he had even come up with the financial compromise to "save him from starving on the streets," as two or three particularly addled teachers had put it. What a joke. What an insult to the homeless and impoverished soul on the street who neither lived on inherited property nor had a reasonable pension. He himself sent a cheque annually to the Old Brewery Mission in Montreal, which housed many a homeless man and woman. If he was "a cockless wonder," to quote one of Ingoldsby's soubriquets for him, he wasn't entirely heartless.

Ingoldsby's art substantially increased his income. How painfully unforgettable that day in the office when the painter had verbally assaulted him so loudly that the voice carried down the hall and through the open doors into the offices of other teachers. After he departed, Ruskow took the brass stiletto letter opener out of its shiny metal sheath and began slitting open his mail. So sharp and swift, it scarcely made a sound. The heavy quartz paperweight, brought back from a trip to Mexico, glinted in a patch of sunlight on the desk.

Barely avoiding smacking his face against one of the branches, he turned abruptly, nearly falling off his aerators. A dark shadow leaped. Murder, murder, murder streaked through his mind like arrows slinging through the air one after the other. An old man unarmed, very susceptible to attack at the moment, but, no, of course he was safe. The dog. One of the McCready's ineffectual watchdogs, a Doberman without menace. These killings put everyone on edge. The killer chose to attack women, in any case, so far not a single man. Who was to say they were not the beginning, but a continuation—a process that began years ago and would continue until somehow psychosis met its match in a garden of the future? Who was to say? Since the death of his retriever several years ago, Ruskow avoided dogs and disliked having one jump up and lick his face.

"Get down."

The dog instantly obeyed as it obeyed any command spoken by friend and stranger alike. Defective training or defective psyche, Ruskow suspected, certainly putting the lie to the notion that dogs obeyed one master. It was getting late and he needed to wash and change before the meeting.

"Go home, boy, go home."

He pointed in the direction, but the dog bounced its head up and down between its front paws, leaping over the lawn, thinking Ruskow had thrown a ball. Dog had no more real sense than, well, Ingoldsby himself, genius notwithstanding. The veins on the right side of his neck tensed and vibrated: let him not think any more about Ingoldsby. Sorry that he had chosen not to go for his morning stroll through town, Ruskow rubbed the back of his neck, staving off a headache. Pensioned off for attacking a student. Well, it was his own idea, but knowing Ingoldsby's mercenary instincts and quelling the nausea, he had advanced it. Think of all the free time Ingoldsby would now have to devote to his own painting. Realizing they would not silence Kate, even the faculty representative had encouraged Ingoldsby, now assuming the pose of martyr, to accept the offer. Kate did not take her case to the outside world. The university had saved face, or believed it had. And now Ruskow was full of regrets. Ingoldsby had been released, handsomely compensated, not punished. Moral compromise, while solving one problem, had created another. He did not feel very good about himself. He had not acted against Ingoldsby when the opportunity arose, had chosen silence and seething over confrontation and prosecution.

One day, though, real justice would be done. Sitting down on a lawn chair to remove his aerating clogs, Ruskow remembered a painting of St. Sebastian tied to a pillar, standing amid classical ruins, pierced by arrows, his mouth open, his face shimmering in the throes of ecstasy. Ingoldsby, though, would not take delight in pain. Among all his defects of character, Ruskow had never perceived masochism. He suspected the painter would scream on the way to the scaffold, proclaiming his innocence. Appealing to and arousing public sympathies, he'd escape the hangman through the efforts of teachers, mounted on fiery steeds, galloping into the town centre, hacking the head off the hangman, slashing through the rope, and carrying Ingoldsby off to safety. No, no, no. Ruskow clapped his aerator sandals together to shake off the earth, noting the spikes designed to pierce the strangled thatching of grass and compacted soils. Skilled in verbal gymnastics, teachers could be so adept at twisting reason to protect their own interests. When justice appeared, it must do so surreptitiously, and not be seen to be done.

12

. . .

QUESTIONS, QUESTIONS, QUESTIONS, and still no arrest. Professor Ingoldsby walked the streets like any law-abiding citizen going about his business. Kate had seen him herself, wielding the sledgehammer, which he had in fact borrowed. What more evidence did the police need? Morris wondered. An eyewitness report, practically. But what was the point of telling them? A man had a right to return borrowed tools, even if they belonged to a murdered woman. Given Kate's history with Ingoldsby, the police would probably assume she was bent on revenge, driven by spite. Look what poor Kate endured at the university, herself accused of maliciously impugning the professor. The faculty representative and counsel described Kate as twisted out of shape by a low mark, and a nymphet who seduced innocent academics for her own perverse satisfaction. Truth and common sense fell by the wayside. God, what that man got away with. Allowing for the generosity of the final agreement, what would Ingoldsby have to gain by harassing Kate? He could just hear the police saying that, skepticism evident in the very motion of their pens writing in their notebooks.

Morris drank his coffee, now cold in the bowl, at a corner table in the front of the café, watching the rain slide down the expansive window glass. It was too wet again to work in the gardens, so he had given the boys the day off, asked Kate to remove the laundry from the dryer and fold it before she left the house. Tarun was picking her up for a date at the Cineplex in the mall, where they could shoot pool or play table hockey before seeing one of twelve movies. He did not protest. Since Kate had returned home safe and sound during the night of the storm last week, later than he would have liked, no sign of drug or other abuse about her person in the morning (and he had perused her face and body movements, trying to sense one kind of violation or another), he couldn't very well continue interfering with her social life. Ignoring a crisis and letting time soften the memory or restore perspective had worked. He could now speak to Kate without feeling the sting on his cheek, without his tongue swelling with embarrassment. He hoped she would construe his silence on the subject as a form of forgiveness. Anyway, after the news about Mrs. McCready's murder, personal problems diminished in importance.

A great evil had invaded his community, a serpent slinking in the shadows of the gardens waiting to strike. Indifferent to religion, scarcely giving God a thought from one day to the next, despite his witnessing of miraculous growth, Morris resorted to quasi-religious terms to explain what he couldn't even begin to understand. Of course murders happened all the time. What made it so different here and now? He wasn't naive, an ostrich with his head stuck in the sand. He hoped Kate would be safe, that some divine agency in which he probably didn't believe would cover his daughter with a protective shield.

He had seen Geraldine McCready at the memorial service for Mrs. Ferroux, remembered a few of the minister's words about light emerging from the darkness, of good arising from evil, of God's mysterious purpose; the church and all it represented had not stayed the hand that had felled poor Mrs. McCready. Kate, gardening at the scene of the outrage only moments before it happened, Kate who could just as well have been the psychopath's victim, although "demon" was the first word that had popped into Morris's mind to describe the killer. Short of forbidding her to leave the house entirely, hoping that his own fortress was secure against assault, his own garden exempt from invasion, he had no means of repelling attack except hope. No matter how often he tried to feel hope, or repeated the word like a magical incantation, hope never changed the weather. And why indeed should the walls of his little house not collapse under any attack by the devil? This lovely place of the earth where he had spent years growing flowers and building and maintaining gardens, bringing beauty where before the eye only saw scrubby patches of lawns and scraggly bushes, was now scarred by violence and smeared with blood.

The senior citizens' residence asked him for an estimate yesterday to cover half the grassy area by the riverside with low-maintenance gardens for the seniors to stroll through, interspersed with Muskoka chairs. Such a scheme would certainly improve the appearance of the neighbourhood. He would undertake the project only if the administration agreed with his choice of plants and his arrangements. Absolutely no petunias or impatiens or red salvia allowed. Agreed, and he had just that morning promised to provide a garden plan and budget by September. Staring at the watery patterns dripping down the café window, after the first sweep of daffodils and tulips (old people loved tulips in the spring—but no red, he had insisted), he was visualizing Russian sage, globe thistles, and coreopsis, and heliopsis and rudbeckia for the fall. Sipping the last of the cold coffee, Morris was not warming to the project. Images of gardens clouded over like mildewed leaves of phlox or bergamot. He had been reading about a dreadful bug, appearing it would seem from nowhere, devastating once resistant lilies in certain parts of the country. When would it attack his terrain? He had never sprayed protective poisons over his gardens, knowing the cure to be worse than the disease. Perhaps extreme situations required extreme measures. He had been known to rip a plant right out of the soil and burn it, so tortured by marauding insects or mangled by disease, if it failed to respond to his treatments and was beyond hope.

Donald Ingoldsby swished into the café with two companions, shaking rain off their closing umbrellas and rustling raincoats. The waitress appeared and blocked him from view. His stomach uneasy still after a sleepless night, Morris had been unable to eat the breakfast Kate kindly offered to prepare. She was being very thoughtful these past few days, no doubt feeling bad over what happened—he knew that—probably worse than he after leaving the house the night of the storm. Ingoldsby and his one female and one male companion laughed and shuffled their way among the chairs to a table in the middle of the café, where he sat with his back to Morris. By turning his head to the left, Morris could see them clearly. He raised the collar of his shirt and held one hand against his left cheek. Two tables separated him from Ingoldsby.

An elderly couple in identical sweaters sat at one of the tables, drinking tea. Perhaps, not expecting to see Kate's father, the professor wouldn't notice him. Morris at first thought he should pay for his coffee immediately and leave, but he ordered another bowl and his usual cheese Danish. The waitress seemed distracted, nervous, always peering above his head out the window, asking Morris in French to repeat his order. He wanted to mention Mrs. McCready—the waitress must have heard—wanted somehow to say that she needn't fear for her personal safety.

"Terrible, isn't it?"

"La pluie, monsieur?"

"I mean what happened. First Mrs. Ferroux, then the McCready woman."

She didn't at first respond, then he explained himself in French. If he wasn't mistaken, the waitress, a middle-aged woman, lived alone in one of the low-rise apartment buildings on the street behind his house. Véronique was her name. She used to work in the cafeteria of the seniors' residence. Pudgy fingers displayed several rings of ornate beaten silver. Pleasant, round face, Morris noted, her brown hair streaked with blond, she knew his name because he was a regular. He had once or twice thought of asking her out, but she seemed resistant or indifferent to overtures. Not that he had ever directly suggested ... but sometimes, after his wife's death and before Nancy came along, he had imagined strolling the boardwalk along the river with Véronique. That was before he had seen her in the Cineplex at the mall in the company of the town's gas station owner.

"Don't remind me."

Remind? How could anyone forget. Should he offer some kind of advice? Lock your windows and doors. Don't open the door to anyone you don't know. Stay home at night. Avoid gardens at all costs. As an apartment dweller, she should find that easy. Didn't she believe the murders affected her life? Everyone was now implicated, everyone at risk. A murder brought down the entire family, devastated everyone—think of poor Mr. McCready.

And Professor Ingoldsby laughing and raising his voice in the middle of the café so everyone could hear him, breaking into the quieter, private conversations people were trying to conduct around their own tables.

"I'll get your coffee and Danish, *pas longtemps*."

"*Merci.*"

The old couple rose together, unsteady on their feet, placed a ten-dollar bill under a plate, and walked out, the woman with the aid of a cane, the man holding an umbrella unfurling over her head as the door opened. Morris didn't remember seeing them before, but the town was not so small that he knew everybody. Perhaps they resided in the senior citizens' residence. The professor couldn't even let them enjoy their tea and pastry in peace, could he? Barged in as if he owned the place. Their voices now high and loud, commandeering the space, the teachers called for cappuccino and pastry, although Véronique had disappeared into the kitchen at the back of the café. Morris didn't want to hear another word about the number of students in their classes who couldn't read or write or think or argue their way out of a paper bag, certainly not meet the standards set by the superior beings who chuckled and guffawed with a molester and possible murderer.

He should have phoned the university the instant Kate had told him about meeting Ingoldsby in the shed. No, she had insisted, that would make matters worse. And he wanted to avoid another fracas between father and daughter, especially after what happened on the night of the storm. He didn't hurt me, she said. Of course he had hurt Kate. She knew that as well as he did. The police's failure to focus on Ingoldsby as a suspect dumbfounded Morris. He turned his head to look out the window through the patterns of water sliding down the windowpanes, and tried to get a look at the stores across the street. Visibility, as the traffic reporters on the radio would say, was poor. Sometimes those in charge didn't see the forest for the trees. Lack of vision. Procedures crippling justice. He saw Ingoldsby all too clearly, his hair now shaved off, the moles on the back of his neck dark as the centres of black-eyed Susans. Shaved his head, indeed. As if he could disguise himself, trying to look like some kind of Eastern guru.

The other two teachers Morris recalled seeing in the university, the woman whispering in Ingoldsby's ear when they both came out of the dean's office. She wore her hair in a thick, leather-strapped braid all the way down to her buttocks and pronounced her name, Laura, in the Italian way, Kate had said, puckering her lips, deepening her voice in imitation, and stretching the name into three syllables. Rimless granny glasses perched on the tip of her nose, although she couldn't be more than forty, and she wore hoop earrings so large he could throw a ball through them. She had spoken as a character witness in defence of Ingoldsby, applauding his anti-puritanism and his Rabelaisian appetite for life, which he encouraged his students to develop. Expressions of sexuality in his classes were a form of creative and educational play, connected with the very wellsprings of genius and art. Kate had misunderstood the signals, had allowed her own personal problems, ego and vanity, her bourgeois anxieties and repression to misinterpret Ingoldsby's comments and actions. This Morris had read in the transcripts of the hearing, which Kate had a right to see. Sexual harassment as a pedagogical tool. Only a professor would resort to that kind of argument. Christ, an ordinary guy on the street didn't have a chance against the geniuses in the café.

The male teacher, dressed in black shirt and black slacks, his grey hair swept in waves from his forehead, the light of the café reflecting in the hairspray, asked Ingoldsby about his plans for the fall semester.

"I envy you, Don, really I do. Not having to get up in front of addle-brained students and try to interest them in art and ideas. You can spend all the time on your own painting. Forget the university. You've got it made."

Now staring at the table as if examining a group of exotic animals, recent acquisitions of a zoo, Morris squinted. Would the teacher in black have done what Ingoldsby had if he could have gotten away with it? Probably admired the painter for acting the way he wanted to act himself, wanted secretly to throw sense and modesty out the window and play the fool with impunity, refuse to contain his impulses and drives because only dull and ordinary people obeyed the rules. Cowardice or lip service to morality prevented the man from acting out his own fantasies. Her case airtight, the eyewitness, all possible loopholes closed, the administration and other teachers eager to use Kate to get rid of Ingoldsby, out he went. For his supporters, Ingoldsby's dismissal not only implied their own guilt, but it also undermined their security. If Ingoldsby could fall, why couldn't they? Morris once suspected and now believed that Ingoldsby's friends in the university derived a secret thrill from his actions, their desires hidden beneath public view like grubs circled around and nibbling at the roots of perennials or moles digging tunnels in the gardens. One never saw a nocturnal, underground creature during the day, unless it had been killed and dragged into the light by a cat. What was that professor's name, the man in black shirt, black jeans, and black cowboy boots with the shimmering grey waves of hair?

"Have you heard about the recent murder?" the woman asked Ingoldsby.

"You mean Geraldine McCready? Annick told me."

"I think that's her name."

"Annick knew her better than I did. She used to work with Annick's mother. I don't want to talk about some old woman found murdered in her garden. As for the students, I loved my classes, man, and I sort of miss them, but I'm thinking of going back to India for a while. Really need a break from this place. Been reading Basho a lot, thinking of taking a trip to Japan as well. Never been, check out the art, and walk in the old pilgrim's footsteps, quoting haiku."

His companions, finding humour in what Morris did not understand, chuckled. Who on earth was Basho? Where did he walk? Taking a trip, indeed. Right. On taxpayers' money. Assault my daughter. Get pensioned off early with a reprimand. Not even uphold your end of the deal. Can't leave Kate alone, can you. Threatened her with a sledgehammer. Must think we're idiots, returning it to the shed. You can fool the police with your lies and alibis. I know what you are. Taking a trip to Japan, are you? We'll see about that.

Véronique returned with his order. Morris couldn't look at the brown, foamy swill of coffee in a bowl or the thick Danish with yellow cheese pushed out the ends like guts squeezed out a navel. He swallowed, fighting the reflex in his throat. Stare out the window. Watch the oily blue patterns of water drip down the glass. So much rain this August. Try not to hear the teachers laughing and envying Ingoldsby's freedom. If Ingoldsby got away ... The police needed more time—a man like Ingoldsby would always overstep the bounds. There had to be a way to block his plans. No action, though, from the police. The man was talking of leaving, of going to Japan where he could disappear in fields of bamboo or take refuge in a Shinto temple, for all Morris knew, have the taxpayers' money transferred to a Tokyo bank so he could diddle girls in the rice paddies for the rest of his life.

A delivery van pulled up by the curb in front of the café, blocking the view of the street. A man in a white coat got out, opened the doors at the back of the truck, and slid out three wire baskets filled with bagels and croissants in clear plastic bags. Véronique held the door for him.

"Ah, Véronique, *ça va bien? Merci.*"

"You really should deliver at the back. You know the rules."

"Don't snitch on me. I'm running late and it'd take more time than I have to manoeuvre the rig at the back. You've got the delivery now. How about a latte to go?"

By the tone of his voice, Morris assumed the delivery man had fallen into the habit of flirting with Véronique, who, judging by the smile, didn't mind one bit. Perhaps he was her love interest, not the gas station owner. Some women liked men with large bellies. Morris sucked in his stomach. Gardening kept him trim and firm, although his waist was running to flab. The teachers stood up, calling for their bill. Ingoldsby was leaving. Just as the professor, whose hands did not reach for his wallet, turned, he caught Morris's eye and paused. It appeared that he was about to speak, but his eyes passed over Morris and looked outside.

"Hell, it's still raining."

The woman retrieved a twenty-dollar bill from a brown leather bag attached to her beaded belt and dropped it on the table.

"That should cover everything, I think."

"Thanks, Laura," and Ingoldsby kissed her cheek, one hand running up and down her spine. She pushed into his body.

Half risen from his own seat, Morris grabbed his coffee bowl and the uneaten Danish. Heave them at Ingoldsby. That would certainly cause him to acknowledge Kate's father. Ingoldsby clearly did not recognize him or pretended not to. Professor Laura stepped between him and the painter, holding out her umbrella, which she opened in the café. Didn't Laura know opening an umbrella indoors brought bad luck? Did she believe herself immune to the course of unnatural events because she taught at the university? The teacher in black slipped his arms into his slicker. Véronique picked up the twenty and placed it, folded, into her apron pocket. What kind of woman associated with Ingoldsby and defended him against justified and proven charges by female students? Morris couldn't fathom that, but then, unlike Professor Laura, he lacked an infallible comprehension of human character and motive, as well as a Rabelaisian appetite for life. Did that mean a teacher had the right to abuse him?

The delivery man brushed beside them, carrying the empty crates, saying something to Véronique that made her respond, *"Je pense que non!"*

Laughing over a private joke, the three teachers ducked under their enormous umbrellas and jostled outside. Morris sat down again, watching them huddle a few moments like curved figures in a Japanese wall painting before they rushed by the watery window.

"Next time, the bastard, I'll get him next time."

"*Est-ce que tu veux autre chose, monsieur?*"

He hadn't heard himself speak.

"*Non, merci,* Véronique."

The police would never arrest, the courts never convict, that man. Of this Morris remained convinced. The intent to "get him" existed where Morris believed it mattered most—not in any clearly formulated plan but in the marrow of his bones, in the very soul of a father, where love of child originated and remained till the very end of his days. He got up and smiled at Véronique, a friendly, decent woman whom any father would be proud of. He left a handsome tip by the coffee bowl.

13

• • •

TELEVISION AND RADIO NEWSCASTS, newspapers, websites, and the scurrying gossip around town all offered their bits of information, their claps of shock and mews of regret, and their murmurs of anxiety about the murders. Wherever Morris walked, he heard acquaintances or strangers speak on the subject of killing. He couldn't drive into Old Town without feeling tension in the air over the gardens and expensive homes, hearing an expectant hum like the distant buzz of midges and bees, and sensing fearful undercurrents in a dark and still sky, the prelude to a major summer storm. In the hardware store, the café, the senior citizens' residence, the gas station, the boutiques, nursery, and grocery store, men and women hunched whispering and speculating, until the town seemed to wobble with the shifting weight of views and analyses, and the self-satisfied relief that someone else had died.

Some people just liked hearing the sound of their voices—it didn't matter if they made sense, as long as they repeated whatever they had heard that morning, adding their own variations and embellishments. Only a few families, trusting in ancient privilege more than modern technology, had installed surveillance cameras on their grounds. Morris did not own a gun or keep a dog. And he had decided to fire Kate, to let her go, forbid her to work in the gardens anymore. Two murders, and she seemed to be closer each time. A third murder? It did not bear thinking about. In some ways he agreed with what he had been hearing all over town: it could happen again. Who was really safe? Only minutes, only minutes, seconds even, the murderer lurking about the McCready grounds ready to attack. What if Geraldine McCready had not returned home? What if the psycho had thought Kate was the lady of the house?

In Georges's hardware store, one of the last of the small, independent *quincailleries* on the west Island, he liked to wander and linger among the rows of nuts and bolts and admire the sheen of new saws and hammers displayed on the wall. Tools were so clear and functional, designed for any imaginable task. With the right tools, the job got done. Mystery evaporated, confusion dissipated, once you understood the purpose of the tool. In his basement, he kept an orderly tool bench and workstation. During the winter he drilled, sawed, hammered—whatever his client needed that he could manage. He always selected the appropriate tool and derived satisfaction not so much from completing the job but from knowing what to do and how to do it. Strength and security lay in understanding the reason for the tools and trusting to his own skill. Georges, Morris was sorry to see, wore the weary look of a man beaten down by fortune. Life had not turned out as he had predicted, which was especially worrisome now that he was approaching retirement age and looked back with some disappointment. His business was also struggling to survive competition from giant hardware outlets at the malls. Morris overheard someone at the cash register offer his opinion in English about the murders.

"One good thing about it, though, you've got to admit—it could have been worse."

Morris had heard that response to bad news so often that it made him want to pull out the hair of the person who said it.

"We could be living in the Middle East. Not even safe to take a bus there or eat a bagel in a restaurant. No telling when someone with a grudge decides to hurl a bomb at your feet or drive his truck right into your kids."

The speaker was a man Morris didn't remember seeing around the town. After thirty years of residence, he had come to know or recognize a great many members of the community, but he hadn't seen this man before. Hefty, with straight and thick black hair parted in the middle and hanging over each ear like wet felt. His hands were on the counter, fingers folded, knuckles red, as if they had been rubbed raw against sandpaper. He seemed very insistent on diminishing the tragedy of what had happened locally. Spoke with a lilt, maybe a touch of the Irish— Morris didn't know. Having the ruddy face of a heavy drinker of indeterminate age, could be fifty, perhaps younger, perhaps older, with patches of red and blue capillaries like tracery on his cheeks, he turned around to face Morris's question. Quite a mass of shoulder, bullish, a man capable of great force, if the need arose.

"How could it have been worse for the women?"

"Well, it's not like they were tortured and raped, for one thing. Surprised they weren't."

"Oh?"

"I mean, that's the common practice. Guys like that usually go in for that sort of thing."

"You make it sound like the murderer missed an opportunity there. What's another thing?"

"What?"

"You said for one thing they weren't tortured and raped. What's another thing that could have made it worse for them?"

Morris didn't like the shape of the man's mouth, a downward slant on one side, giving him the expression of permanent chagrin.

Ignoring the tone in Morris's voice, the man shrugged in his blue bomber jacket.

"Just expressing my opinion."

He turned his broad back to Morris and finished his transaction. At the cash register, Georges bagged what looked like screwdrivers and chisel. Georges thanked the client for his custom, but the stranger said nothing and almost stepped on Morris's toes with his grass-stained rubber boots, the kind firefighters wore.

"Ever see him before, Georges?"

"Mais non, jamais." Georges then switched to English. "Can't say that I have, Morris. Must have come in from the city."

"All the way from the city to shop at your hardware store?"

"Maybe he remembered needing something and pulled off the highway to drive into town. No law against someone from the outside buying goods in town, is there? Did you want something, Morris?"

"No, just came in to check on the pruning shears. The spring of my favourite pair keeps popping out."

"Sorry, I don't have the springs in stock, Morris."

"Pas de problème, Georges. *Salut."*

He decided to leave his truck parked in the town's public lot and walk to the senior citizens' residence, where the chief administrator waited to hear his plans for the waterfront gardens. He had been clicking through gardening websites on Kate's computer, websites she had discovered and bookmarked to save him time. He also flipped through magazines to sharpen his sense of what plants would work best, to derive inspiration, to steal ideas, and to stop staring at the clocks in his house, glad that another hour had ticked by without incident, that his daughter had not come closer to catastrophe for another day. What did it matter that it could have been worse? How did that in any way alter the actual circumstances in which the townspeople found themselves, and in which he, Morris, found himself? From the bushes, the murderer could have been watching every move Kate had made in the McCready gardens. He could have stepped out of the shadows, cudgel in hand, or whatever it was he had used—Morris couldn't remember—and only slunk back because Geraldine McCready appeared on the garden steps. What had happened, in a way, involved Morris. He was part of the story. He was not part of a nightmare on the other side of the world. These terrible killings—present and real—were tangible like the cracked concrete on which he now walked. In world terms, the atrocity was small; more horrifying news erupted elsewhere on a daily basis, no one needed to remind him, but this particular atrocity had knocked him off his feet. It was not happening elsewhere, it was happening here. Proximity bred anxiety, anxiety fear.

Standing on a corner under one of the arched street lamps from which hung a wire-and-peat basket of trailing geraniums and silvery blue verbena—very well watered, Morris was pleased to see, unlike some municipalities that let their floral displays wilt and wither in the sun—he made a special point of looking both ways before crossing. Not much sun this past week in any case, the sky a flat smoky grey, although the temperature had risen to normal levels for August. He considered entering Manon's café for a coffee and chat before proceeding to the old folks' home.

Because Mr. Szerkasy, the chief administrator, liked plans laid out in black and white—difficult for him to imagine something as imprecise as a garden—Morris regretted not bringing his rough sketches. But he had brought along his notebook with plants and proposed cost estimates. Like most men encased in suits and strangled by neckties, Szerkasy hesitated to believe in the expertise of a man wearing a T-shirt and jeans. If he kept the talk to costs, measurements, the layout of the grounds, the materials required for the pathways and edging, Morris suspected Szerkasy would relax in his high-backed, hunter green leather chair on casters and trust him to complete the task according to plan. Talk of flowers and beauty made an executive nervous. Too airy. Keep it low to the ground, Morris reminded himself.

Staring through the café window, he saw a blue bomber jacket in the middle table where Professor Ingoldsby had sat with his friends. Véronique seemed to be taking his order as the stranger looked up and returned Morris's stare. Because the face appeared darker in the café than in the hardware store, Morris could not see the blue capillaries of the man's cheeks. Véronique disappeared into the back. Three customers sitting by the window frowned at Morris; one of the women waved him away. Morris continued looking over their heads at the man in the blue jacket with the mass of black hair down each side of his head. The eyes were invisible from this distance; all that could be seen was just a bullish head covered in black and a face that did not smile, did not flinch before Morris's rude stare.

If it weren't for the time—Szerkasy frowned on tardiness— Morris would have entered the café, sat at another table, watched the stranger, left when he did, and followed him. What would happen when the stranger stopped and objected? This was a free country, wasn't it? A man could go where he pleased. The stranger stood up. Morris stepped away from the window, much to the relief of the three women trying to enjoy their tea and *pâtisseries*. Behind him a motorcycle roared by, its raucous engine rattling the eardrums and café window. The stranger stepped outside and approached Morris, who immediately put a hand in his back pocket before remembering he carried no weapon.

The man just didn't look right to Morris, not the kind of man you'd expect to see in this town—something about how he carried himself, the roughness of his complexion, the parting of his hair, and when he opened his mouth wide to smile a mirthless smile at

Morris, the wide gaps showed more gum than teeth. Maybe he was crazy to think so, but Morris lately had begun separating people into those who looked right and those who didn't, the division based on his intuition and their manner. He crossed the street before Morris could speak to him and entered another shop, Les Caresses, a boutique specializing in lingerie that, so far, Morris only dreamed about buying for Nancy. The time. Only five minutes to reach Szerkasy's office. What on earth would a man like that want in a women's boutique specializing in fine under-garments? He wanted watching, that man, he wanted surveillance. The world was too dangerous a place to let strange people walk the streets unobserved. Time was not on Morris's side today.

Entering the lobby of the old folks' home, which smelled of lemon-scented cleaning liquids, Morris noted the pots of aspidis-tra and sansevieria in front of the mirrored wall. Two old men were slumped over unattended in wheelchairs beside a table on which checker pieces lay untouched. In front of the wall opposite the mirror stretched a long red leather sofa, so high-backed and square that Morris couldn't imagine sitting on it. Szerkazy's office was down the corridor leading away from the two elevators with the scratched, green doors. Across the street he could see the gas station. A truck pulled up, very similar to his own, and even from this distance, Morris recognized the stranger behind the wheel. His head was turned toward the residence. Once again their gazes met, although Morris didn't believe the stranger could identify who was standing in the lobby across the street watching his every move—ridiculous to even think the man could see him.

"Ah, there you are, Mr. Bunter. I've been waiting for you."

Szerkasy wore a beige suit of summer wool and a chestnut brown tie spotted with yellow bees. Uncomfortable in suits himself, Morris assumed a deferential air toward men who wore them to work, like bankers and lawyers and university administrators. Given the noose they willingly strung around their necks, such men deserved at least the respect one gave to the dying. The truck pulled away from the gas pumps but stopped and idled before entering the lane. Morris could have sworn he saw the toothless smile in the shadow of the cab, the stranger pointedly daring Morris to come out and follow him, Morris was sure, but the truck turned into the lane of oncoming traffic. An arm waved out the window.

"This way, Mr. Bunter. My office is down the hall."

Such a young man to be head of an institution for the aged and decrepit, with his solid black hair so rigorously trimmed and shaped that it looked painted on the skull. Morris examined his own scruffy running shoes and wondered if he should have dressed up for the occasion, as he followed Szerkasy, regretting that he had not pursued the stranger in the red truck.

14

. . .

"ALL I'M SAYING is you gotta give Kate some slack."

"Look who's the expert."

"Just common sense, man."

Morris didn't mind Émile telling him how to deal with Kate because like most childless people Émile believed he knew all about parenthood. Standing on the outside of paternal responsibilities and emotions, he assumed inexperience conferred insight. Never tried and tested, Émile offered advice and nourished two of the most common delusions of men without children: he would have been a great father if he had chosen to be, or he would have been terrible, so it was just as well not to be a father at all. Morris recognized both positions as forms of vanity and self-congratulation. But he loved Émile, an all-purpose maintenance man who drove trucks, opened sewers, drilled concrete, painted yellow stripes on the streets, strung Christmas decorations from lamppost to post, watered community flower boxes, acted as a volunteer firefighter and major organizer of the annual food drive for the region's indigent and dispossessed, which included a few citizens of their town. And twice a week he visited his frail mother, now residing in a chronic care facility for Alzheimer's patients on the south shore.

When he noticed Émile's somewhat wrinkled face, Morris thought of the astonishing flight of time. They had known each other for so long that neither one of the men could remember when they had not. Émile had turned fifty today. His skin was darkened and leathered by a lifetime of work outdoors. Morris joked that he hadn't aged at all for an old man. Which of course meant that Morris himself hadn't aged. Looking to his friend for confirmation that youth had not entirely fled, that fifty meant little more than a configuration of arbitrary numbers, having nothing to do with mortality, he found little to sustain his own illusions. He invited Émile over for supper with Nancy and his friend Bogdan to celebrate the birthday. Kate refused to stay home for the meal Morris cooked to honour the half-century mark of his friend's life. Something simple, just a recognition of the necessity of the ordinary to keep back the bloody terror at the edge of things. Morris could have insisted but realized he risked watching Kate leave the house angry again. They were trying to maintain the hesitant, still-embarrassed peace. Kate knew Émile very well, but spending a Saturday evening with her father and his friends was not her idea of a good time. Not with Tarun revving his rusted junk heap outside.

"Half a century! I can't believe it."

"Can't believe what, Morris?" Bogdan asked.

"Émile's fifty today."

"Yeah, well, you were forty-nine in the spring. What's the big deal?"

Morris was bent over the oven, pulling out a heavy ceramic pan of roasted vegetables from the lower shelf—rutabagas, carrots, potatoes, and leeks sprinkled with spices. He tested the rutabagas with a fork.

"I think I'll add the mushrooms now. This should be ready in a few more minutes."

On the upper shelf of the oven, the boneless chicken breasts were browning in their seasoning of rosemary and lemon juice.

Bogdan shredded endive and radicchio over a wooden bowl. Morris did not expect Bogdan to ruminate about the passage of time. "I like to keep my feet on the ground," he always said whenever conversation turned toward the ineffable. Because he stood so rooted to the earth, Bogdan was a good man to know. If he promised you something, consider it done. He did not waste time wondering about the whys and wherefores. If he could perform a task for a friend, he did. No questions asked. When Maria died, Émile had, in a manner of speaking, embraced Morris in sympathetic tears, but Bogdan had appeared the morning after her death and taken the phone from Morris's hand.

"I will do this. Kate needs you. Tell me what you want."

And he'd made all the arrangements. His body crowding the space between kitchen table and sink, Bogdan kept his eyes straight ahead and let time take care of itself. He didn't play softball, but he often came to watch the games, then go out with the team for a beer and ribs. Having escaped from the U.S.S.R. as a young man, he never once mentioned Russia and seldom talked politics or world events. When asked what he thought or felt about the recent murders in their community, Bogdan turned his head aside as if some facts did not bear thinking about or were too overwhelming to consider. He had left his own family behind in the now defunct Soviet Union. Chances of being reunited had diminished with each year of separation. They used to talk to him about his three children, now young adults, and his wife. Communication between them had ceased years ago. Bogdan still mailed letters and gifts to his home address in Moscow, and never received a reply. Details of how he escaped, but not his family, remained cloudy, so his friends did not pursue painful memories.

A security guard at the university, Bogdan knew stories about Ingoldsby and had even witnessed a compromising scene involving the professor and a young woman ("maybe a student—I didn't stay long enough to ask") in Ingoldsby's office one night while doing his routine walkabout, checking office doors. The harassment hearing and its consequences did not surprise him. "It's good he not touch my daughter. I kill the fucker," was Bogdan's only comment when Morris told him that the administration had fired Ingoldsby. Bogdan lived in the same apartment complex as Véronique, the waitress at the café, and Morris sometimes thought he should arrange to bring the two of them together, Véronique being so clearly attracted to big men. Bogdan bought his clothes at a store in the city that specialized in extra-large sizes. Still firm, he did not jiggle and wobble when he walked. He spoke a somewhat undiomatic but comprehensible French with a throaty Russian accent.

Morris uncorked another bottle of Bogdan's passable red wine, which he pressed and aged in the basement of his apartment building. Every year Bogdan drove to the Atwater market in Montreal, where he bought several wooden boxes of grapes wholesale. For the birthday celebration, he brought four bottles, presumably one for each person, including Nancy, as well as a litre of his favourite vodka, which he drank on weekends like water. He and his Russian friend had already emptied one bottle of wine while working in the kitchen. Morris liked the sensation of mild inebriation, the warming of his blood, the viewing of life through the pulverized grape. Émile was watching a baseball game on Morris's thirty-six-inch television screen. Nancy, expected any minute now, had volunteered to buy a strawberry cheesecake, Émile's favourite, at the bakery-delicatessen in the mall. Morris and Bogdan had contributed twelve dollars apiece toward the cost of the cake.

The last Saturday of August, gardening work mounting, wet weather causing delays, and the residents of Old Town stupefied with anxiety over the murders, they all deserved a celebration.

Nancy didn't want to talk about the killings, fearful that discussion would somehow bring the murderer to her door. When her boys were out for the evening, she locked all the doors and sat up with the lights on, even though the women of Old Town had been murdered during the day. She called Morris two or three times to come over and sit with her. Which he didn't mind because, well, he liked the smell of her hair and softness of her thighs pressed against his when they sat together on the sofa watching television. Both Émile and Bogdan admired Nancy very much, and Morris suspected that Émile was more than casually interested. He sat too close to her after the ball games and often asked if she wanted anything, and Nancy responded flirtatiously. Morris wasn't sure how he felt about this, because Nancy and he had slept together. He assumed making love indicated serious, not merely recreational, interest. He had also changed her kitchen taps in mid-July, but Émile had installed a basement shower for the boys a week later. They were all such good friends—pity to undermine it with sexual tension and jealousies. He would just have to make his intentions clear to Émile, who would back off.

When Nancy pushed open the kitchen's screen door with her backside, carrying a huge white cake box, Morris also noticed Bogdan's face. Three men in the middle of their middle age without a woman, and Nancy with voluptuous backside and smelling of flowers and spice, her red hair catching light, and glowing with slivers of copper and gold, her luscious lips so red, red as the strawberries on top of the cheesecake that she carefully removed from the box while Morris found a plate in the cupboard large enough to carry it. Bogdan stood behind her, opening another bottle of wine. Morris steadied himself, the aroma of the vegetables and chicken making him dizzy with hunger. So hot in the kitchen. As he gulped down half a glass of wine to suppress the hunger pangs, the wine shot right to his head like an arrow of light. His legs loosened, his mind, easy and free, rose and dipped like a canoe riding high and bright above the rapids. Mmm, what a woman.

He tried to forget murder and murdered victims, the murderer at large, the insecurity of life, and the awful passing of time, because here was Nancy of the strawberries. Bogdan plucked a fat one off the cheesecake and held it between her open lips. More alone than not, her sons pushing at the edges of manhood, a woman whose garden he had designed and helped to grow so she could have a place to sit, surrounded by the beauty of lilies and roses, Nancy seemed to be beckoning to him like a mermaid in a mirage, wavering and distantly golden in the sunset. He drank the last of the bottle and his head spun. He shouldn't drink too much wine—it didn't sit well and could lead him to lose control of the occasion, and this was a very special time. The oven timer dinged, and Morris almost heaved head-first like the wicked witch into the oven, except Bogdan pulled him back and grabbed the roasting pan of chicken before it slid to the floor.

"Steady there, comrade."

"Morris! We haven't eaten and already you've had too much." But Nancy's tone was amused, not critical.

"You're too much, sweetheart," he said, affecting his unconvincing Humphrey Bogart voice, wishing he had a cigarette.

Émile came into the kitchen, proclaiming the state of emptiness of his stomach.

"Hey, Nancy, this is great."

Morris winced as Émile greeted her with a kiss on the strawberry lips. He immediately looked for something to carry. The kiss seemed longer than it needed to be.

"We're eating in the dining room. Table's set courtesy of Kate before she left."

"Kate's a good kid, Morris. I always said."

"I know she is, Nancy." And then he placed his arms around her waist and pulled her toward him, right in front of the heat pouring out of the still-open oven door, in front of Bogdan and Émile, and kissed her full on the lips, tasting of syrupy strawberry and creamy lipstick, his tongue wet with wine inside her surprised, unresisting mouth. As long as he held her, she was not alone and therefore always safe.

"Okay, Morris, give the girl a break. Take the salad in."

Bogdan placed Morris's hand on the bowl and turned him toward the dining room.

"I'll serve the chicken and vegetables. Émile, you pour the wine. Nancy, please sit at the end opposite birthday boy here. Great-looking cake."

"That bakery makes the best cheesecake, I tell you, worth every calorie."

As if testing for excess weight, she ran her hands down her thighs covered with pink capri pants like Kate's, and the eyes of all three men followed her fingers. The green top tied with a bow beneath her breasts, above a puckered navel, revealed the deliciously freckled skin of her abdomen, full and soft and inviting the head to rest and the tongue to taste. Her long feet in high white cork sandals, her toenails painted red like dabs of blood. Red berries, berries, berries: Morris did not want to think about blood.

"I'm famished. Let's eat."

Nancy brushed by them like a perfumed breeze, and the three men stood in the kitchen, not looking at each other, and each considering the degree of lust they felt for the woman they all loved. Morris's stomach turned and twisted from excitement and pleasure, not from apprehension and murders. This party would set him right, remind him of goodness and love, the wine a means to joy, not a suppression of fear.

They all sat around the table, covered with Maria's lacy white cloth and her best blue willow dishes, and raised their glasses, toasting Émile hunched in the candlelight, smiling like a gnome, then sang "Happy Birthday" completely out of tune, and raised their glasses again, and began serving themselves. Their heads appeared bright like moons above the light of the cluster of candles on the table, their skin flushed from wine, and all eyes turned to Nancy. Morris had left the doors to the deck open. The late-summer evening flowed into the room and so did mosquitoes. Clapping and slapping after a few, he got up to shut the doors. Stepping across the threshold, he inhaled deeply and glanced at the sky. The white August moon spread a smoky pearl light over his golden grasses, now whispering in the night breeze. A place of peace and refuge, the garden. Not a body to be seen in the perennial beds, although he stared hard at the pergola as if seeking a presence, a fleeting shape, silly really, nothing, the rustling of leaves, spectral illusions, the play of shadows in the moonlight and the swilling of the wine in his imagination.

He stepped back into the room and closed the doors behind him. Here, in his house, they were safe, although it was indeed warm enough to drink on the deck under the moon if he lit the containers of citronella candles to discourage insects suicidally attracted to the flames. Nancy in pink would glow in the moonlight. After dinner, he would suggest they lounge on the deck. Unsteady on his feet, Morris was relieved to sit and drink again. He reached over the table and forked another breast of chicken from the serving platter onto his plate and filled his wineglass again. How many times? As many as it took to quell the riot in his head. Nancy was chattering about her work and the boys and the softball team, not chattering at all, her voice too sweet, how could he think it, because to Morris's ears her voice sang, rising and falling like a melody of love, an aria from one of Maria's favourite operas, oh, let him not remember

Maria at this moment, not now. Nancy's face wavered behind the glowing candles like a luminous fish in gold water, and he shook his head. Her face swam away into the darkness of the room, then appeared again like a goldfish in the still waters of a Japanese pond. Behind the candles, how shimmering red her lips, red as bloody berries wet with rain, red as her bloody toes polished like gems, and her hair in the candlelight soft fire rinsed with water and blood. Out of the sudden darkness Mrs. McCready's ghostly head opened above the centre platter of chicken breasts and roasted vegetables and blood poured from her gashed skull like red sauce over the food. Morris's stomach leaped and rolled.

"Morris!" His three guests all shouted his name at once.

The chair fell over backwards as he stood, clutching the edge of the table with both hands to keep from falling, his glass tumbling over, the wine spilling and spreading like thin blood, and Morris shouting over the candles, their flames sputtering.

"Who did this?"

He had yet to eat a slice of the cake, but the red, syrupy thickness of the cake's topping seemed to catch in his throat and he retched.

"Oh my God, he's going to be sick." Nancy's singing voice.

"I got him. Morris, you've had too much to drink, comrade."

Bogdan grabbed him from behind, preventing him from stretching his arm over the table to point. Did they not see? The head rocketed up and through the ceiling, which he could not see, leaving a spume of blood streaking and disappearing like a comet's tail. Nancy disappeared in the darkness, and Émile shrank beneath the table. His own body buckled and jumped in Bogdan's arms. He gasped, his lungs heaved, then collapsed, and there was no breath at all left in his shaking body, and no light in his swirling head, and no sound in the red light of the room. Only the reflection of the moon, round and dead in the glass of the closed doors, as the heart swirled and the body slumped into the black cushion of Bogdan's arms.

15

· · ·

RINSING OUT his favourite coffee mug—a gift from Kate the first Christmas after Maria's death—he remembered falling asleep in front of the tree, lights ablaze, hugging Maria's nightgown until Kate had wakened him just before dawn.

"Is it time to open the presents, Dad?"

Maria and he had always got up before Kate, who surprisingly slept well past dawn on Christmas morning during her early childhood years. She had pudgy feet and pink toes, and she loved to wear a white eyelet gown Maria had sewn, dragging Gumption, a rag doll clothed in dungarees and mackinaw, a straw hat permanently attached to his soft brown head, also sewn by Maria. Whatever happened to Gumption? Kate had loved that doll so much that she'd never let it out of her sight, sleeping with it, nestling it on her lap at the dinner table, stuffing it in her school bag, only letting Gumption out of her hands when Maria insisted on washing it. Of course she had outgrown both gown and doll.

Kate had been keeping secrets from him, or he had been too blind to notice. He didn't believe Kate decided to move in with Tarun on the spur of an angry moment. Such a move entailed some previous commitment and planning. Did Kate really expect her father to approve? She'd come home last night after midnight to see her father heave his stomach's contents into the toilet bowl,

Nancy and Bogdan holding his head and wiping his face, his brain sodden porridge, and Kate had shouted, "You're drunk!" What happened later, once he'd turned his head over the rim of the bowl and seen his daughter point a finger at him from the doorway, Morris did not recall. Except Kate's scathing tone: "Honestly, Dad!" Through the kitchen window, he saw the purple finches and nuthatches dipping for the black sunflowers seeds in the feeder. He made note of what needed to be done in his gardens. It was still too early to cut anything down; he preferred letting the stalks, stems, leaves, and late blooms dry and brown in the late summer and early autumn. The leaf clusters of his foxtail lilies were yellowing, the plants entering their dormant stage, the splendid spires, sheltered from the winds, having disappeared. The end of things also had their beauty. Oh boy, his head, dense as an iron ball, was about to roll off his shoulders. Eyes bleary, tongue thick with the residue of last night's debauch, coated with slug slime despite the toothpaste and mouthwash, Morris didn't know whether to stand, sit, or lie down, except that lying down sent him twirling through the coils of a headachy spiral.

Early morning, the dew still visible on his garden pathways and the broad leaves of the hostas, the sun woven in spiderwebs spun overnight from frond to frond, leaf to leaf, he thought of taking a cup of coffee and sitting on the top step of his deck, surveying his tiny kingdom, letting the coolish breeze clear away the dankness of his head. Maria had loved sitting outside in the early mornings of summer. He'd come out with two cups of coffee and join her. They often discussed the plans for the day, who had to do what. Always something to do. How was boredom possible? And the plans for the residence needed to be finalized—Mr. Szerkasy expected a detailed cost analysis by Wednesday.

Morris couldn't eat the omelette Kate had made. Over her breakfast, as he chewed unbuttered toast to the consistency of wet blotting paper, she blithely told him, waving aside objections with a fork, that she had decided to move into an apartment with Tarun, almost daring him to protest by the way she stood up with her hands on her hips. The toast congealed in his mouth, refused to budge. He drank orange juice to help wash it down, but a piece lodged in his throat, forcing him to leave the table and cough it up in the bathroom. Splashing water on his face, Morris knew Kate's news would knock him off balance for the rest of the day and lead to a bitter quarrel. His body too insecure to withstand major disturbance—it would crumble on the first impact—he had to respond carefully. Returning to the breakfast table, he sat down and drank more coffee, asking Kate when and where in a voice that he hoped did not betray anger and sorry disappointment laced with incipient panic. Today, a place in town, she answered, meaning Montreal, five minutes from the Berri Métro station. Not far, but on the other side of the world. The distance between father and child could not be measured in miles. Why did she believe it necessary to leave? Living with Tarun didn't solve anything. Was life at home so insupportable that Kate had no choice but to vacate the premises? Not only move, but move into an apartment with her boyfriend, for Chrissake!

"You sure you can't eat the omelette, Dad? Pity to waste it."

"No, really, Kate, I'm sorry, my stomach's not up to it, but thanks for going to the trouble …"

"It was nothing, Dad, just a few eggs and mushrooms."

Today! Morris tried to pretend he minded Kate's leaving because he disliked or disapproved of Tarun, but he would have disapproved of any guy; he minded because, simply and horribly, Kate had decided to move out of the house—leaving their home, leaving her widowed father, leaving what he had always believed was their happy life together. He cringed at the idea of living in an apartment. No land, no garden, no stepping directly outside into the full and fragrant air—he'd feel crushed and suffocated by the smallness and convenience of apartment living. Not that he had come to depend on his daughter to fill the space widening in his life, month by month, year by year, since Maria's death; shock diminished, initial grief passed, but sorrow sank deep like a long taproot to the very bottom of his heart, regardless of how he went about his daily business.

Life continued, of course. No one needed to beat him over the head with a platitude. No one could pour herself into Maria's place, least of all a child who had every right to go out into the world and begin her own life, separate from the demands of a parent. When Kate left, the vacancy would be more than he could endure. At one time, he regretted the smallness of the house, inadequate for Kate's burgeoning personality and adolescent tastes. Despising her music, Morris did not look forward to the silence of her room. He watched her clear the table. Kate was capable of looking after herself. No harm would come to his daughter in this sometimes terrifying world. Morris hoped that repeating a deeply held wish, genetically sealed in the very core of his being, made it true.

Did she really have to leave today, of all days? Why today meant more than any other, Morris couldn't say, aside from general dilapidation of body and soul, and the self-pitying urge to cry. Just where did Kate and Tarun plan to live together? A place in town, she had said, near the Berri Métro, offering no concrete details of size, condition, costs, although she called it a flat. Kate should have prepared him: in a year's time, say, she planned to move. And now with this lunatic killer on the loose, how could he guarantee his daughter's safety? How could he even trust Tarun to protect Kate from Ingoldsby? The kitchen wall phone rang. Wiping her hands, Kate picked up the receiver.

"Yes, he is," she answered. "It's for you, Dad."

He rose too quickly; his head whirled, the air flickered with phosphorescent pins and evanescent stars like the momentary flash of fireflies among pine tree boughs.

"Ah, hello … hello?"

Kate draped damp tea towels over the rod and, humming, walked out of the kitchen, her head obviously bursting with song, and his heart a rotten rhizome. God, she couldn't be packed already and leaving without saying goodbye. At least let him recover from last night's binge so he could hug his daughter like a sane and sober man and say no matter what happened she'd always have a home. After he convinced her that moving in with Tarun was a very bad idea. This house, you see, he wanted to make clear to Kate, this house is yours in ways perhaps you don't understand now, but you will. One day, if not today, one day. Please don't leave now.

"Mr. Grant? Yes, of course, Monday?"

Difficult to hear Grant's muted voice at the other end.

"Pardon me? Trees? I don't cut down trees."

Covering the receiver while Grant maundered and mumbled about a forest on his lawn, Morris called his daughter.

"Kate? You're not leaving yet, are you?"

"No, Dad. I'm reading the paper. Tarun's picking me up at two."

The familiar way she mentioned the name made him gag into the receiver. Already there was a history between his daughter and this boy about which Morris knew little. He wanted to know everything about their relationship and nothing, nothing at all, lest the knowledge veer in directions he didn't want it to go.

Morris had promised to play softball this afternoon. Kate's leaving was momentous; he'd have to cancel first thing he got off the phone with Mr. Grant. The Grant place, one of the largest properties on the highest point of Old Town, well above the level where he had discovered Geraldine McCready's body. He drove by the estate almost every day. Ignoring local expertise and labour, the Grants relied on professional landscaping companies.

"Yes, sure, I can stop by late Monday, after I finish with my customers. Okay? Great, goodbye." He hung up and waited until his brain stopping racing after its tail.

"Kate, where are you?"

"Here, in the living room. What's the problem?"

"No … no problem. That was old Mr. Grant who called. You know the Grants?"

"Not personally, but I know they live in the big mansion on top of the hill in Old Town."

"He'd like my advice."

She did not reply, sitting on his favourite chair, one leg hanging over the arm, sections of the newspaper in disarray at her bare feet. The last thing Morris wanted was an argument, although it did seem necessary, yes, that for her own safety he forbid her to move. Psychopaths on the loose—whose daughter was safe from harm? Had she even packed? He simply refused to allow her to live with a man, a boy, really, as if that made any difference. Dating was one thing, even sleeping together, although he stopped short of pursuing that line of thought—the less he knew the better—and trusted to Kate's common sense about health and protection, but living together—Tarun scarcely twenty— why take on the burden and commitment so young? Anyway, if Kate really planned to go this afternoon, she didn't have time to laze about on his favourite chair, so perhaps he hadn't heard correctly. There was still time to persuade her to take a moment to think about what she was doing.

What a mess she made of the newspaper, which he liked to read first, opening one section at a time, refolding it, then neatly insert- ing the sections one into another in their proper order. What had once irritated now endeared her to him. Kate could always be the first to read the paper and scatter the sheets all over the house, if only she would stay. To walk into the house and not hear her music, the sheer awfulness of silence left by her departure—oh, let her raise the roof with alternative cacophony.

"Kate?"

"Yes, Dad?"

"I really believe you ought to give this some thought."

"What?"

"Moving in with Tarun. I don't think you're ready for an adult relationship. I don't see why you feel you have to move."

"I am an adult, and my relationship with Tarun is really my business, not yours."

"Of course it's my business—I'm your father. Aren't you happy here?"

"Sure, that's not the point."

"It's not?"

"I want to be free to come and go as I please."

"That doesn't make any sense—you *are* free."

"No, Dad, I know you mean well, I'm nineteen already and … sometimes …"

She didn't finish the sentence and he bit his tongue.

Only nineteen, too young, although she made it sound old. That was precisely his point. Too young, too inexperienced, unready for the world, the dangerous, murderous world, his child still. Parenting did not end on a birthday. What absurd logic plucked nineteen out of the air and declared that age the irrefutable argument for independence and security?

"I don't like the idea of you moving out."

"You will, soon enough. Tarun's great—take my word for it."

"I don't give a shit how great he is. You're too young. Kate, I don't want you to leave."

· 172 ·

She snapped open the sports section of the newspaper, pretended to read, then folded the paper, letting it slide to the floor.

"I guess I should get ready."

"Did you hear me?"

Removing her leg from the arm of the chair, she stood up. Morris stepped aside.

"Yes, I heard, but there's no point arguing about this."

"We're not arguing."

"We will."

"Why can't we have a serious heart-to-heart, father-daughter talk?"

"That usually means why can't I do what you want."

"No it doesn't."

"Yes it does, and it almost always means an argument."

"But this is a serious decision, Kate, it's not like buying a pair of jeans."

"Tarun's a great guy, Dad, don't worry about it."

"It's not just Tarun …"

"What, then?"

"You're still a young—"

"You mean a child, I'm still a child?"

"I have such a headache."

"You shouldn't drink so much."

"No, I guess I shouldn't. What I mean to say is, do you think you'll be safe shacking up with Tarun?"

"We're not shacking up. You make it sound dirty. Of course I'll be safe. Why wouldn't I be?"

"You read the newspapers, Kate, you know as well as I do, and think about what's been happening around here … Ingoldsby …"

"Are you always going to bring that jerk into every one of our conversations?"

"Not just him … I mean … the ladies … Mrs. Ferroux and …"

"Jesus, Dad … you can't let that sort of thing run your life."

"It's your life I'm thinking about."

"Well, then, you can't let it run my life."

It wasn't going well. The tightness in his chest, the roots of his heart pot-bound and strangled, the thickness of his tongue, the distant but murmuring pain at the back of his head—not all attributable to the consequences of drink. If he continued to protest, he could tell by the slight rise in her voice, Kate would back away, perhaps lose her temper, slam the door in his face, pack in anger, and wait seething on the edge of the bed until Tarun honked his horn.

"You'll be back, then, tomorrow for some other things?"

"Yeah."

"Do you have what you'll need … a kettle?"

"We're okay. It's not like we're getting married, you know."

"No … that's good … I mean … well, it's better having convenient things than not."

"We'll manage, Dad."

Her voice dropped. She kissed him on the cheek before going to her room. Morris sank into his chair, warm from Kate's body, relieved that they had not fought, that she would not be storming out of the house. He became aware of his own smell, a sour, musty smell exuding from all parts of his body. If Tarun happened to enter the house today, Morris thought it wise to meet the lad looking less seedy than he now felt. A shower would cleanse his body and refresh his spirit, sure, and prime him to play ball, flirt with Nancy behind home base in the early afternoon, perhaps clear his head. Then he remembered the game scheduled for the afternoon and groaned. He called Émile, who acted as coordinator and business manager of the softball team, to cancel.

"I just can't see myself swinging a bat or running around bases today, Émile … Sure, last night was great fun … We all wanted to celebrate your birthday. Bogdan and Nancy ... Well ... I'm glad ... No, my head's about to burst—any movement, you know how it is. So I'm really sorry, but you know what state I was in ... Have a great game. I'll call later. Bye."

In the shower upstairs, the water sluiced down his aching body, each movement of his arms, especially when he raised them above his shoulders, flooded his head with pain, the aspirins not working very well. Served him right—red wine always had that effect, especially bottles of Bogdan's homemade poison. Morris stood behind the glass door of the shower stall, head bent, hands cupped across his belly, marked by the appendicitis scar, water pooling around his feet because the washcloth covered the drain. The force of the shower splashed against the back of his neck like a massage, less painful, somehow soothing anxiety as much as cleaning away the odour of stale vomit. Soaping his genitals, he remembered the showers with Maria, and surprised, he felt a stirring. Let him not imagine Maria, not now. He shampooed his hair with one of Kate's several brands. Conditions and leaves hair shining and manageable. God, Kate and Tarun in the shower together! After she moved out, what shampoo would he buy? Kate chose all the hygiene products of the household, except for his personal deodorant: soaps and toothpaste, shampoos and eau de cologne, even for him. Five, mostly full, bottles of men's cologne remained in the medicine cabinet. Only under duress, which was to say Kate's insistence, did he ever splash himself with fragrances of any kind. His hands in muck and mire more often than not, hoisting bags of fertilizer and turning soil; perfumes didn't stand a chance against manure.

Stepping out of the shower stall, he did feel better, his head less weighted, his bones less rubbery. A knock on the door.

"Dad? I'm going out for a bit, but I'll be back for my things later, so don't worry."

"You're leaving now?"

"No, I'm not leaving. Chantal's downstairs—we're going to a jeans sale in the mall. I'll be home before Tarun gets here."

He continued wiping himself dry to subdue the panic in his voice.

"You sure? You promise?"

"I'll be back at one, I promise. Okay?"

"Yes, if you promise, okay … You be careful now."

The famous parental warnings that guaranteed nothing except an illusory peace of mind. Chantal owned a car; almost all of Kate's friends drove. Insofar as he knew, Chantal drove well and had never been involved in an accident. But knowledge and safety did not always coincide.

"Where did you say you were going?"

"Stopping for gas first, then to the mall for a while. Bye."

She ran down the stairs, Morris could tell. The front door clicked shut. Rubbing the steamy washroom window, he saw Kate get into Chantal's Toyota. As it pulled out, signalling a left—good girl, Chantal—a red truck slowed down and gave it the right of way. From this perspective, Morris couldn't see the driver. The red truck picked up speed behind Chantal's Toyota, and both vehicles disappeared from view. Morris quickly dressed in his bedroom, taking a reasonable view of things: red was a common colour for pickups, probably the first colour people imagined when someone said *truck*.

He grabbed his car keys and wallet off the tallboy, hurried to his own truck parked in the driveway, pulled out without stopping at the end to check for oncoming traffic, and squealing the tires, drove toward the gas station. His truck was also low on gas. He'd be there in time to see Chantal's car, look out for the other red truck and, if need be, go all the way to the mall himself. If need be. It all depended on a little red truck.

Pulling into the gas station, he saw no Toyota and no truck. Why he assumed Chantal would choose this station, Morris didn't know. She could easily have driven straight to the gas station outside of town, just before the access ramp leading to the highway. Getting out and unhooking the gas line, unscrewing the lid to his tank, he persuaded himself not to follow the girls to the mall. If Kate ever discovered him, she wouldn't talk to him for Lord knows how long. That girl had perfected the silent treatment to a fine art, drove him crazy when she wouldn't speak to him. The red truck drove by, not travelling in the direction of the girls but going west along Riverside. He thought he saw the driver—a blue jacket—but couldn't be sure. Anyway, what if the driver of the red truck was the man in the hardware store? Just what absurd connection was he trying to make?

Morris checked the gas gauge and released the handle of the hose. The same truck, though, no mistake about it, and clearly not following Chantal's Toyota. What made him think the stranger had any interest in doing so? The lawn mower in the back—just another landscape worker—so many casual hired hands this time of the year. Not everyone required his services. He didn't know the guy from Adam. There, the next car, a green Pontiac, the man driving also a stranger. People had a right to come and go as they pleased. Morris tried to convince himself of the logic of that commonly held assumption. Since the murders, he really didn't believe it was true anymore. Kate would return by one o'clock. She was a good girl. In goodness lay safety. Right? Morris paid the twenty bucks, muttering to himself at the counter, sniffing the combustible materials in the gas station.

16

. . .

KATE WOULDN'T APPROVE of his sitting up at night like a guardian at the gate, waiting for her to come home. Against his wishes, she had gone out again, after she'd returned from the shopping trip with Chantal. She had called earlier on her cellphone, the background babble of voices and music so loud that he had scarcely heard what she said. Not to worry, she was fine, Tarun wouldn't be picking her up today after all, a change of plans. No, she was still moving out, but tomorrow ... on her way home soon ... don't wait up. He knew it, Tarun couldn't be trusted to look after his little girl. He had dozed off in his favourite chair. Rising from a semi-conscious fug like a heavy tortoise surfacing for air, he noticed the lateness of the hour. So late, so silent in the house, except for the ticking of clocks and the whirring of the refrigerator motor. The room lit only by the reflected glow of the moon, Morris fought against the urge to wander the streets, looking for Kate. Of course, she knew the neighbourhood; familiarity surely offered a guarantee of sorts. Exhausted, he could not sleep, so he stepped outside, stood in a pool of porch light. Meet her at the bus stop, well after midnight. Where was she?

Between the bus stop and their house ran the two streets of low-rise apartment blocks, each square unit separated from the others by driveways. Unremarkable rectangular grass plots in front, standard cedars, brown from winterkill, plunked in the middle, or half-naked spirea bushes marking the property borders, leggy petunias spilling over their boxes attached to the iron railings of the little balconies. Rigid red salvia and searing orange marigolds sat up in their narrow beds under basement windows, timid white impatiens, sometimes pink or salmon, circled tree trunks, and limp hostas edged along walks like green mounds of indifference to the front door of the apartment buildings. Landlords rarely rose to heights of horticultural splendour.

The moon cast a flattering, bluish white hue over the banal landscape. A few apartment lights showing in windows, flood-lights pouring down driveways, the street lamps lowering their yellow glow, the darkness attenuated by the lights of the town, and the stars in their millions scarcely visible above the city, Kate, having often walked this route from the bus stop, ordinarily would have felt no anxiety. She had never feared the dark as a child. In any case, here, darkness for the most part had fled. Who really lived in the dark anymore in this day and age, the night sky blanched by electricity? Maria used to tell Kate tales of a world when the night sky was purple black like the queen-of-the-night tulip, and you could trace the lifeline of your palms beneath the immortal beauty of the perennially glinting stars. In that world, fearsome creatures lurked behind hoary trees and moonlight revealed their shadows, if you had an eye for such things.

He didn't want to remember Maria's stories because then he'd remember how Kate had snuggled against her mother's breasts and felt safe under the covers as she heard the most appalling crimes and punishments—her favourite being the false princess sealed up alive in a barrel studded with nails and rolled through the streets. Morris disapproved of her taking the late bus home—call me, he always said, no matter the time; why didn't she call?

She could at least try to understand his position, but no, she probably chose to stay downtown with her friends until after midnight in a *brasserie* or smoked meat deli. It was a forty-five-minute rocking bus ride along the main highway and through a few suburban streets, and she'd be walking home in the late evening—early morning actually, when he checked his watch. Morris went outside. Shadows under the moon shifted, assumed shapes that could frighten a child.

To reach their street, Kate would have to walk down the lengthy block of avenue des Merisiers, which met a crossroad, St-Zotique, where she would turn right, continue for another block, then turn right onto Paris Street, one block up, half as long as des Merisiers, cross over to Curé Cholet, a cul-de-sac that led nowhere. He could almost visualize Kate's movements, stopped himself from getting his car keys and driving to meet her. But there was a lighted path between two bungalows, leading from the curve of Curé Cholet, through a small park where toddlers played in sandboxes or climbed the moulded blue-and-yellow plastic monkey bars, and out to her own street. Not far—the terrain was so familiar that she could walk blindfolded. The lay of the land did not reassure Morris. So many places to hide, out of which to leap upon the unwary.

A warm evening with a breeze blowing from the east. So little traffic this time of the night, quiet except for the unceasing hum of the highway and the swishing leaves. When she reached the corner of des Merisiers and St-Zotique, suppose that red truck pulled up beside the curb, the passenger door swung open, and a man leaped out. Why hadn't Kate called again? He walked faster down the middle of the road. Yes, anyone could attack his daughter in the night. She would kick, kick and scream. The shadows looked like arms reaching out to strangle a passerby.

Morris began to run—not enough time to turn back, look for keys, and back the car out of the garage. Thank God for baseball, kept his legs strong, although lately he had become more conscious of his soft stomach when he ran. He thought he heard a scream—couldn't be—just the night-cracking voice of a screech owl. Was it Kate's scream, muffled and broken? The man with black hair—Morris remembered it hung thick and straight on either side of his head—could easily slip back into the truck, move like a giant cat in the night. Why didn't anyone look out a window? Forcing his legs, Morris ran faster, feeling pressure in his chest. Running under the nightmarish shapes and shadows of the trees, he shouted Kate's name.

Although most windows of the apartment buildings were dark, the light above the doors and the floodlights bathed the lawns in yellow-white. He could determine the colour of the impatiens around the diseased birch tree—he discouraged his clients from putting too much faith in birch saplings. Daddy, Daddy—he heard his daughter's voice as clearly as the screeching owl tangled in the tree branches. He pushed his body to run faster, his lungs scarcely able to supply it with oxygen, his stomach swilling and welling up. A roaring in the head—why didn't the neighbourhood wake up?

That man, that man, Morris kept remembering, afraid of a man he didn't know, and yet knowing as surely as his body protested against the run. The stretch from first to second base, far enough at the best of times, no more than a hop, skip, and jump compared with this, leaving him only mildly winded. He stumbled, his lungs breaking—his daughter was caught in a terrible danger. Use your cellphone. He had given it to her as a birthday present, insisting she carry it around with her at all times. Even the white stones edging walkways and garden beds loomed in the moonlight. One of them could be a broken cellphone, its insides spilling out like the fine and tiny intestines of a very small animal flattened by the wheel of a car. Poor Kate, frantic, scrabbling on the street, searching for her father's present.

The man with the black hair looked as if he could willingly snap a neck. He meant business. Under the barely perceptible stars over their hometown, a peaceful community, worse was coming. But the worst had not yet happened—there was time to stop it. He had run fast enough, his spirit pushing his muscle and bones beyond endurance itself. He raised his eyes to the sky, the smile of the pockmarked man in the moon chilling and horrible like the grimace of a petrified, bloodless head. And there Kate was, alive and walking toward him, so relieved to see her father. He had frightened off the marauder, he had saved his daughter. She was all right.

"Dad! What the hell are you doing? Are you crazy or something?"

Doubled over, trying to catch his breath, Kate standing above him on a moonlit street corner, a pink boutique bag rustling by her legs, heartbeats thumping in his head, Morris couldn't speak through the gasps. Crazy, maybe, but Kate was safe.

17

• • •

NANCY AND KATE walked on either side of the grocery cart as Morris pushed it down the wide aisles of the bulk food warehouse at one end of the mall. Kate seemed to have forgiven him for running down the street that night. Tarun was a closed subject between them. Kate had moped and cried in her bedroom for a few days over the collapsed plans to move in with him. He apparently had suddenly changed his mind about sharing a flat in Montreal. Morris offered what comfort he could, but his deep pleasure in the news would have compromised his solicitude. It was wise to let Kate have her cry. With marriage on his mind, Morris forgot about teenage infatuation and concentrated on the woman he loved. When Nancy agreed to spend Saturday morning with them, lunch together after shopping, he just knew in his heart that Nancy really did want him. By enjoying the pleasures of the moment and focusing on food, perhaps he'd be able to control his worries and pretend normality where none existed. At her door she pecked his cheek like a nun kissing a cross, and Morris kept his hands to himself. Give her time. Of course she was hesitant, worried (what woman wouldn't be these days?), afraid of her own emotions, wary of commitment, not the sort of woman to engage her deepest feelings without reflection.

Here they were, though, his daughter and his future wife, passing up and down the aisles, selecting economy packages of detergent and toilet paper. The volume of goods and foods, piled almost to the ceiling, raised his spirits. He didn't want to strut, but any man would be proud to be seen with Nancy, whose curves filled out her denim jeans in the most enticing ways. Her hair was loosely piled and pinned, curls waiting to be brushed off her cheeks by a lover's fingers. To his surprise, Kate had also agreed to accompany them, so here they were together—exactly the way they should be—his two women chatting, exclaiming over one product or another in the manner of women in stores. Not for a moment did they sense his uneasiness, his body and mind fragile—one knock and they would shatter.

Debating between a case of vegetable beef or tomato soup, Morris wondered about the appropriate moment to propose. He didn't want to be too premature and insistent, or make Nancy feel pressured. Overeagerness exuded a bad smell like fritillaria in the spring, repellent to rodents, however spectacular the blossom. Timing was everything, but the times, being so bad, required some decisive action. What better opportunity to show what a regular guy he was, how interested in the ordinary things of this world that made life comfortable and satisfying than shopping for groceries? Not that Nancy needed proof that he was a man to be trusted; she had known him long enough, had played softball with him.

His daughter did not resent the presence of another woman in his life. Marrying Nancy might also make Kate feel more secure at home, less eager to move out, should Tarun change his mind again. Nancy admired his house, often said it had a homey feel to it. As for her two boys, why, there would be room for everyone if he built an addition, an extra room for them. He liked her sons, they liked him, everyone liked one another. They would all be quite happy together in his house like properly placed *Dictamnus fraxinella* in a richly composted bed of earth. Left undisturbed, the gas plant sent down long taproots, growing stronger and fuller as the years passed, its fragrant leaves and white blossoms smelling of citrus.

Choosing the twelve-tin case of vegetable beef, he tried not to let his fears for the safety of his girls cloud the morning. But like voles tunneling toward the bulbs of his favourite tulips, worry and tension, memory and dread, undermined his confidence. Two women murdered, the police ineffective, unable to provide guarantees that it wouldn't happen again. And his nightmare vision of Kate under attack. He had difficulty explaining why she had met him running down the street at night, and she seemed only half persuaded that he had been overcome with concern for her safety.

"Morris, please buy this jar of olives. I love black olives."

He almost blurted out, Maria, you prefer going to the market for olives, but his daughter saved him.

"If you eat a dozen a day, that jar will last a year, Nancy."

"Don't you love black olives, too, Kate?"

"Not gallons' worth, but Dad, look, sweet pickled peppers."

She placed the humongous jar of red peppers next to the olives. The women started chatting about shoes they had seen in one of the mall boutiques. Peppers and olives, rye bread and havarti or Swiss cheese or both, sweet vidalia onions, kippers or smoked salmon: they would eat a splendid lunch. He'd prepare everything in his kitchen. Call her boys to come over if they weren't working or otherwise engaged. As he looked toward the end of this particular aisle, which led into one of the three central corridors of the warehouse, the jar of low-fat mayonnaise nearly slipped out of his hand. Attired in black wraps and straps, Annick crossed his line of vision and, Jesus! No! Ingoldsby, sporting a deep blue long-sleeved shirt, blue as a delphinium, pushing a grocery cart himself as if he were an ordinary guy like everyone else, with nothing on his conscience. Morris didn't think the girls saw, so preoccupied with the stacks of food behind him, talking about shoes, pickles, and eating lunch in the food court of the mall, which was not his intention at all, as he had planned a perfectly wonderful lunch for the entire family at home.

If he turned left into the corridor, he'd be going in the opposite direction and avoid running into Ingoldsby, but they could meet over the fish counter or in the bakery section or at the cash register. Anyway, he hadn't completed his own shopping. Why should he hurry out of the store because Ingoldsby stalked its premises? He didn't know what Kate would do, though, if their carts bumped into each other. His instinct impelling him to attack, avoidance nonetheless solved so many problems. If you don't want rampant goutweed to take over your garden, don't plant it in the first place, or rigorously set up borders through or under which it cannot grow. To reduce the risk of mildew, give your phlox breathing space and don't hose down the leaves. Even then, with the best gardening in the world, problems arose.

His breath ran a little short, and his heartbeat jumped, sensations he blamed on the atmosphere of the store. However air conditioned and climate controlled it was, he still disliked being inside on a lovely, cool day, ideal for digging in his garden. The warehouse space with its stacks of metal shelves burdened with boxes and tins suddenly shrank. More shoppers milled about, clicking and clanking their metal carts. There wasn't enough space for him and the professor, who passed out of view with Annick. Mustn't panic, mustn't let Nancy see distress in any way upset his composure. Control, focus, as athletes always said. Good. He returned Nancy's smile and breathed easily. Reaching the end of the aisle, Kate pointed to the right.

"Let's buy a cake, Nancy. The mocha chocolate is to die for."

"Kate, the cheeses are to the left."

"Oh, we can work our way back, Dad. Nancy wants cake."

"Sure, go ahead, blame me!"

To argue about direction would arouse suspicion. Damn Ingoldsby! Ruining a perfect morning. The man didn't have to do a single thing and still posed a threat. Watching his two women confabulate and chuckle, Morris began thinking what an excellent opportunity Ingoldsby presented. What better way to show Nancy how necessary to seek shelter in Morris's home and love. If Ingoldsby so much as flickered the slightest bit of interest in her direction, so much as sneered at Kate, he, Morris, would confront, challenge, and, not to put too fine a point on it, combat. Yes, show Nancy that she loved a man on whom she could rely, who'd never desert her in her hour of need. It was better to avoid a scene altogether—Morris understood that perfectly well—but unpleasantness, not of his own seeking, might be inevitable.

There, just ahead, clearly spotted by Kate, who stopped chatting with Nancy and turned to her father, was Annick of the spiky hair and the blue brightness of Ingoldsby, having reversed direction, now pushing a cart toward them, laughing and brushing up against each other like ridiculous lovers. They paid no attention to other shoppers, as if the world had to part like a biblical sea to let them pass. Just like Ingoldsby not to make allowances in a crowd, not to acknowledge anyone else's existence. He barged, rather than walked, using his body like a plow through the fields of lesser beings. The arrogance of the man set Morris fuming, his eyes squinting with irritation the way they did when he saw grasshoppers and their depredations in his garden. As a man of peace, wanting to sidestep confrontation, immediately turn down the next aisle before Ingoldsby noticed him, he was no coward. To avoid the meeting meant calling after the girls and knowing he'd retreated, giving the professor victory without so much as lifting a hand of protest. No, courage was called for.

"Dad? Please don't say anything. Just walk by."

"What should I do, Kate?"

"Just don't start anything."

"Start what?"

"Kate's right, Morris. Let's just move on."

"You don't know what he's done, Nancy."

"Oh, give it a rest, Morris, that's over and done with."

"I mean, you don't know everything he's done, Nancy."

"Dad, please, don't even speak to him."

They had stopped in front of a display of silver-and-gold tins of olive oil. Annick glanced at Morris and nodded her unsmiling head. Ingoldsby rattled the cart past without looking at Morris or Kate, although Morris sensed the professor's appraisal of Nancy, that furtive, swift shifting of the eyes of men toward women they wanted but couldn't have. How dared he even think of Nancy! Morris's palms were sweaty on the olive oil tin. He didn't need a gallon, but it showed Ingoldsby that he hadn't flinched. He could tell Kate was uneasy, embarrassed, but she touched Nancy's shoulder. The oil was heavy in his hand, heavy enough to smack against the side of a head and cause damage. Nancy let Kate lead her up the aisle. The moment to prove his prowess had disappeared as quickly as it had arisen. The professor was now out of reach of a swinging arm, probably laughing to himself.

"The cakes are over here," Kate called.

Pushing his cart, Morris looked back. The painter also looked back. The eyes of the two men locked. Was that a smirk, a sneer, a self-satisfied smile on the professor's face? Did he think he had gotten away with something, believed that he frightened Morris in front of the extra-virgin olive oil?

"Dad?"

"Okay, okay, I'm coming."

He needed to compose himself, concentrate, focus, recover his good spirits, try to remember his feelings of satisfaction as he drove to the mall with his wife-to-be and his daughter. In the front seat of the car, Nancy had relaxed and slid closer to him, their bodies touching. Ingoldsby should not be allowed to invade and destroy. It was always better to wrench a diseased plant out of the ground, uproot it entirely, than to waste effort coddling and nursing. Gardening taught ruthlessness. Hacking and deracinating worked wonders. He had lost this chance to impress Nancy. Would she think he had weakened at the crucial moment? But she herself had encouraged him to move on, to avoid confrontation. Was Kate to be always embarrassed by Ingoldsby? Would he never leave the neighbourhood? Two women dead, already. The police befuddled or at their wits' end. No arrests made—he should talk to them about his suspicions.

The blue-black and spiky hair disappeared down another aisle. What a pity Annick had saddled herself with a man like Ingoldsby. Her mother must have been turning in her grave. Morris tried to believe that his girls were right—better to ignore and pass on. He pushed his cart toward Nancy and Kate, who were waiting. Relying on him for protection, so willing to avoid conflict, they didn't really see the necessity of the task that lay ahead. He wanted Nancy to know that he'd do anything to win her love.

As she stood in front of a display counter of cakes and pies, each one large enough to give a generous portion to a dozen people, Kate's voice rose a pitch higher at a tempo faster than usual.

"I really like mocha, but look at the banana cream pie and this Black Forest cake with the maraschino cherries, the biggest cherries I've ever seen on a cake. Do you like apple pie, Nancy? Have you ever seen one so big? Dad, let's get a cake or pie."

"They're so large, honey, we couldn't eat it all."

His voice reverberated in his head. Cakes and pies, sweets and desserts. Just deserts.

"They freeze very well, Morris. Just cut it in half and freeze it."

"Nancy's right, Dad, it's a great pie at a great price."

"Well, then, choose what you like."

After some debate, they picked up the mocha cake sitting on a black plastic tray under a clear plastic dome, and continued along an aisle leading led to the fruit and vegetable section. Kate seemed to be settling down again, talking with Nancy in a more normal tone of voice. Even Morris was recovering his good spirits, so pleased to see his girls happily exclaiming over the size of honey-dew melons, the braids of garlic, the onions bulging in twenty-pound red-mesh sacks, tomatoes wrapped in purple tissue and arranged in cardboard trays of fifteen, and expensive black juicy grapes from California. His own garden produced most of what they would want at the moment, except for potatoes and squash. How could the world be so wrong when cherries from British Columbia tumbled like rubies, and sweet orange and yellow bell peppers, six to a bag, beckoned the eye?

The store was getting crowded. Carts clanged into each other, traffic jams of shoppers blocked the aisles. Piled on a free-standing counter in the middle of the produce aisle, the melons rose as high as his head, carefully but precariously stacked. One injudicious selection and the entire mountain would tumble down, he imagined, melons like bowling balls rolling all over the floor, except for the ones that exploded on impact. A young child stood up among the groceries in her mother's cart and reached out to tap a melon. The mother snatched away her hand but tapped the melon herself, even holding it to her ear as if listening for interior voices. An old couple, wearing white sweatshirts, wedged themselves between his cart and the counter. Morris shifted position, deciding to work his way through the traffic to the other side of the melon display. Kate gently rested a bag of black grapes on top of the other purchases in the cart. "Help me choose a melon, Nancy. I can never tell whether they're ripe."

Oh, the curl on her forehead, just a slip of loose hair, and maybe their fingers would touch over the melons. He'd propose instantly, without hesitation, without giving Nancy a chance to reflect. Forced by spontaneity and love of melons, by the inescapable desire in his eyes and voice, she'd have to say yes, yes, forever yes. She deserved the very best of possible worlds, which only he could provide. Nancy and Kate again flanked him as he pushed the cart around the counter. Morris let the murmuring of love and the fantasy of proposing in a public place—didn't they do such things in romantic movies that Nancy liked to watch on video?—detract from his manoeuvring skills. Should he embrace Nancy in front of Kate, in the store in front of all the snarl of shopping carts and melons? Seal her agreement with a kiss?

"Morris, be careful."

"What, Nancy?"

On the other side of the counter, his cart bumped into Ingoldsby's backside.

"Christ, why don't you watch where you're going?"

Collapse came quickly, like bearded irises flattened by heavy rain. For a moment, all Morris saw was blue, a field of Ingoldsby's blue shirt, until he forced himself to stare into the professor's brown eyes, a face as hard as the blade of a plow. He thought he heard Nancy say something. Kate's hand covered his on the handlebar of the shopping cart. Behind Ingoldsby, Annick picked up one melon, then another, three or four rolling dangerously down to the bottom. Although the professor's face remained immobile, Morris saw anger in his eyes, contempt, and just a hint of fear. He clearly recognized Morris. The eyes did not lie.

"We don't need a melon after all, Morris."

Well, yes, we do, Nancy, although he didn't say anything, and he certainly didn't approve of the look Ingoldsby gave Nancy. Impossible to avert his gaze, now that he stared Ingoldsby in the face, now that Ingoldsby had rudely spoken to him, now that he enjoyed an opportunity to perform, to show Nancy that she needn't fear Ingoldsby. How cool and far-seeing his rage in this instance, more like meditation than madness; not tumultuous screeching, lamentation, not a lunatic lashing out, but cool, collected, a man secure in the rightness of his beliefs, standing his ground, deliberate. One did not garden in a rage, did not wrench out weeds, decapitate grasshoppers, or dispose of unproductive or unsatisfactory plants in anger. Purpose, patience, and some sense of ultimate design prevented mere arbitrary or senseless actions.

"Dad, please."

Kate didn't fully understand what he had to do. He had obeyed her wishes in the past not to cause a scene with Ingoldsby, not to participate in the university hearings, not to embarrass her at the university. A man who was a protective and dedicated parent, something Kate could never fully comprehend, moved mountains for his children. His life was no longer his own. That was the price any loving parent willingly paid for having children: the responsibility beyond measure, not for the faint-hearted, the rewards incalculable. Was Ingoldsby backing away or jostling for a better position from which to strike? How capable was the professor of striking secretly, without conscience? Here, in a public place, Morris could force his hand and solve everyone's problem.

"Morris, let's go."

If he retreated, Nancy would see him as weak, ineffectual. What woman wanted to marry a man who couldn't defend her? The world hadn't changed so much that Morris no longer knew his duty. So clear his head, empty as a baseball field after an evening game and still flooded by the giant lights. He could see everything. Ingoldsby's wrinkled shirt, buttoned right up to the neck and down to the wrists, the contempt so evident in his yellowy brown eyes, paint-stained fingers on the bar of the shopping cart, white and green, even the black pearl studs in Annick's earlobes. He saw the stain of blood in a shade garden, mixed with and darkened by the soil. Feeling Nancy's restraining hand or Kate's on his shoulder, he gently shrugged it off. The professor's Adam's apple, on which Morris focused his attention and imagined pressing his thumbs hard, so hard that the man's goddamned eyes would pop out of his head.

"Dad—" Kate whispering in his ear "—Dad, let's go."

"No, Kate, not this time."

"I'll never forgive you, Father, I mean it. He's not worth the trouble."

"No, *I* mean it."

"Dad, please."

Morris understood what he must do but realized the means to achieve it were missing. He wasn't a man to walk the streets with a weapon in his hands. Who among the crowd would condemn him for his actions once they learned the truth? Leaping over the cart and grabbing the professor by the throat was his only option. Too many people and too many carts now pushing at them from all sides made that procedure awkward and ineffective. Still, circumstances forced his hand. Step calmly aside and around the carts without speaking, approach the professor, who had still not looked away, his eyes darkening with evil intentions, Morris could tell. A good strong punch in the face. Nancy, momentarily stunned and angered, would eventually be proud and grateful. She would marry her hero.

"Donald, help!"

Annick's voice fluttered above their heads like a terrified bird. Her arms swept the air like ineffective wings, flapping against the slipping, sliding, tumbling melons. The first to hit the floor split apart, so did the second and third, forcing everyone's eyes downward, until Morris could no longer count the number of melons rolling down and thudding on the concrete floor, smashing among the wheels of the shopping carts and the feet of shoppers who jumped aside, Annick screaming for help. Ingoldsby, cursing, threw himself against the avalanche. How was it possible for Morris to gain a safe foothold among the melons and attack? Melons mounding up before the painter's outspread arms, melons leaping his shoulders, Ingoldsby was so vulnerable to attack that Morris considered it unfair and cowardly to act. Nancy would not approve. Now was not the time to strangle Ingoldsby or to propose marriage to Nancy. The professor pressed his body against the counter, his arms collecting and stalling the landslide in their embrace.

"Would someone help me, for fuck sake?"

One or two customers, their way blocked by carts, joined Ingoldsby at the counter. Annick busied herself picking unsmashed fruit off the floor. The child in the cart clapped her hands and pointed, jumping up and down, and the old couple both bent down to retrieve melons.

"Thank God," Kate said. "Let's go, Dad."

"Morris, should we help?"

More shoppers joined Ingoldsby, forming a retaining wall against the slide. The melons stopped their tumble.

"No, Nancy, we shouldn't. Let's get some cheese."

She seemed hesitant to leave. Extricating his cart from the general crush, his anger temporarily subdued, Morris looked back. For a moment he imagined Ingoldsby turned his head to throw daggers with his eyes, but it was no more than convolutions at the melon counter, a pleasing colour combination, pale green melons and delphinium blue shirt. Consider yourself a very lucky man, Morris thought. He did not feel the weight of the cart, heavy with the goods of the earth, as he surged forward, his mind brisk and clear, his women safe by his side.

PART THREE

· ·

The back-door region and back-yard of many a small house may be a model of tidy dullness, or it may be a warning of sordid neglect, but a cataract of Rose bloom will in the one case give added happiness to the well-trained servants of the good housewife, and in the other may redeem the squalor by its gracious presence, and even by its clean, fresh beauty put better thoughts into the minds of slatternly people.

—GERTRUDE JEKYLL, *ROSES FOR ENGLISH GARDENS*

18

. . .

LIKE GREEN-SHINGLED ROOFS, masses of leaves blocked the rising
sun and muted the whistling of birds. Morris couldn't put a name
to it, as he often interrupted his work in the early morning,
straightened up, scanned the trees, expecting something to land at
his feet. Between the tangle of branches, he saw little of the sky
except patches of smoky blue, the sun a yellow smudge. Even the
air hung heavily, lacking the light fragrances often stirred about
by the breeze. Old Town smelled, yes, but not of flowers and
herbs, not of mown grass and decomposing compost; nor did it
smell of money, privilege, the deep security of stone foundations
and spacious houses that had stood for a hundred years. Not
even of the pressure-treated lumber and excavated earth in the
newer section of the community with its bright brick monster
homes, bleached landscapes where saplings struggled to root
themselves in the sandy soil; a sulphurous scent, possibly septic,
was in the atmosphere.

He had worked on several gardens in the morning. Now,
well past his usual supper hour, he devoted himself to this last
job of the day. On the grounds of the oldest and darkest home
of the neighbourhood, a multi-gabled, neo-Gothic, gingerbread-
trimmed brownstone and copper-roofed mansion once inhabited
by a prime minister, Morris moved like a man wading through a

waist-high marsh. The reeds attempting to bind his legs, he could feel bottom, but every step met resistance. He was half-heartedly raking through the undergrowth around the base of sun-starved pines overshadowed by larch and balsam. In darker corners, bushes of belladonna offered clusters of poisonous berries, the redness of many deepened to purple, some of the berries so dark that they looked black. Morris grew deadly nightshade among his own poisonous plants. Because of its reputed properties, it was a difficult plant to find in the nurseries. He never ripped a plant out of its natural habitat to transplant in his cultivated beds.

The prime minister's descendants occupied the house, living, according to rumour, more on tradition and privilege than on financial means, the family fortune having diminished from one generation to the next. This section of Old Town stood on a plateau, Riverside Road rising two hundred yards above lake level. The Grant mansion, much of it damaged by fire in the mid-nineteenth century and reconstructed in the 1880s, occupied the summit. Once past the lion-gated entrance—two supposedly fearsome stone lions with cracked eyeballs and chipped noses, chunks of concrete broken off their manes—the driveway snaked through a forest of hoary willows and various evergreens like Norfolk pine, larch, and balsam. Weeds and moss spread between them. Morris's practised eye could determine that the enormous trunks of the willows, their branches trailing the damp ground like the tresses of a giant woman, had already reached the state of advanced rot, the interiors softened by age and decay.

Potentially dangerous, these messy old willows, forever dropping off twigs and leaves, not to mention gathering places for annoying insects. He'd never grow a willow in his yard. Their roots seeking water, they latched on to and squeezed underground pipes. In a small space, they needed cutting back and chopping down: removal of the putrefaction for safety's sake. It was not unknown for a rotten willow branch to drop on the head of an unwary romantic. A sward of grass stretched behind the Grant house to the bluffs rising above the beach. Even that expanse of treeless green, though, was more plantain, creeping charlie, and moss than grass. The wire-mesh fence around an old tennis court to one side of the property had disappeared behind thickets of eglantines, the sweet-briar rose that grew, if left unattended as these bushes had been, into impenetrable screening that one needed a machete to hack through. He didn't think many roses bloomed on the thorny canes anymore. The nets of the courts had shredded ages ago. An old carriage cannon from the First World War, aimed at the empty air over the lake and poised to fire, was fixed on a cement dais on the edge of the cliff, its wheels chained to iron hasps, a symbolic defence of the mansion and all who dwelled therein from naval attack by the enemy.

Mrs. Grant, whom Morris had seen a few times, refused to set foot off her property since knocking her head against a stone after her horse had shied on the road and bucked her off the saddle. Besides leaving her with a cracked skull and a concussion, the fall had also damaged her brain. She wandered from room to room of her mansion, screaming through the intercom at any uninvited person who dared to ring her front doorbell. The stables sagged from neglect and rotten beams. Many of the terra-cotta tiles, similar to those of the university, had slipped out of place, fallen, and now lay in shards at the base of the buildings. The horses and stable hands had long since disappeared. Mr. Grant trundled about the property on his tractor, shifting piles of branches and debris from one place to another. Morris had heard around town that the Grants still insisted on dressing for dinner as if the world had not changed since Mr. Grant's great-great-grandfather's time, when people knew their place and minimally paid servants did their bidding. Morris charged the going rate for his services.

He did not know the people well. Old Mr. Grant, a pink-and-brown-mottled man, wafted down the curving stone driveway in brown carpet slippers and a navy blue velvet smoking jacket when Morris arrived in his truck in the afternoon. Mr. Grant had phoned the day after the infamous birthday party. Speaking in a low voice, almost inaudible beneath layers of privilege and padded indifference to the world at large, he asked Morris to stop by to consider the landscape problem of excessive shade. Mr. Grant knew Morris's reputation. He called because he had lost confidence in the landscaping contractors who traditionally cared for his property. Morris did not consider himself an expert on trees. He did not climb ladders with power tools to saw off branches, but he could offer advice on what trees should be trimmed and what light that would allow in, cut lower branches himself and suggest how to garden the terrain, if Mr. Grant was thinking of gardens. Already Morris was deciding what to plant after properly cleaning and amending the soil: shade-tolerant plants like bishop's hat or lamium, swaths of pachysandra or creeping Jenny, judiciously arranged ferns, astilbe, and tradescantia. Although they would take a while to develop and spread, Solomon's seal would do well in various parts of the woods. Even the much despised, rapaciously rampant goutweed would be preferable to bare earth and patchy grass under the pines.

An old rose garden on the property, famous for its English cultivars, used to be the pride of the neighbourhood, Morris knew, and had even found its way into a coffee-table book about heritage gardens. Through lack of attention, improper protection over the winter, the indifference of later generations, the bushes and their glorious blooms had died from exposure to severe cold, blackened under disease, or dwindled to scraggly, undernourished cultivars struggling above dandelions. Their original identity still not obscured, he recognized a *Rose de Meaux* and a *Blanc double de*

Coubert, even the climbing Dr. W. Van Fleet, massed over a bronze trellis, well past its flowering time in the spring. Morris doubted if the twisted, strangled canes produced much in the way of fleshy pink and white blooms. Maintaining perfection required consistent dedication. And love. If no one loved the rose, it struggled alone, then ultimately shrivelled.

There was some distant kinship between Mr. Grant and the McCready woman, exactly what Morris didn't know. Driving along Riverside, he met two different police cruisers within ten minutes of each other. Reversing direction, one of them followed him past the Ingoldsby house, until Morris stopped in the driveway of his first client, who waved to the police officer, shouting, "It's okay, it's Morris Bunter, the gardener."

The next thing they'd be asking for some kind of passport or identification just to enter the neighbourhood. Still, military presence, in a manner of speaking, offered reassurance. Terrible crimes had been committed. Of course people expected protection and reassurance. Morris liked to see police cars patrolling the streets of the entire community. He didn't enjoy being followed to a client's door as if he, Morris, were the maniac. Georges at the hardware store told him that residents of Old Town had gathered in the Grants' music room. It contained a defunct fireplace a man could stand in. Something about a neighbourhood watch, Georges had been told by someone who had attended, organizing patrols of armed civilians, seeing to it that no woman was left alone and paying attention to unfamiliar faces. Rumour had it that the wealthier members suggested hiring a kind of mercenary group of private guards, licensed to bear arms, conventional methods being inadequate to meet the crisis. That idea, though, faced overriding opposition from people who were afraid defensive measures could themselves cause greater, unforeseen problems. What was greater than the hidden terror creeping about their neighbourhood, attacking at will? Who wanted to step outside alone these days? The local authorities disapproved of vigilante groups, however law-abiding. Georges said Mrs. Grant had erupted into screaming fits until she was removed from the room. Morris asked Georges if Ingoldsby participated. Georges couldn't rightly say.

Raking allowed Morris to acquire a knowledge of the terrain. He suspected the soil was very acidic, given the number of conifers. The brown needles mounted. Tomorrow he planned to return with an outline of his suggestions for Mr. Grant to approve. Velveteen Rabbit, Morris recalled, watching Grant enter his house, the character from a children's story Kate used to love hearing her mother read. In the meantime Morris should feel free to wander where he pleased and gather what impressions he needed for his purposes. Morris threw the rake in the back of his truck. Removing his work gloves, he pulled on a black sweatshirt kept bundled in the wooden toolbox. Sunset brought cooler temperatures. He followed the broken cobblestone path leading to the sward behind the house, or "the field," as Mr. Grant called it, the great open lawn at one time so perfectly smooth and manicured that children played marbles on it. Now rutted and matted, circles of fungus visible in various sections, stubborn burdocks and stinging nettles poking up here and there, smothering crabgrass and purslane taking hold, it did look more like a neglected field than a lawn where once the Grants hosted garden parties under canopies for guests who clicked croquet balls through silvery hoops.

A ray of the setting sun glinted off the cannon's rusted iron as its light trawled along the surface of the water and sank behind the treed horizon of the opposite shore. Several sailboats, two with blood red sails, seemed anchored in the middle of the lake. Barn swallows swerved after early evening mosquitoes. Bats would soon rustle out from under the branches of the tallest trees, dive and dip for insects as well. The neo-Gothic spread of the Grant mansion caught the light of the sun in its many mullioned windows. The residence appeared to glow, trembling with a hundred fires behind glass. How effective could that cannon ever have been? Morris wondered, peering into its mouth after scraping out pebbles, fossilized gum, dead beetles, and the skeleton of a bird's head. Georges, something of a local historian and chief repository of historical gossip, remembered when old Mr. Grant, meaning the father of the present old Mr. Grant, had excavated the grounds to sink several tanks filled with oil illegally purchased during the last war as a guarantee against his family's privation during times of scarcity. Now covered with sod and bushes, possibly wrapped and squeezed by the insistent roots of willows searching for subterranean moisture, their metal sides corroded, their seams rotting, the tanks were probably leaking oil under the very foundations of the house, seeping through the earth beneath the estate, polluting for generations what the eye could not see. Morris hoped Georges exaggerated. The man told many tales, occasionally woven with the truth, about the rich families of Old Town.

Morris raised a hand over his brow to shade his eyes, watching the last visible perimeter of the setting sun sink below the treeline on the other side of the lake. The land on which he stood somehow also belonged to him, in a manner of speaking; he shared in its story, its ruination, its possibility for recovery. Like the cannon, he stood sentinel, however momentarily fixed on the spot, surveying the horizon for possible attack, peering over the cliff down to the pebbly beach to espy any secret invader. A wobbly wooden stairwell, precariously secured to the face of the cliff, led to the beach. No one trusted it anymore. The Grants never descended.

With the dusk deepening, Morris scanned the stand of hickories on the eastern verge of the lawn—shadows shifting as day bled into evening, small creatures scuttling among the lower branches of overgrown spirea, sumac and white-berried symphoricarpus bushes crowding around the trunks of the tall trees. Soon it would be the hour of nocturnal excursions and quests, of the instinctual urge to forage, to consume, to tunnel into dark and damp places for buried, yet living, food like grubs, themselves blindly nibbling away at tender roots. Foxes and rabbits, raccoons and squirrels— larger animals could cause that rustling and tossing of middle branches of the sumac patch. He stared long, not expecting, hoping not to spot the unusual, his eyes from this distance unable to make necessary distinctions.

His spirits oppressed by the dullness of the day, unnatural exhaustion in his bones, his nerves surged and snapped behind his eyes. There—again—a quick rush through the undergrowth, now darker in the evening, a shadowy, wavering form, the height of a man, say, pausing to avoid detection. A bat looped swift as a thought in front of Morris's face. His brain wired with worry, Morris unaccountably bolted and raced toward the dark sycamores, his hands tightening into fists, regretting that he had left his tool belt in the car.

"Damn you!" he shouted. Then he stopped and considered what he was doing. Was he mad? Chasing phantoms? What weapon had he? To strike at what? At whom? How to deflect a counterattack? Himself alone arrayed against the invisible forces of evil? He did not expect divine assistance. Aware of the craziness of his action, adrenalin and anger blunting common sense, his arms raised like some kind of shield, Morris positioned himself to meet the assault. He understood instantly the futility of the stance, concentrating as hard on controlling his terrified bowels as on dodging the assailant. The branches clicked, the leaves brushed aside. Out of the bush waddled a King Charles spaniel, burrs attached to its floppy ears. The Grants' dog, wagging its tail, sniffed around Morris's workboots, then ambled across the lawn toward the house. Stupid, stupid, bloody fool. The heaviness of his head sharpened into pain on the right side, similar to what he had felt during his hangover. Served him right, Kate had sneered, having returned home to discover Nancy and Bogdan helping her father vomit in the toilet bowl, and Émile beaming like a red-faced idiot, picking berries off his cheesecake. Kate really shouldn't speak about his friends that way. But Émile could look idiotic without trying too hard, Morris had to admit. "Honestly, Dad" was the phrase Kate used to indicate how terribly wrong he happened to be. The young seldom showed mercy toward the failings of their parents. Exactly where had she been that night and with whom? What had she drunk or smoked with Tarun? Not that he had asked those questions before he dozed off at the breakfast table.

The sun had slipped beneath the horizon. Morris stepped back at the sound of more rustling in the bushes. Leaves fluttered like lids over dark eyes, dark as belladonna, eyes peering at him between sumac leaves, a shadowy head, the play of shadows. For Chrissake, Morris, get a grip. He saw nothing, heard breath, breath, the noisy, heart-driven breathing of tension before the leap, the attack, panic breathing—his breathing. He heard his own breathing in the dusking-down of the day and wiped his moist palms on his jeans. The sky swooped with bats. The chill rose up from the oily damp of the grounds. Nothing more in the under-brush unless he cared, unless he dared, to poke about himself. Nothing, nothing at all. Fool that he was, he had seen things before. This wasn't the first time his imagination had shaken him loose from sense and probabilities.

His ancient, beautiful home shivered with quiet panic. Except it did not belong to him, in fact—no matter. Where he stood belonged to him in spirit as much as it did to the Grants in law. It was an inextricable part of his world, whether the Grants under-stood or not. He did not check out the continuing rustle of the leaves. Trusting his back to the darkening bushes, Morris pushed himself up toward the house, his legs leaden, his spirits heavier still. Sober and collected, he did not flinch when, down from the house, rushing toward him, came a woman in white cloth wafting behind her arms and head like the broken wings of a terrified snow goose. Old Mrs. Grant, flying down the field, Mr. Grant, now attired in a long, gold-trimmed black robe, following, calling her name: Eleanor, Eleanor. The spaniel flipped and flopped, barking after his master.

Mrs. Grant rushed straight for Morris's head, screeching, "No more of that! No more of that!" She surrounded him. Morris didn't know what to do except softly deflect her harmless blows as the woman beat him about the head with her ineffective wings, gibbering at high pitch, until Mr. Grant restrained her arms.

"You'll have to forgive her," Mr. Grant whispered, "she has not been well."

Morris patted the old man's soft shoulder. Mrs. Grant went limp and silent, veiling her black, terrified eyes with what Morris now recognized as a white shawl the size of a tablecloth thrown over a white peignoir. Mr. Grant led her back to the house. One leaning against the other, the Grants merged into a single black-and-white hobbled creature before they disappeared through a dark doorway. Sensing a chase, the dog scurried into the stand of hickory trees. Morris walked back to the carriage cannon and leaned against a chained wheel, his head solid as a cannonball, his neck sore and straining under the weight of the day's feelings.

When it struck again, this terrible thing, Morris knew it would not sneak across the water. No, hearing the dog in the brush, he believed it was already here. A frightening thought flickered through his mind, swift as a sparrow's flight through the mead hall. It wouldn't do anymore to shoot the enemy at one spot, to explode one thing, for the enemy was everywhere; defence meant the destruction of everything. The idea, too horrible to harbour, flew out of his brain. It vanished. The light of the early moon slipped into the lake, and the sailboat with the blood red sail slowly glided across the water. Listening long in the sunset silence, Morris cocked his head, as the wings of bats swept the air, and low-hanging tresses of willows, stirred by the breeze, brushed the ground.

19

• • •

BLACK SPOT ... dreaded disfiguring disease ... pockmarks scarring a queen's lovely complexion ... her lovely roses ... so necessary to spray and ward off infestation ... she squirted the bushes ... the can empty ... a whoosh of air spurting out of the dozen tiny holes of the spray nozzle ... force enough to shiver some of the thinner twigs and weaker canes of the dead bushes, mottled brown and black, brittle to the touch, easily snapped off ... a few desiccated blossoms on one or two bushes like dead flowers in a year-old bridal bouquet ... beautiful as the pink dawn her roses or the rising gold of the morning sun or the white glitter of first snow before Christmas or the red glint of the ruby pendant she kept in her teak jewel box on the top shelf in her wardrobe ... a teardrop of glassy blood ... another squirt for salvation ... so many roses undone ... *rose o'morte, rose o'morte* ...

Behind the tennis court fence, hidden by thickets of rose, he had been watching her for an hour flit from bush to bush, hovering over each blackened branch and wizened flower with the spray can. Having scouted the property, he decided to wait in the tennis court for his next move and was about to approach the house when he saw the woman between the interlocking canes coming down the path to the rose garden. Her twittering voice like a series of bird calls truncated and strangled from this distance—

half muffled by the breeze picking up the chill of the lake. Relieved that she had come outside, he preferred to work in the open. His fingers caressed the large knob of the iron post. Red dust from the court grounds coated his boots. Behind the thicket of wild eglantine he was hidden, imperceptible, and safe.

Nettles and burdock, creeping charlie and purslane, so many weeds strangling the roots of her favourite roses ... without air without space they do not thrive ... and suckers shooting up from the root stock weakening the plant ... attenuated unproductive suckers crowding and sucking the life out of the bush ... inferior things ... low life ... rising up where they did not belong ... oh, how splendid to train the *Rosa eglanteria* ... spreading and arching its branches over and hiding the steel-mesh fence of the tennis court ... long flexible vibrant cane each bearing blossoms without end ... the apple fragrance of its leaves on hot muggy August days wafting into the open windows of the house, thousands of pink clusters in the early summer blooming so profusely they surrounded the tennis court like pink clouds ... you could not see the ball whacked over the net ... a thicket of thorns and twisted briars ...

He parted a few branches that poked through the fence, pricking his flesh on the pre-eminent thorns, a spot of blood like a red button sewn on the tip of his finger. Sniffing, he disliked the odour of rotting apples, sickly sweet and overpowering, but the bush covered the fence like a wall and rose higher than his head, matted so thickly with canes and briars that the man did not think he was seen. Peering through the canes as carefully as possible without nicking the skin of his nose, he nonetheless inhaled the perfume of decay. The woman in white bent over smaller bushes, reaching out a hand as if to pet a cat, then straightened up and flitted to another bush. The rose garden was enclosed by a windbreak of cedars on the northeast and southwest sides of the garden, from where the worst winds and the coldest weather blasted in winter or rolled withering hot waves on a summer's day. Together, they were in a kind of room in the garden, a garden room with walls and no windows. He should have worn gardening gloves. They lay like severed hands in the shed. He sucked on his bleeding finger, savouring the glutinous texture and salty taste.

She flashed the cutting tool among the blackened canes, snipping and cutting, sometimes pulling at the bush as if to uproot the entire plant. Fussing over stupid dead bushes and brown flowers he didn't see the sense of, but he kept his eye on that cutting thing to see where she put it when she stopped. Stop she must. All things stopped sooner or later; he should know. His blood stopped flowing. The air no colder than the chill in his bones. Getting late. Time to move on. Time to scout new territory. Experience always told him the right moment to move on. Singing to herself like a madwoman in the garden. Lunatics sang to themselves. That crazy old bitch. No one would ever catch him singing—no way. What was the hag doing now?

Down the path in a circle of round stones several Frau Dagmar Hartopp ... a sturdy Germanic princess ... elegant but profuse ... the touch of perfume or the fragrance of silk ... pink dashed with silver ... how it bloomed it seemed all summer ... snip, snip, snip; dead branches gone ... suckers ... but where was the spade ... dig beneath the soil to cut the suckers off the root stock at source ... oh, gardeners, gardeners where are you ... I have commands ... too much ... too much time, too much loss ... who killed my roses ...

What the fuck? The old woman now dancing in the middle of a circle of stones, her dress caught and torn by the dead branches of the rose bushes. He had to get a move on. His stomach growled: almost a day since he had last eaten. Too dangerous to linger around here anymore. More and more difficult to move about undetected; his time here was over. On to the next thing, not before finishing his business here. Opportunities presented themselves, some he made. Waiting, watching, he always found what he wanted. Where did she put those damn cutters? He didn't want her to see him. He didn't like his ladies to see his approach. The joy lay in the surprise—the mysterious, sublime moment of unsuspected contact. Approach from behind, carrying the rusted iron post, fallen off its moorings in the tennis court, a few strands of the rotted net still attached like desiccated entrails.

Assured of his own invisibility, he had escaped detection. The old man in the house had not seen him, and he had left a while back, had driven off the estate. No servants in the house that he knew. So they were alone. Some occasions spontaneously presented themselves and he acted on the spur of the moment, taking advantage of the lucky opportunity. Other moments required patience, the laying-down of the groundwork. For this one he had been patient. Who would have spotted him anyway on this property so covered with bushes and woods and outbuildings like the pumphouse where he had hidden himself on the other side of the hickory grove? His body still smelling of the dank, almost septic odour of the pumphouse, where the central generator sucked up and conducted well water through underground pipes leading to the house. Police patrolled the neighbourhood, but where there was a will there was a way to sneak through any barrier. Helicopters flying over the lake had not spotted him, nor had that man the old lady flapped about the head a couple of days ago. The iron pole was heavy. It would do very well. He peeked through the briars one last time to check if she had moved from her position, sitting like a giant mushroom in the middle of dead rose bushes. She had not. It was time. Famished, he was so hungry for a steak soaked in its brownish red juice.

Where are my rose-cutters ... a bouquet for the house ... a bouquet of dead buds for the house ... the house of dreams and parties and so many fine things ...

Twigs and dried leaves crackled under his booted feet. Like a cat, he never crossed any space in a straight line. He paused. So far he had not engaged in a struggle of any kind. Not here. Other places, yes, with other women, but not here. He preferred a clean touch. Over and done with. The cutters—he saw her cutting tool on the perimeter of the circle. The woman stirred but kept her back toward him, staring up at the western screen of browning cedars, her hand shading her eyes. She singing-whimpering like a kitten mewing for its mother's teat. Her head looked so small, porcelain like a doll's head, wisps of silvery white hair a net of spiderwebs. More power than necessary, the iron pole—he almost regretted the swing above his head and the force of the drag down over the old woman's skull. The cracking thud took flight above the trees. His heart screeched like a gibbering monkey in a cage. And red, red, red splashed over the porcelain like rose petals covering the head of a doll.

20

. . .

NANCY CLIPPED THE LAST SHEET on her line with blue and pink plastic pins, reeling it away from the post on her porch toward the post standing at the back of the yard opposite the two trees. With no wind today, the laundry hung like flat shrouds in the cool sunlight waiting to be spread over dying vegetable plants and flowers. Morris had shown Jonathan, her older son, how to prune the lower branches of the maple trees, thereby liberating space in her small yard. Together they had planted her bed of day lilies. The season now over, only browning strips of narrow leaves remained, spilling over the brick edging onto the grass like clusters of papery ribbons. Morris had suggested the boys could spade up the turf to create even more possibilities for gardening, but Nancy liked the cooling sensation of summer grass on her bare feet. She now had all the garden she could conveniently manage. At least the yard had ceased being a repository for rusty pipes, old boards, mattress springs, and broken chairs.

So chilly this September day, despite a sky clear as a scoured fish bowl. Another load of laundry, mostly the boys' jeans and socks, tumbled inside the automatic dryer. Nothing surpassed the scent of bedding blown dry by a sunny wind. If the wind failed to co-operate, the blue and yellow sheets would nonetheless absorb the refreshing light of the sun. As it was her day off work, she had spent the morning washing, dusting, vacuuming, anything to move her body and focus her attention. From this perspective behind the porch railing, she saw everything—and anyone—in her garden, nothing large or dark enough to conceal a dog, least of all a man with murderous intentions. She didn't wish to think about him, but domesticity had dropped its protective shield. Nancy shivered in the sun. Between those poor ladies and herself stood only chance. Why not *her body* on the lily leaves? Imagination ran wild. Shaking her head and clucking her tongue did little to help. The perspective from her porch offering no consolation, she picked up the wicker laundry basket and went through the back door into the kitchen. Remembering Morris's insistence, she locked the door. The rumble of the dryer steadied her nerves. So many chores left to do—no end of keeping a home in spotless condition. Housecleaning, though, like hanging, concentrated the mind wonderfully.

During their spring break from school, she and the boys had painted the kitchen a creamy yellow with white trim. She had also bought a new canister set to match. With two windows on the east and west walls, the kitchen received almost a full day of light and was the brightest, most welcoming room in the house. Not large, the oval, Colonial-style dining table accommodated all four of them at mealtime. Space enough remained for the butcher block on wheels on which she chopped off the heads of red snapper (her favourite fish). They could all sit or work at the counters without stepping on each other's toes. A cardinal rule of the household was that everyone pulled his fair weight.

She liked her house. This was her domain, paid for with tears and blood, arguments over money with her former mate, the father of the boys, a man prone to drinking and promises of reform. Then he walked out in an alcoholic stupor after punching her in the face, and disappeared like an evil spirit in the mists of

· 216 ·

the night. Cory, the younger boy, was still waddling in diapers. Since then she had never heard from the man again, to this day refusing to say his name or speak about him to the boys. He drank, he deserted us, she had told them, confessing no more than the truth, hoping the truth would end further curiosity. It was a mercy they had not married. If her former lover had dropped off the edge of the universe, wherever that might happen to be, or been sucked into and obliterated by a black hole in space, he could not have disappeared more completely. If only the killer would do as much. She had seen a program on *Nova* and was surprised to learn that the black hole was not a depth at all, but a surface, a dead star of incredibly dense gravitational force, trapping light. Smashed and splattered like a bug against a windshield rather than sucked into a tunnel would be more accurate. The desired effect was achieved either way.

Morris had proposed almost in the same breath as telling her the dreadful news about Mrs. Grant. Her knees gave way, and she fell back on the loveseat in her tiny living room, an arm almost slapping the imitation Tiffany lamp off the end table. Now, plugging in the kettle, Nancy wondered if her body collapsed from the shock of yet another murder, or from the spectre of marriage. She thought she loved Morris, was indeed afraid in a vague sort of way, but she also distrusted marriage. Quandaries upset her stomach. Or the effort of suppressing the information that Ingoldsby and she had met in the café, more than once, had talked agreeably over coffee. She knew his reputation, knew how much Morris disliked the man, but Kate's past was, well, past, and it had nothing to do with her, nor did it lessen the pleasure she experienced in Ingoldsby's company. As for Ingoldsby's sexual escapades, Nancy thought little of them. Now was not the time to tell Morris that she had agreed to visit the botanical garden in Montreal with the painter. And no, he did not invite her up to his place to look at his etchings. She certainly didn't wish to hurt Morris, dear man who, she knew, cared deeply for her. He had proposed first, then informed her about the most recent murder, the horrible fact slipping out of his mouth so closely after a confession of love that one became indistinguishable from the other. At the kitchen table over a cup of instant coffee, knocking over the pepper grinder, Morris held both her hands together.

"I have something to ask you."

Instantly Nancy knew what. Men always spoke in a peculiar tone when they introduced the topic of marriage. A sudden, soft plummet in the timbre of the voice, like a canoe poised momentarily on the top of a waterfall before plunging down in the spray. A look of panic and supplication in the eyes, which seemed to darken their natural colour. Not her first proposal. Other men, of whose advances Morris knew nothing, had expressed an interest, had pursued to some degree, even Émile. Each declaration of love made her more hesitant and nervous about accepting than the last. Such callused hands, stubby fingers with scrubbed and trimmed nails. Oddly soft, though, soft like deerskin gloves. Morris used a special cream, designed primarily for farmers and cow udders— bag balm, he called it. Her hands slipped out of his. She did not withdraw the arm entirely, to avoid giving offence. A sweet man, Morris, a good man, a perfect husband, if such a thing existed. In the depths of his brown eyes, she noticed glints of gold. Now and then he grew a moustache, which added a touch of handsomeness to an otherwise unremarkable face. He did not sport a moustache now, which was just as well, because kissing had been a problem last winter, the hairs of his thick moustache tickling the tender insides of nostrils, making her sneeze in the midst of an embrace.

"Let's go into the living room, Morris."

He followed her and wrapped his arms around her. Although the Jane Fonda exercise regimen had helped to tighten the waist,

Nancy enjoyed the middle-aged relaxation of the muscles. The exquisite liberation of no longer trying to look young, of toning and firming the body according to magazine standards; she loved the smooth ridge of fat between her fingers. Judging by his caresses, so did Morris. Ingoldsby's attention was flattering. She had not yet lost allure.

"Oh, you smell like cinnamon and fruit peel."

Nancy supposed that had been a compliment of sorts, although she thought of a hot-cross bun puffing up in the oven. He turned her around and kissed her on the lips. Still holding her in his arms, brushing her cheeks and lips, he whispered the horrible story of Mrs. Grant as if lowering the voice lessened the gravity of the news. She was beginning to find breathing difficult, smothered by closeness, Morris holding her too tightly.

"I don't know what to say, Nancy. It's awful what's been happening. You know old Mrs. Grant, the mansion on the hill ... They found her ... God ... in the rose garden ... this afternoon ... I want to protect you, Nancy, keep you safe ... Dead ... another murder ..."

"Mrs. Grant, the crazy old woman, murdered?"

"Yes, I want you to marry me ... I love you, Nancy ... Will you marry me?"

"Murdered? Marry?"

She pushed his arms away, suddenly short of breath. Morris crowded her so, the news ... too much ... and her knees buckled ... Sitting, feeling faint, seeking support, she fell back onto the loveseat, her left hand flicking off the lower rim of the lamp, which wobbled on the table. Morris immediately sat next to her, again grabbing her hand when she so much wanted to be left alone, not have a man touch her at this point, not mention marriage in the same breath as murder. What teary, moaning, sad eyes Morris had. His timing, though, left a lot to be desired.

Flustered by the proposal in the first place, she felt the added shock of slaughter sizzle along her nerves beyond bearing.

"Are you all right, Nancy? Would you like something to drink? It's terrible … Something has to be done about this … We can't go on living this way."

Nodding, she appeared to agree without speaking.

"I want to marry you, Nancy, protect you."

Something wasn't clear—too much overwhelming information befuddled her senses, heated her blood and drained her head at the same time. If she attempted to stand, she would fall. She stared at dear Morris, wishing to kiss the tears on his cheeks, wishing him away at the same time. Was she in danger? Did she need protection? Was she the next victim? Why was the room so dark? The lights were on. Was she going blind, incipient panic dropping scales over eyes?

"Poor Mrs. Grant."

"She didn't deserve to die that way, Nancy. Are the boys home today?"

"Not now, but they will be for lunch."

"Then I won't stay?"

It was a question begging for a positive response. She liked waking up next to Morris's body, its very ordinariness more appealing than all the male bodies she saw in movies or advertisements. For a man whose hands dug into the dirt so much, Morris paid particular attention to personal hygiene. Nancy couldn't bear the thought of sharing a meal with dirty fingernails or the smell of fertilizer. The paint on Ingoldsby's fingers, though, had not bothered her. Not today, it was better Morris not remain today, not with the promise of marriage on his lips and the news of Mrs. Grant's murder. The boys liked Morris well enough. They did not object to the few times, somewhat shamefaced, he had greeted them at breakfast. If she encouraged him to stay the afternoon and overnight, would that signify yes to his proposal? He would protect her. Yet another woman slaughtered. He loved her.

"No, Morris, not now ... the news ... I can't ..."

"Of course I understand."

He leaned over to kiss her on the cheek. On the porch step, he had also kissed her goodbye, then said something about buying new pruning shears at Georges's hardware store.

"You lock the door, mind."

Drinking her coffee after hanging the sheets on the line, Nancy didn't think Morris understood at all. How could he? It was a relief to take a break from Morris's enveloping love, to go out with Ingoldsby, who clearly would not threaten her with eternal devotion. She did love Morris after a fashion, despite the sometimes crushing weight of his concern and thoughtfulness. Love had led her to renounce a lot for the boys' father. In Morris she had infinite trust, in marriage she did not. She liked a night of lovemaking, Morris being so sensitive and adventurous at the same time, an utterly thrilling combination, followed by unbroken, dreamless sleep, breakfast together, then saying goodbye. Once he left, she found herself in her own house, still her own woman, and essentially free from entanglements, or if entangled, quickly able to disengage.

Morris, however, would protect her. If she remembered correctly, all the murdered women had been married. What protection had their current or former husbands provided? Nancy had difficulty understanding how Morris equated marriage with protection when the evidence suggested the contrary. How did a ceremony before clergy or judge guarantee safety? Here he was, her knight in shining tin charging at full tilt on a weak-kneed nag to rescue the well-seasoned maiden, past her first youth by more than a few years, somewhat after the fact. Nancy didn't know why Morris's goodness pushed her into a corner, nor what the images of a horse with buckling knees heaving the rider off its back suggested about her feelings for the man. She loved Morris, she really did. She put on a sweater inside her warm kitchen, thinking of poor Mrs. Grant—not even craziness had protected that old lady from the horrors of the real world. She listened to the drum of the dryer whirl and rumble like her thoughts, without beginning or end, going round and round and round.

21

· · ·

MORRIS PRETENDED to examine cellophane bags of cedar closet deodorizers on the counter as Georges struggled with yet another coughing fit. Before pulling down the shade of his front door and turning over the *Fermé*/Closed placard, painted in black, he had allowed Morris to enter the store.

"Closing early, Georges? Not many people about this morning."

Traffic was indeed light that morning. The day was eerily quiet, the people Morris did see somehow distant, unapproachable, looking like friends he had known all his life, but now moving in unfamiliar, strained ways. Strange pedestrians walked by as if they had parked their spirit or soul elsewhere, like that movie, he remembered, about aliens who appropriated the bodies and assumed the personalities of the town's citizens, their brains invaded by … was it mushroom spores? They sure as hell acted and sounded as if they were all pretending to be something they weren't, certainly their focus no longer on the life they used to live. Sort of how he was feeling, waiting for poor Georges's lungs to get a load of reviving air.

Clutching his chest, Georges choked on a stifled cough. Morris looked across the street to the Hôtel de Ville. The town's flag and Quebec's fleur-de-lys were lowered to half-mast. A building with shingles and green shutters flanking the windows on two floors, the town hall had originally been a Grant residence, one of the Grants anyway, possibly the current Mr. Grant's great-uncle, who had lived there at the turn of the last century. Deeded to the town in the 1920s. Not for Mrs. Ferroux or Mrs. McCready was Georges shutting up shop for the day, but this recent, this third, murder. Morris couldn't rightly blame him—so difficult to go about ordinary business anymore. Poor Georges. Sick and wanting to retire, Georges had once offered to sell him the hardware business, given his knowledge of tools and his carpentry skills, but Morris preferred his own line of work, although hardware had its seductive charms. If he couldn't endure dripping faucets, he replaced the washers. If he couldn't abide squeaking doors, he oiled the hinges. If he couldn't tolerate drafty windows, he caulked and sealed or, ultimately, replaced the rotting frames and installed new double-glazed panes. Hardware provided answers to life's inconveniences. He had a problem, the right tool solved it.

"Yes, Morris," Georges said in English, "I'm closing early today, maybe tomorrow as well—depends on how I feel. Couldn't get Mrs. Grant out of my mind since I saw the news on television. Terrible. Breaks my heart. I knew the dear old lady. Known her for years."

"I know how you feel, Georges."

Georges had another coughing fit over the cash register. Morris stared at the town hall as if expecting answers and assistance from local politicians. After the old man had spent a lifetime smoking, his lungs had blackened, pulmonary tracts clogged with tar and nicotine. Emphysema, Georges had told him; the pernicious but comforting habit had worked its secret devastation. What was the point, though, of quitting smoking after the damage had already been done? Couldn't see the logic of it, Georges had said. He searched his pockets for a cigarette package, then found it under the counter.

"Finally, people are getting worried, Georges. What does it take? I ask you. Something's got to be done about it."

At town hall meetings, he himself was among the first to demand that something be done about unsafe playground equipment. Something had to be done about delivery trucks blocking the main thoroughfare. Something had to be done about testing the drinking water. Something had to be done about increasing funds for the local library.

"What do you have in mind, Morris?"

"Well, I need new pruning shears. My spring's shot to hell and the blade's so old that it's getting thin from all the sharpening over the years. A few other things, but seeing as how you're closing … Why don't we go outside for a moment, Georges, for a breath of fresh air."

"That's a good idea, Morris—could do with some air."

He lit the cigarette, cupping his hands against a breeze as they stepped onto the sidewalk. At that moment, Professor Ingoldsby and Annick walked by, the professor wearing white cotton jeans and a white shirt with a pinkish tinge on the collar like the colour of an iceberg rose. The phosphorescent spokes of Annick's hair prodded the air. Her long black dress crinkled like tissue paper around her legs as she sauntered by, letting go of the professor's hand when she saw Morris. Her greeting was friendly, with not a hint of embarrassment.

"Good morning, Mr. Bunter."

"Good morning, Miss Ferroux.'

Ingoldsby glanced, then dropped his eyes, probably remembering, Morris thought, the avalanche of melons and how much reason he had to fear Kate's father. He clearly recognized Morris and feared for his life. Let him fear. Let him learn caution. Morris saw instantly that the professor, averting his eyes, only pretended not to regard him any more than he would a fire hydrant.

This time Morris would be the plow and refuse to give way. Hoping for a confrontation, he was disappointed to see Ingoldsby step off the sidewalk and continue along the curbside, followed by Annick, who retrieved the professor's hand once they had passed. She didn't appear at all to be a woman in mourning for a mother found slaughtered in her garden not so long ago. Perhaps he expected seclusion, a grim attitude, a proper distance at the very least, between her and Ingoldsby.

"You know much about that guy, Georges?"

"Well, I've heard tell a few rumours … seen him once or twice drunk in the pub … Quite a ladies' man—can't seem to keep his hands off the girls at the university, so I've heard. I know he caused your Kate some problems. Been in the store a few times, always been pleasant to me. Wasn't he fired?"

"Yes, he was. I sometimes wonder about him."

"Wonder what?"

"I mean he's always there, isn't he?"

"Can't say I follow, Morris. Where's there?"

"Never mind. How are you feeling, Georges? This business is pretty unsettling, getting on all our nerves. Let me buy you a coffee and we can talk."

"Thanks, Morris, but I think I'd like to be alone awhile. Not feeling my best these days—the chest, you know. If you still want to look around, I'll keep the store open for you."

"No, thanks, Georges, don't bother—some other time. The shears can wait. You take care of yourself. You get some rest. I've got to see the administrator of the seniors' residence about a garden. And Kate hasn't been feeling too well herself lately. She says it's probably a flu bug going around. I think she's really worried, Georges. I mean, who wouldn't be?"

Georges began coughing again. Morris debated between patting the man on the shoulder and leaving him to clear his lungs in private. He touched Georges's shoulder, then left. On the way to the residence he saw Ingoldsby and Annick through the café window. He should enter and say something, or just order a coffee and watch the professor become nervous, possibly frightened by Morris's presence. Annick was laughing so hard that she threw her head back. Ingoldsby's smiling stopped when he noticed Morris staring at him. Szerkasy was waiting. No time to confront the professor.

Szerkasy informed Morris that he had issued specific instructions to the staff not to leave the television on the news channel in the community lounge. It was difficult enough to ease anxieties and calm nerves among the elderly without contending with misinformation and public panic. His memo notwithstanding, many of the residents had seen or heard the report of Mrs. Grant's murder, repeated throughout the day during his absence at a downtown meeting with the minister of health. The news coverage this time mentioned gruesome details—brains skewered on rose thorns.

"Now, I ask you, Morris, is that kind of reporting called for?"

"It's no more than the truth, Mr. Szerkasy."

"Yes, well, some truths simply don't have to be told, do they?"

Uneasy over a question that called for a complicated response, Morris remained silent. When he had entered the lobby, a dozen benighted souls flocked around him, their attenuated, fleshless arms grabbing on to his sweatshirt. Gently disengaging himself, he offered soothing words: "There, there, you have had nothing to worry about—the authorities have everything under control."

Sitting in his office behind his steel desk where he signed several letters of admission while Morris stood and waited, the final garden plans and cost estimate at last in hand, Szerkasy muttered under his breath. Despite the sheen of his light wool suit, he looked harried and exasperated. Much too young to understand the fears of the old, Morris thought. Certainly lacking imagination when it came to gardens, which required a greater vision than a rigid budget provided. During their discussions, Szerkasy had repeated the term "cost effectiveness." What was the difficulty? Put in a path and a few flowers. Szerkasy regretted even agreeing to the idea of redesigned riverside grounds, but the gift of money stipulated precisely that: new gardens for the elderly to totter about in. He had no choice. This particular gift, courtesy of the Ferroux foundation last year, could only be used for the designated purpose. After scaling down Morris's ambitions for the terrain, he even suggested that leftover cash could be applied to the laundry in the basement that required new washing machines. Kitchen staff also complained about antiquated appliances. Not that he had spoken so bluntly within Morris's hearing, but the gardener sensed that Szerkasy hoped for the possibility of unspent dollars, after paying for visible and, to his mind, unnecessary changes on the riverfront property.

He asked for Morris's proposal by raising his right arm over the desk and gesturing. Perusing Morris's proposal for a few minutes, he then looked up and agreed with the plans. The new garden must proceed. He turned the green leather swivel chair and stared out the window overlooking the river. Speaking to the glass, he reminded Morris that Mrs. Ferroux had been a staunch supporter of the residence, raised money for the forty-eight-inch television set in the lounge and donated cash toward the purchase of new linens. Along with her benevolence, though, had come vigilance. She had always reserved the right to see her purposes fulfilled, even—and here Morris thought he heard a kind of snort—"berating me for buying cheap sheets with an inferior thread count."

He turned around to face Morris.

"But, sorry to say, she is no longer with us, and I've been doing my best these past three years of my administration to cut costs without sacrificing the quality of care."

He paused, as if waiting for agreement and approval. Morris said he imagined it couldn't be a very easy job. Through the dirty glass of the window, he could see the brown river. A few sailboats relieved the monotony of the unremarkable view, cottages and skimpy trees scattered on the opposite shore. Apparently keeping costs down meant refusing to hire window washers, the budget not allowing for more visibility than streaked and grimy glass. Outside the office door, a mixture of French and English rose from a low hubbub to loud whining.

"What on earth? I hear Kwaku outside."

Szerkasy got up to open the door. Checking his watch and worrying about Kate, Morris prepared to leave. A wizened fist, no larger than a baby's, struck the administrator's chest. The blow landed softly against his lapel. Then another blow, and an old woman with a flaky, brown-mottled scalp began heaving and crying without tears. Two other old women and one man, their bodies curved like question marks, the stench of sleep, urine, and baby powder reaching Morris's nose and making him sneeze, gibbered together, so he understood very little.

"What are they doing here? Kwaku, what's the meaning of this?"

Kwaku, born and raised in Senegal before immigrating to Quebec as a teenager, answered in French. "Sorry, sir, the news on television …"

Kwaku was urging the old man to sit in the wheelchair, and he responded in a combination of English and French. "I got legs. Don't need no wheelchair. You sit in fucking wheelchair *toi-même. Touche pas,* don't touch me. *Chaise roulante? Pas pour moi.* What, am I crippled? *Laisse-moi seul.* I hit you!"

"Now, now, Bertie, you've got to relax. I'll take you to the sunroom."

"I don't want no fucking sunroom. Roast like hell, *comme l'enfer.* Don't touch me, *maudit bâtard!*"

"Mr. Lloyd. We do not permit foul language in this institution."

Kwaku grabbed his shoulders and pushed him into the chair, then strapped a wide leather belt around the old man's waist. The buckle clicked shut behind the back.

"There, there, isn't that better? They are much afraid, sir … The stories …"

"Didn't I issue a memo about the news programs on television?"

"Yes sir, you did, but we cannot watch them every moment in the lounge."

"Well, calm them down. They've nothing to worry about. Everything's under control."

"They get an idea in their head and just can't let go of it."

"Yes, of course, disturbing news for everyone. All the more reason to protect our clients. Listen to me, you're perfectly safe here—whatever you've heard on the news has nothing to do with you."

Kwaku wheeled Bertie down the corridor. Szerkasy looked, he hoped, imploringly at Morris. Did the director want assistance? What was Morris supposed to do?

"Come with me, ladies. Time for tea," Kwaku announced.

Hobbling and tottering, mewing and muttering, they gathered around and followed Kwaku in his starched white uniform.

"I guess the poor dears are frightened, Mr. Bunter." Szerkasy switched to English, although he knew perfectly well that Morris spoke French. "You're seeing them on a very bad day." Frightened and hopelessly dependent—a terrible vulnerability. Morris for a moment tried to imagine himself in their position but could not. Szerkasy forced a smile when Morris, still in the office, put on his short-billed baseball cap. The director's crisp, expensive suit made him self-conscious in his working clothes. Not every place was a compost heap or tool shed; he should have dressed for the occasion. At least his nails were clean.

"I'm sure you'll do the right thing by us, Mr. Bunter." He held the door open as Morris left the office.

"*Merci, Monsieur Szerkasy. Je vous souhaite une bonne journée. Salut.*"

"Thank you, Mr. Bunter. Good day to you, too."

22

• • •

MARIA HAD BEEN ESPECIALLY FOND of tea roses, although Morris regarded them as demanding and fussy, breathtakingly beautiful, but fleeting and fragile. Every year since her death, he returned to the Jardin botanique de Montréal in early September, on the anniversary of their wedding, to stroll among the winding beds of the rose garden. Protected from harsh winds by trees and shrubs, the bushes thrived. Requiring considerable attention, not to mention protection against the winter months, the floribunda and grandiflora rose bushes still presented a lovely show of their blossoms, many having lost their first splendour by the end of the summer. The tea roses had for the most part retired for the season. In the middle of the garden stood the statue of a young girl holding a necklace. After the wedding ceremony, they had come here to pose for their pictures. Although the practice was not encouraged, Morris nonetheless caressed a few fading blooms, remembering how Maria had so loved the rose, touching as much as looking. He had only grown them in their garden because it was something he wanted to do for Maria. He looked up as a flock of birds careered overhead, perhaps purple finches. He thought he heard Maria's voice, but recognized the imaginary sound as a trick of nostalgia.

Morris did not linger long among the glory of the rose because he wanted to wander through the Japanese garden before returning home. A noisy wedding party rushed onto the path behind him. The bride wore a gown so lavishly decorated with overlapping petals of organza and folds of tulle that it reminded Morris of a giant inverted white artichoke, the groom a pillar of mourning-dove grey beside her, several bridesmaids laughing in pastel sheaths of shimmering satin and carrying bouquets of yellow roses in tufts of lady's mantle, their male counterparts more subdued in hunter green suits. A crowd of family and friends bustled around, not listening to the harried photographer's instructions. Maria had preferred a quiet, less ornate style of wedding, attended only by a maid of honour and his best man, a few friends and relatives. Their wedding party, too, had been positioned among the roses by a photographer to stunning effect. She had worn an elegant, ankle-length dress of creamy beige silk with faint blushes of yellow in the skirt and bodice, her unveiled hair coiled in braids like a Welsh princess and woven with amber beads. He had himself cultivated the flowers for her bouquet: aromatic soft yellow day lilies with arching and tapered white blossoms of gooseneck, all surrounded by peony leaves tinged with late-summer bronze. Their wedding day had been warm but overcast, not sunny and somewhat chilly like today. The arms of today's bride were sheathed to the elbow in gloves. Her veil puffed up and away from her pearl tiara, slipping down to the ground where it trailed like the flower-bedecked branches of the bridal veil spirea bush.

Impatient for his bride, he had driven to Maria's apartment in the east end of Montreal on the morning of the ceremony and climbed the wobbling iron staircase to the second floor to present her with the bouquet. Several times he had himself phoned her landlord to complain about the precarious condition of the stairs. Wearing a terry-cloth robe, Maria had just wound the beads in her braids before he knocked. The sun sparked off the coiling amber as she opened the door. Oh my, Morris remembered saying, the feelings of his heart soft as a rose. He had waited in his blue suit, drinking tea in the kitchen, while Maria and Nicole, her maid of honour, mockingly protested in French over his appearing and bustled Maria back into the bedroom down the hall. In all his life, Morris had never experienced such profound contentment and anxiety at the same time, happy over his good fortune to have found, loved, proposed to, and been accepted by Maria.

How was it possible for him to continue living happily without the committed companionship of a woman? Having loved and lost once, he could surely love and win again. Nancy only needed time to think about his proposal. She would soon realize the depth of his feelings. Her heart would lead her to accept the security and happiness he promised. There was nothing he wouldn't have done for Maria. She had only to ask. Walking out of the serpentine pathways of the rose garden and heading for the Japanese garden, Morris fondly recalled that he would have attempted the impossible for her, just as he would attempt the impossible for Nancy, if only she would agree to marry him.

Too many people at one time ruffled and strained the serene loveliness of the Japanese garden, one of the most popular spots. It was difficult to meditate on the harmonious, artful arrangement of water, stone, and plants in a crowd. Not particularly attuned to the cosmic or spiritual significance of things, Morris nonetheless appreciated the underlying skill of the Japanese garden more than its symbolic import. He knew that stones and boulders, deliberately placed, symbolizing duration and the forces of nature, provided a foundation for the garden; that water cascading down stone or rippling in the large pond indicated renewal and continuity, the various levels or elevations of the stones allowing for free and rejuvenating circulation. All the plants, of course, this being a Japanese garden, were chosen for stunning visual display and philosophical potential. Each plant possessed significance, referring to something other, something more profound, than itself. Unlike the many varied perennials and seeming chaos of his own kind of garden where he felt most at home, letting nature take its spontaneous course with only minimal human interference, the Japanese garden depended on relatively few and carefully selected species and cultivars of flowers, bushes, and trees. All of them were subtly manipulated and pruned, subjected to the dictates of philosophy and art. Morris loved the genius of the place, although to his way of thinking human control and deliberation were too much in evidence.

At this time of the year, Morris did not expect to see irises, among his favourite flowers, their transient beauty having been succeeded by chrysanthemums. The rhododendron bushes had long passed their flowering time. The crabapple trees, more durable in a Quebec climate than the traditional Japanese cherry tree, were already turning colour. With their stunning bronze-red leaves, the Japanese maples attracted and amazed the eye. Here the pine trees were also shaped according to aesthetic criteria. He had planted bishop's hat and other acid-loving ground cover under pine trees, but aside from sawing off bothersome lower branches, he had not thought to prune and shape the entire tree. He stopped to study the vista, for the Japanese garden always encouraged the prolonged, contemplative pause.

A slight, cooling breeze caressed the surface of the pond, on the other side of which rose a pile of aesthetically arranged boulders. The quiet music of water finding its natural level reached his ears. A young couple with a howling baby in a carriage jostled with packages, strolled up behind, then beside, Morris along the path. They argued in French about the distance between them and their car; they shouldn't have walked so far. *"Bébé a faim, et il est misérable,"* the mother said, blaming the father for the child's hunger. Their voices cracked the spirit of the place, distracting Morris from horticultural reverie. To one side of the path ahead, the white stony beach curved along the edges of the pond, deeply reflecting the September blue sky. He waited until the couple, turning off the main path and on to the grass, disappeared, their voices no more than the squeaking of distant birds.

With Maria he had strolled through the Botanical Gardens to see the different plantings on many a Sunday in spring and summer, as late as October, even in the winter, which provided its own kind of austere, frosty beauty. After Kate's birth, they continued to visit the garden. As a baby, Kate had also cried and perhaps they had argued, although Morris didn't remember arguments in the gardens. They must have had their share, but a man who had loved and still missed his wife didn't recall the unpleasant moments about their life together. Pushing Kate in a carriage before she began walking on her own, his dark-haired wife beside him, gardens galore, the peace-and-quiet thrills afforded by botany, he had, like the flawless rose, achieved perfect bliss.

Perhaps Nancy would enjoy touring the gardens as well. She was already developing an interest in her own yard, admiring his work. Happily, people were few today, despite the boys clambering over the rocks farther along the path on the other side of the bridge. Quarried and hauled from Thetford Mines, he knew, the peridotite rock had been chosen by the landscape architect for its greenish glaze. There were rigorous procedures of placement according to Japanese theories of gardening. The rocks had to be both male and female, a concept Morris failed to comprehend, although, desiring Nancy, he recognized the logic of the theory. The boys shouldn't be so disrespectful. He would speak to them. From this perspective on the bridge, looking over the pond, he could see the splendid *Yukimi-gata,* the Japanese snow lantern carved out of stone at one end of the curving beach.

The water shallow, so clear that the shapes and patterns of pebbles were visible on the bottom, the koi, the Japanese golden carp, slithered and swept under the surface like living yellow-and-orange flowers. Of varying sizes, some of the carp displayed white spots and black patterns on their fins and scales. The broad-leafed pads of water lilies rested on the surface of the pond. The carp disappeared momentarily under the leaves, only to reappear, their backs flashing in refracted sunlight. He would love to show the koi to Nancy. One Sunday afternoon in July he had embraced Maria in the monastery garden, where he kissed her in front of a bed of poisonous blue aconite, Montreal traffic whizzing behind the trees and garden walls. It was always better to walk through the Botanical Gardens with someone you loved. Raising his head again, he noticed a couple standing on the stony beach next to the lantern, a practice also not encouraged because human feet had the disconcerting habit of disarranging significant patterns. Like the raked sands in the Zen garden, the designs were supposed to be looked at and contemplated, not ignored and trampled.

The sun tangled in Nancy's red hair just before glittering on the orange fins of the koi. How brightly the lovely woman shone! Too startled to call her name, Morris waved until he realized Nancy did not see him. She was too preoccupied, laughing with the man in a shirt the colour of the detested, overused red salvia. A tall, slender man in a red shirt folding his long arm around Nancy's shoulder like a lover. Morris put his own arm down. He stepped back to the middle of the shaded bridge, then aside, to allow three older women in walking shoes and sweatpants, talking one over the other about *les pêches d'or* and *les mets japonais,* to pass him by. *"Merci, monsieur. Il fait beau, n'est-ce pas?"* they said, not expecting a response. He smiled, but his teeth grated. Surprise deepening to shock, chill in his veins like the first heavy frost striking a tender perennial, he would not be the first to show Nancy the splendours of the garden after all. Ingoldsby had darted ahead like a serpent striking for its target from the dark damp undergrowth of deadly nightshade. Why was she with Ingoldsby? A curiosity, no more than a stray thought like common weedy mullein, which never appeared in the same spot from one year to the next. He pulled the plant out when he did not want it. Morris did not pursue the logic of the question.

The Japanese garden induced calm, reflection, the meditative state of mind, where hurry became stilled, disquiet quieted, rage mollified, and loathing diluted to philosophic acceptance of the mysteries and complexities of the universe, beyond human control or understanding. Be calm. Morris stared down at the koi. He tried to remember Maria. But the image of his wife disappeared like a golden carp under the bridge. Why would Nancy have chosen to accompany Ingoldsby to the Botanical Gardens? He wouldn't lay blame at her feet, for he loved her too much. It was more apparent, though, why Ingoldsby would trouble himself with Nancy. He was a stalker and violator, the natural enemy of trust, decency, and love. Morris stared at the rippling of the pond's surface and the floating of the living flowers beneath to maintain equilibrium. Such an easy and natural flowing there. Anger knotted his stomach. It could have swept him off the bridge if he had allowed it, forcing him to bound through the water, kicking at the fish, splashing lilies aside, until he could throw himself at Ingoldsby. And? Do what, precisely?

Raising his eyes, he almost shouted out. Ingoldsby kissed Nancy on the cheek by the snow lantern. Morris's fingers folded into fists of their own volition, then opened; the fingers spread, then shaped themselves into the kind of tool required for strangulation, thumbs touching, hands spread far enough apart to enclose Ingoldsby's neck and press inward, both thumbs hard against the Adam's apple. How to save Nancy, for saved she must be from the predator. She didn't understand the danger. No woman was safe around the professor. Look at the way he grabbed at Nancy's hand, forcing her body next to his, his arm like a chain across her back.

Nancy didn't understand how her natural good spirits and trust in people could lead her astray. She didn't realize yet how much she needed Morris to keep her safe. Be calm, study the male-female arrangement of rocks, how one blends into, rests on, depends on the other, the principles of the universe, the harmonious arrangement of separate units into a pleasing whole. Nancy must marry him. She could depend on him forever.

They were headed up the path for the Japanese tea pavilion that housed the Zen and bonsai gardens, neither of which particularly appealed to Morris. He did not understand a garden without green and growing things. Rocks were splendid in any garden. He had arranged many himself. To stay on a wooden porch and survey the fine raking of sand around consciously placed rocks, however, was not his idea of horticultural happiness. Appreciative of the skill and patience required for bonsai, Morris nonetheless disliked such dwarfed, crabbed, and confined trees, never allowed to reach their inherent potential for growth and expansion. To think some of the bonsai trees rooted in ceramic pots were decades old and no taller than a foot!

He struggled against blaming her for being with Ingoldsby. She lacked a complete understanding of the risks. Was Nancy safe? She was clearly laughing, although Morris couldn't hear her voice. A lot of people laughed when they were nervous. Ingoldsby wouldn't try anything in a public place. It was wise policy to follow. A man also did that for his beloved, putting his time at her disposal. Ingoldsby forced Nancy next to his body, his red shirt a dark contrast with her white-fringed beige shawl dangling down the back of her designer-jeans-clad thighs.

Resisting the urge to whip stones at Ingoldsby's head, Morris hurried along the path toward the rock pile over which water cascaded like a miniature waterfall, the boys having disappeared and escaping his reprimand. Surely Nancy couldn't have been taken here by force. There had to have been some measure of free will on her part. She was such an open-hearted, friendly person. He had waited too long to take her to the gardens, which she had never visited before today, so who could blame her for coming here with the first man who asked her? Ingoldsby, everyone knew, could be as charming and friendly as he pleased with women. Yet Nancy knew about his disgusting behaviour with Kate. Was it possible that she could forget that and agree to go out with a man whom Morris had every reason to hate?

Partly obscured by the flaming branches of a Japanese maple, the rocks and waterfall behind him, Morris didn't think they would see him if they troubled to look. Ingoldsby and Nancy entered the Japanese pavilion, presumably for the tea ceremony and to contemplate the Zen garden. He spotted a bed of russet chrysanthemums; how fine they looked when touched by a light frost. Now was the season for potted chrysanthemums in the supermarkets. He would buy a pot of gold or purple for Nancy. If he followed them inside, it would be difficult to hide. Bonsai trees were not ideal for concealment. He tried to imagine the stillness of the stones in the Zen garden, focusing intently on the arrangements of boulders to soothe the anger, to help reconcile conflicting feelings. A sense of shame and foolishness overrode his resentment of Ingoldsby as Morris approached the gate to the pavilion. His stomach hurt. She would blush if she saw him. He must spare her the embarrassment. One could sit and meditate, and the garden taught harmony, perspective, peace, humility, perhaps ultimate forgiveness of the contradictions and deceptions of life. It induced a proper frame of mind. Morris turned back. Inside, Nancy and Ingoldsby sipped tea from porcelain cups, just as Maria and he had done on her last visit, just as he was meant to do with Nancy before Ingoldsby spoiled his plans. Before returning home, Morris walked to the monastery garden, where he considered its wide array of deadly plants.

23

· · ·

THE EFFECTS OF ANY ONE POISON varied from person to person. The lore about the particular plants in his garden described a prolonged, agonizing death. Morris suspected stomachaches and diarrhea were closer to the truth. Tempted, he did not wish at the moment to kill, just to inconvenience Ingoldsby, or make him sick for a few days with unremitting cramps or nausea. Clicking through websites, searching his books and magazines of plant life, consulting his memory and knowledge, he researched one plant, discarded it for another, determining its properties and efficaciousness. Sitting in the darkness of his pergola under an early autumn moon, the cool breeze whispering among his still-standing grasses and flowers, the vegetable patch a bit the worse for wear, he wore a grey cotton sweater depicting a totem pole, bought years ago when Maria, five-year-old Kate, and he had toured the gardens of British Columbia. They had camped in the Pacific Rim National Park between Tofino and Port Renfrew on Vancouver Island. Kate screeching revulsion or delight, he was never sure which, when she saw banana slugs slither on the tent flaps, her mouth stained with salmonberry juice.

So concentrated on method and means, Morris did not wonder about the chances of pursuing his line of thinking to its conclusion and consequences. Ingoldsby, though, must pay. Like spittle bugs foaming on leaf nodes, some things were inevitable. Death camas, not unlike a wild onion in appearance, for which it was often mistaken, or camassia, the Indian hyacinth: the ingestion of its bulb or flower caused diarrhea, vomiting, coma, then death. That was good. In his garden, death camas was not to be found. Count that one out. Jimsonweed: only five grams of its leaves or seeds, he had learned, were fatal for a child. Used in herbal medicines to treat madness and depression at one time, it was related to the lush datura bush growing by his compost pile. Lacking jimsonweed, he could substitute the leaves and seeds of datura. A magnificent trumpet-shaped flower—angel's trumpet, everyone called it—laced with noxious atropine, causing hallucinations, then coma. Well, he didn't need to encourage Ingoldsby's hallucinatory states of mind. The painter was already famous for regaling his startled students in class with tales of artistic visions induced by peyote or mescaline or whatever drug the underground provided. Quite an elegant blossom; did a blast of the angel's trumpet guarantee death?

What else did he grow, never for a moment imagining that one day he would seriously be considering taking advantage of the maleficent properties of his plants, cultivated out of curiosity and love of beauty. Now, yes, of course, his splendid drift of monkshood, the flowers so blue that you'd think they had absorbed the sky. Leaves and roots, all parts of the plant were also imbued with poisonous alkaloids like aconitine, which paralyzed before it killed within two hours, according to theory and one or two authenticated accounts. A merciful man, Morris wanted to avoid prolonged suffering. He rocked himself on the bench. One shot put an animal out of its misery. The same courtesy should be extended to the artist.

Across the road, his neighbour planted ornamental castor shrubs that grew rapidly as sin, wide and tall like weedy sumac. Morris disliked castor plants as a rule, but you take its seeds, scratch the coats to damage them enough to allow water to seep inside, and they produced ricin, he believed, a toxin used for suicide and assassination. Only two-millionths of a man's body weight constituted a lethal dose. Bulgarian police, Morris had discovered, assassinated a broadcaster by using a 1.53 millimetre pellet containing three- or four-hundred-millionths of a gram of ricin.

The moonlight was a transparent veil of silvery pearl over his whispering grasses. Castor, though, also posed a problem. If it was not injected directly—and what was the likelihood of that?—one had to chew the seeds. Morris couldn't even begin to imagine how he'd get Ingoldsby to chew poisonous seeds, unless he broke into the house and somehow mixed the seeds with his granola. A man like Ingoldsby probably didn't eat breakfast.

What else? What else? What did he grow in his garden? Mary, Mary, quite contrary, how does your garden grow? Cockleshells? No, but *Digitalis purpurea,* yes. Now past their prime in his garden, of course, the foxglove stalks had dried, the flowers withered and dropped most of their seeds. Steeped in a teapot, their leaves led to death. A source of heart medicine, digoxin, which if taken in excess could also kill, the digitalis presented a distinct possibility for Morris as he shifted on the bench, reminding himself it wasn't death he really had in mind. What was not so simple, as Morris listened to the grasses breathing under the light of the moon, was implementation. To strike at Ingoldsby by means of poisonous plants did not seem to be as certain or convenient as he would have liked.

The toxic glycoalkaloids in the green, immature berries of black nightshade, according to the records, killed children who ate them. The berries of his *Solanum nigrum* had ripened to black and were now harmless. In drifts along the edges of his perennial beds, autumn crocus in their flamingo pink loveliness, their colour even apparent in the moonlight, reminded Morris of cattle asphyxiated after consuming the crocus growing wild in the meadows, pulling the plants up by the bulb, where the poisonous colchicum gathered in most deadly concentration. He remembered that benefits were derived from this poison. The crocus also provided colchicin to alleviate gout. His father had suffered from gout in his later years, and Morris sometimes wondered if the ailment were hereditary. He wiggled his big toes. No pain. In his garden, if not the cure, then some comfort grew.

The roots, berries, and flowers of the lily of the valley, also poisonous, caused problems, especially if one drank the water plants were kept in. Successful poisoning, it seemed, depended on the childishness or stupidity of the intended victim. In the corner of his lot behind the pergola, rising five to six feet high, grew several false hellebore. Large doses of it led to death, as did the oxalic acids in rhubarb leaves if they were mistakenly eaten as a vegetable. Similar to aconitine of monkshood, the dugaldin of sneezeweed, also among his perennials, caused spasms, vomiting, convulsions, then death. Their flowers such a vibrant orange, copper, vermilion, and yellow in the autumn that they put the sunset to shame, hellenium was recommended by Morris to all his clients in search of autumn glory for the garden. For all their sturdy beauty, they remained among the most dangerous of plants for cattle ranging low, wet meadows. Since it hadn't rained for two weeks, the soil in which his sneezeweed grew could do with a good soaking.

Belladonna, cowbane, northern water hemlock, black henbane, wormwood: the names of poisonous plants tumbled over each other in his mind like numbered balls in a bingo lottery game. Cyanide or arsenic would be easier. He didn't have a clue where to purchase cyanide and didn't know how to extract it from almonds. In the nineteenth century, a farmer or housewife could buy arsenic over the counter. Imperceptibly the poison worked on the victims over a period of time, years even, until they fell into a coma resembling death, their pulse and heartbeat undetectable by the medical technology of the day. Buried alive.

Boiling aconite or artemisia did not meet his purposes. Anyway, once forensic investigators discovered and identified the poison in Ingoldsby's stomach, the police would arrest him within days. People knew about his knowledge and cultivation of poisonous plants. After rejecting death by poisoning, Morris sauntered along the pathways between his perennial beds. Somewhat shocked by the notion, he persuaded himself he wasn't planning murder—he didn't believe he was the murdering sort of man—but, oh, let him not see Nancy and Ingoldsby together again. Anything but that.

The next day he and his temporary workers would begin the digging and building of the new gardens for the old folks' home. Szerkasy had not been entirely thrilled with the final proposals, always asking for ways of cutting costs, even suggesting to Morris's dismay that they buy cheap flats of marigolds at the mall's home-renovation garden centre. A deal had been reached, however, the terms agreed on, the contract signed. A few compromises, a bit of scaling down along the way, but the riverside park would be quite an eye-catching place after he had finished. An inviting, soul-soothing garden should be more than a bed of petunias and red salvia the colour of Ingoldsby's shirt, something Szerkasy didn't seem to grasp.

No murderer could really hide in his own garden, so Kate was safe. Another town hall meeting was announced. Complaints about police inefficiency and procrastination he heard daily. In the residence, the elderly had worked themselves into a panic. Who could blame people for biting their nails? Poor Mrs. Grant was murdered on the very day that police cars patrolled in front of her house. Like everyone else, Morris repeated the phrase "Something has to be done" or "Someone should do something." Always the undefined, the imprecise, the vague someone and something. More vicious guard dogs and sensor lights appeared on the properties of the rich. Doors double-bolted, perhaps electrified. No one lingered alone in the garden. He had heard that a few of the residents of Old Town employed private security guards to roam their acreage twenty-four hours a day. All that security and still Mrs. Grant was clubbed to death amid her derelict roses.

Morris stopped in the middle of his yard, listening to the grasses, inhaling the autumn fragrance of dying plants, rotting leaves, and the heady, sweet smell of decay. No, poison was out of the question. It was getting cooler. He dug his hands deep into his corduroy trousers and hunched his shoulders. How was it possible that he should be thinking of ways of harming a man? Murder, like a contagious virus, polluted the air. You breathed it in and were infected. That was another of Ingoldsby's crimes: his influence turned good people into bad. Once stricken by his charm or blinded by his genius, they helped him, for which they received his moment's attention, grateful for notice from their idol. He did not imagine that Nancy regarded Ingoldsby as her idol. But was she immune? Those who tried to hinder him fell victim to the painter's mockery of their qualms and scruples. Either way, his very existence tainted their lives, just as the existence of the secret killer stalking the gardens destroyed the peace and beauty of his town.

How, for the sake of argument, could Ingoldsby be eliminated? Decapitation appealed: a clean snip the way he sometimes whisked off grasshopper heads with pruning shears. That required larger shears, however, than Morris possessed, and could create more mess than he was prepared to clean up. Besides, decapitation to some degree depended on the willing or enforced co-operation of the victim. Please be so good as to sit still while I chop off your head, or now that I've captured you, allow me to bind you like a bundle of straw. No, no, Morris could not see his way clear to that method of disposal, if he permitted himself to pursue the matter. He had not deadheaded the coneflowers this season, deciding to let them stand over the winter.

Knives, of course, were always useful. Step right up to the unsuspecting professor as he got out of the car and plunge—what?—a paring or bread or butcher knife into his chest. A knife struck Morris as rather too close and personal. He wouldn't want to see or hear the man, risk blood splattering on his clothes. How difficult it was to get rid of bloodstained clothes, which never seemed to burn or stay buried, judging by the murder mysteries on television he had seen. Gunshots necessitated the purchase of a firearm that would leave a paper trail right to his door. Hide in the bushes or on top of a roof, get the bastard in his sights, then pull the trigger. Morris had never shot a firearm in his life. He knew nothing about the underworld or illegal traffic in arms and couldn't even begin to imagine how to locate one. Plant a bomb in the professor's car? He was a gardener, not a munitions expert, instructions on the internet notwithstanding. Hire an assassin? One of those black-hooded, lithe and swift, wall-climbing creatures he saw in kung fu movies, adept at whizzing shiny blades through the air or strangling a sleeping man with a silver wire. What were the chances? Aside from not having a clue about how to hire a killer, he knew his own safety lay in keeping intentions and plans to himself, not in contracting a professional. But, Morris reminded himself, his thoughts about Ingoldsby were punitive, not murderous.

How difficult for a good man to arrange an evil deed. Morris avoided stepping in a mound of German shepherd dog turds deposited by Captain, a dog down the street who, unleashed, had lately begun roaming and leaving his deposits in neighbourhood backyards. Doing something about that was well within his power. Other neighbours had complained, just as they publicly worried about the murderer still on the loose and criticized the seeming incompetence of the authorities. Morris coughed, shivered with the beginnings of a cold or the flu in his bones. Boiled roots of his purple echinacea supposedly boosted the immune system. If only the terror at hand were so easily treated. Desperate ills required desperate remedies. People sounded desperate at the meetings he had attended. Yes, well, people reacted only when blood splattered their faces, not before. He didn't remember the town getting terribly upset over the first murder, only mildly interested after the second, gossiping and exchanging anecdotes as though Mrs. McCready's death were a passing phenomenon of no lasting significance or relevance to their lives. After all, she had once been a member of the rich and powerful, so people need not expend their sympathies on that crowd. And now, as if hit over their own heads with Mrs. Grant's death, the town reeled and spun from the blow.

If he could not kill, however compelling the thought, he would then have to do something to release his justifiable anger and to warn Ingoldsby away from his women. Do something clear and direct so Ingoldsby, left alive, would be appalled and permanently affected for the rest of his life. What, though? Something lasting. The action had to touch the soul, if soul Ingoldsby possessed.

24

• • •

FOR THANKSGIVING DINNER the following Monday, her father had invited Nancy, her sons, Bogdan, and his new sweetheart, Galina, a recent Russian immigrant. Her English non-existent, she spoke French like a jackhammer. Only Bogdan understood a word she said. Respecting Kate's vegetarian principles, acquired under Tarun's influence, Morris planned an entirely vegetarian meal: seasoned, roasted tofu shaped to look like a turkey. At least they would have their traditional cranberry sauce boiled down from real berries, not that congealed stuff out of a can. Kate supposed she could wait until after Thanksgiving to inform her father about quitting university. Morris worked so hard, and packed her a lunch every day (at a loss on how to replace cold cuts, he made either cheese and lettuce, or peanut butter and banana sandwiches). He didn't even complain about the loudness of her music or the amount of time she spent on the internet.

One week of pretending to go to school should not be too difficult to manage, now that Morris spent most of the day with his helpers digging up the riverside park attached to the old folks' home. To soften the blow, she had managed to find full-time, if not handsomely paid, employment at the art supply store in the mall. From Ingoldsby she had learned a useful thing or two about bristles, oils, acrylics, charcoal, and canvases. Still uneasy about her decision, she had no intention of reversing it. However rewarding the work, gardening did not figure in her plans for the future. Nor did Tarun anymore. From her father she had learned to eliminate what did not satisfy.

Her registration for the fall semester accomplished at home by means of the internet, Kate had experienced some anxiety about returning to the scene of the crime, as she now referred to the university. On the day after Labour Day, she had set foot on campus, distracted by the initial rush of hurried students until she sat on the stool behind her assigned easel in the class Oil Painting III, taught by one of Ingoldsby's staunchest supporters. Hilary Van Leeuvenshotte peered over her rimless glasses when Kate entered the studio. For a woman who enthused about the liberated body, the professor still bound her hair in one long braid strangled by tightly woven leather straps. The teacher spoke briefly in general terms about oil painting and the relationship between this class and the previous two prerequisite oil classes. She began calling out the students' names from her registration list. Classes were kept small, only twenty students allowed to enroll in any one painting course. The teacher's voice tightened when she mentioned Kate's name. Kate raised her hand, and Van Leeuvenshotte paused and stared.

"Yes, of course, Ms. Bunter. The name is familiar."

The professor affected either jeans with sequins running up and down the seams or long, black, body-clinging dresses that reached to her feet, always strapped into black, thick-soled sandals, regardless of the season. Today she wore a black dress spotted with oil paint. Her toenails were painted purple. Rumour said that she and Ingoldsby were lovers, but rumour had placed half the female faculty in bed with Ingoldsby. After the roll call, she assigned a drawing task, speaking about mastering the fundamental truth of line and the integrity of form before superimposing colour and texture. As students drew, she hovered over them, commenting on their work, completely ignoring Kate's line drawing of her own hand. At the end of the two-hour session, the professor glanced at the paper without comment.

The rest of the day passed more quickly than Kate had hoped, most of the classes dismissed after brief introductory remarks and validation of enrollment. Many of her friends and former classmates had registered in other classes. Kate met only one or two who were too rushed for a chat. She ate her havarti cheese sandwiches on the Common, sitting alone on the grassy field in front of the university's main building, the day warm and blue and student voices raucous and cheerful. Morris had also packed a banana and Oreo cookies.

Another class in the afternoon with Van Leeuvenshotte, who introduced the live model, a young man with skin the colour of mocha coffee beans. Nude, he draped himself over a plaster of Paris pillar rising above the folds of red velvet cloth. Professor Van Leeuvenshotte said they were experimenting today. Students must paint quickly from life without benefit of preliminary drawing, on which, judging from what she had seen last class, they need spend no more time, with one or two exceptions. She lowered her granny glasses and stared in Kate's direction. Kate now understood why teachers chose rimless reading glasses perched like giant sequins on their nostrils. They became a prop, a means to display contempt, condescension, or superiority. Kate spent the next hour painting the model's dusky neck and shoulders, ignored by the professor, who leaned over one or two male students, admiring the vigorous form depicted on canvas. She folded her hand over theirs, guiding the brush and lingering over their depiction of the genitalia.

"Do you think everything's in proportion? Proportion and perspective are everything. Here, let me show you what I mean."

Passing over Kate's work again without looking, she stopped at the next easel and loudly proclaimed the virtues of that student's efforts.

At the beginning of the second week of classes, Kate met the academic dean outside the registrar's office, where she tried unsuccessfully to transfer out of Van Leeuvenshotte's painting class. A man with agate blue eyes and a thick neck so squeezed by collar and tie that his head looked like a helium balloon about to burst, he acknowledged Kate with a barely perceptible smile. Before the final deliberations of the hearing, the dean still expressed regret over the proceedings.

In her next class, the History of Western Art, Part III, which used to be taught by Ruskow before he retired, she took notes as Professor Goyette, famous for his love of computerized teaching methods, using PowerPoint in the darkened classroom, droning on like a recording without rhythmic variations about the Age of Reason, dividing and subdividing, categorizing and schematizing, reducing painting and ideas to convenient modules and outlines, and making "points," until Kate's own reason soured, then stultified. Great paintings reduced to artifacts and corpses, classified and autopsied via computer technology, their beauty rendered into mere patterns by Professor Goyette's bloodless emphasis on diagonals, perspective, and chiaroscuro.

Polite and gracious, he said hello when Kate entered the classroom, and hoped she'd had a good summer. His manner was at least friendly. He was not her enemy. Goyette had calmly argued, not hysterically like the faculty representative, against Ruskow's compromise solution, insisting on "the consideration of issues greater than personal misdemeanour." He had suggested a reprimand and apology rather than dismissal. One had to grant artists certain latitudes, didn't one? Ingoldsby was too important an artist, too gifted a teacher, to be sacrificed, according to Goyette, on the altar of political correctness. However lamentable his behaviour, however deserving of censure, the university, the student body, needed his unique talents.

Kate avoided spending breaks between classes with the few friends who still attended the university. On the way to the library, she wedged her way through the crowds of students in the corridors, many of them with cellphones glued to their ears. Carrying satchels and sacks, they wore shorts and sandals, cutoff jeans and T-shirts, some of the guys in loose-leg jeans with the seat of their pants dropping behind their knees, khakis and skin-tight capris, vampirish black skirts, a few in department-store coordinated wear. Girls stomped or teetered on platform shoes. Hairstyles ranged from military crewcut to shaggy bush, from long and lank to brushes and spikes dyed in colours of the rainbow. However familiar, the students nonetheless struck Kate as alien, almost a different species. Her own choice of clothing for the first day of classes, jeans, tennis shoes, and a yellow cotton sweater set, blended in well with the sartorial mishmash crowding the halls.

Standing in front of a terminal of the computerized catalogue, she clicked on the search icon, not really looking for anything in particular but trying to fill her time until the next class. She was beginning to feel hollow, disconnected, as if her brain and heart, liver and bones had dwindled into mounds of dust. Rising three floors, the central atrium opening all the way to the vaulted ceiling, plants draping over the banisters of the second and third floors like the hanging gardens of Babylon, the library used to be one of her favourite places in the university. During the winter especially, she loved to see the darkening of the day outside the tall windows when she was studying for an examination or doing research. There was always a student carrel where she could be alone with her books and write papers, or confabulate in hushed voices with one or two friends. She stared at the terminal screen. Although it was noisy for a library, with too many students and too few staff telling them to keep quiet, Kate heard nothing except the swift rushing whisper a garter snake makes over grass. Her hand froze on the mouse. She held her breath.

No, not this time. No cause to worry. She quickly looked around, expecting Ingoldsby's supporters to appear and threaten. Just the stacks, hanging plants, a few teachers, tables, and dozens of students jostling for space. Professor Van Leeuvenshotte stood at the circulation desk talking to a librarian. Even in the midst of this seemingly harmless gathering of people, Kate thought, someone could be preparing to attack and strike.

Coming to school this morning, Kate had tried to suppress those little rushes of fear and worry, blaming them on her father's own anxiety. Feelings of safety withered as she entered the Arts Building, where Ingoldsby had taught his classes. She wondered if Mrs. Grant's murder had anything to do with this unease, this eerie sense that she was both on the earth and out of it at the same time, the way, she imagined, an out-of-body experience felt. Very few of the students worried about the local murders, as far as she could tell, so many of them living in Montreal and commuting to the university. The bad news here had little impact on their view of things, as it didn't touch their lives. How truly stunned had anyone ever been, including herself, over any atrocity not directly involving him or her, especially if it happened elsewhere? A momentary gasp of shock, a transient thrill of horror, then their lives, like hers, continued a briefly interrupted course. People forgot as quickly as they commiserated.

She entered "murder" in the Search by Subject box. Websites with "murder" with one qualification or another appeared by the legion. Kate scanned the library. She didn't belong here. Not only had Tarun broken faith, but the university had also broken faith, even though it had done the just and proper thing in the end.

"Can I help you, miss? Are you having trouble with the catalogue?"

The library staff had always been helpful.

"No, thank you. I've found what I was looking for."

"Were you looking for a particular website? I can suggest efficient ways of searching the internet."

The same height as she, not at all the same age. The woman in the blue serge suit, a cameo brooch pinned on its right lapel, hair curled like snail shells, looked forty, if she was a day. Today Kate was forty and nineteen at the same time. Her father wouldn't be happy about her decision. She really didn't want to disappoint Morris or cause him pain, especially now that he seemed so easily distracted and often upset. Given time, he would understand and offer support. She wasn't, though, about to collapse. When her father saw decay or disease in a garden bed, he wrenched the plants out by the roots and trashed them, excavated the ground again, added new soil enriched with fresh, uncontaminated fertilizer. Perhaps she was only deceiving herself, pretending to be stronger than she really was. Did that matter anyway? She had made the right decision, however unsteady her nerves. Kate hoisted the satchel, heavy with the anthology of Western art, conscious of moving one leg in front of the other, and walked out of the university library.

25

. . .

WORK EXHAUSTED BUT FAILED to console. Morris concentrated on the tasks at hand, checking his plans against information on various gardening and landscaping websites on Kate's computer. He organized his hired help to do exactly what he wanted—youth was strong but inconsistent—and was trying very hard to keep the pieces of his heart together. A lengthy paisley-shaped perennial bed curved under his booted feet the last Friday before Thanksgiving, deep enough for all the old people who stood on the edges watching the workers to lie down and be covered with sweet-smelling rich loam. Preparing for spring growth with each spadeful of earth, keeping his body fixed to the ground, Morris nonetheless wandered into speculative fields of purpose and mortality. All these senior citizens swaddled in sweaters and coats, mufflers and hats, against the brisk October breeze, some in wheelchairs, some supporting their frail bodies with walkers and chairs—remove the scaffolding and they'd all tumble down in a pile of creaking and cracking bones—commenting on the labour, offering incomprehensible or irrelevant advice.

How many would survive the winter to see the flowering of the first bulbs? How many would live long enough to witness the completion of the new riverside gardens, which, according to Morris's best estimates, needed three to five years to reach maximum fullness and beauty? The average life expectation of a resident in the home, Szerkasy had once told him, was less than two years. Mrs. Grant had been younger than the youngest resident here, which was older than Morris cared to live, and had died in her garden, murdered. Growing old had not troubled Morris before Nancy's refusal to marry him. He had sworn "till death do us part" when he married Maria. He had died a little each day while her once shapely body wasted away. Death had unfairly parted them too soon but had not diminished his desire to grow old with one woman and devote his life to her well-being. One didn't meet the right woman, though, and fall in love with the regularity of autumn leaves blowing off the trees. He figured it miraculous that Maria had ever fallen in love with and married him. The world was now distinctly short of miracles. Morris would settle for a bit of luck, but what were the chances? All this energy to give, his hands open, his heart full of tenderness and solicitude, and no one on the receiving end. Was it so impossible for Nancy to imagine spending the rest of her life with him? He wanted more than a mere frolic in bed. He wasn't a horny eighteen-year-old like the two hired workers. Sooner than they realized, they'd both be fragile and forgetful. What was she waiting for? Surely not a proposal from Ingoldsby.

"Looks like a grave."

One of the old men stepped into the plot. He started shuffling around, scuffing his slippers and dirtying the bottoms of his pyjamas under the pea green army coat, so heavy and thick that it forced his already bent body into a question mark. Didn't these people ever wear anything besides pyjamas?

"Yeah, well, it looks like you're ready for one," one of the young workers said under his breath, which annoyed Morris. Show a little respect, but he decided to ignore it as he helped the ancient gentleman out of the "grave."

"Bury me now and be done with it. Save a hell of a lot of fuss later."

Edging closer to the shallow pit, the other residents tottered like arthritic herons. Morris prevented the gentleman from trying to lie down.

"I don't think you really want to mess up your clothes. Why don't I help you out? Just wait until spring, sir, you'll be surprised by what you see."

"Spring! He should be so lucky," one of the women blurted.

Morris understood the comparison. He had imagined digging his own grave, "both long and narrow" according to the old song, "the grave of my hopes," he lamented in his self-pitying moods, more frequent of late. Double-digging a new garden required a lot of back muscle—the rewards splendiferous—but the more he bent his back to the task, the more the world weighed him down. Shit, he loved Nancy. Why had she slipped away from him—he didn't want to use the word "recoil"—when he had proposed? Perhaps he had been too hasty, too insistent, driven more by fear than desire. For a few days he blamed her refusal on Mrs. Grant's death. Another murder, people were anxious, it was a stupid move, what was he thinking of? Love and murder in the same breath—no wonder Nancy hesitated.

She had been frightened. He didn't mean to frighten her but to offer a sense of security, however frail, in an arbitrary and incomprehensible world. Of course, Nancy's previous experience with commitment left a lot to be desired. All men, though, were not the same. When he made a promise, Morris kept it. When he vowed fidelity, he did not break the vow. When he loved, goddamn it—his spade struck a rock beneath the soil—he loved with his whole his body and soul—fucking stone—forever. How could he make Nancy accept, believe, and, more to the purpose, want that? Want him? Didn't she, sweet lady, desire him as he desired her? He tried not to pursue unsavoury thoughts about her visit to the Japanese garden with Ingoldsby.

Applying a pickaxe as a wedge, Morris lifted the rock out of the soil, more a small boulder than a rock, quite finely veined with purple and gold. Inspired by the Japanese garden, perhaps he could add it to the configuration of giant boulders he had ordered. He stood up and rubbed his lower back. On the river, so polluted that it no longer reflected sun or sky, sailboats still glided under the October sun. Next spring, he and a few other concerned citizens planned to put the condition of the river on the town hall's agenda. It was time to do something about the pollution of the water. Of all the seasons, Morris loved the light in autumn the best. Humidity-free, cool and clear, the sun less of an opaque yellow, strength-sucking force, and more of wonderfully invigorating presence in the sky, October usually provided perfect weather for gardening work. If the rains held off, he'd have the new beds and pathways laid, the first plants in place, before the end of the month. If Szerkasy balked over the expense of the Asian and Oriental lily cultivars, he had at least agreed with the lavender, Russian sage, and globe thistles.

From the middle of the river, music and laughing voices sounding like the shrieks of garbage-seeking gulls interrupted his reverie. Since lifting the boulder, Morris hadn't moved, leaning on the shovel, one end of the pickaxe stuck in the soil like a blade in flesh. Fifty yards from the embankment, the small yacht seemed to have dropped anchor directly in front of the riverside garden. His two workers were unrolling the wire over the recently laid stones of the meandering path. The old folks, gathered in groups of three or four, now overseen by Kwaku and other attendants, turned their attention to the river. What a lovely idea—Nancy surely would say yes to a cruise on the river. Boats could be rented at a kiosk down the boardwalk next to one of the town's more popular pubs.

When he saw Ingoldsby in a black T-shirt, standing at the bow and stretching his arms wide, Morris reached for the axe. He didn't recognize the music, but it was louder than it had to be. Everyone now knew that Ingoldsby floated by on his barge, laughter and music from the boat bellowing in the wind, which had just picked up. That man was having too much fun, Morris decided, wiping the earth off the blade of the pickaxe with his gardening gloves. Dirty tools rusted, entailing inconvenience and unnecessary expense. Simple preventive measures averted so many potential problems. Ingoldsby looked toward the embankment where Morris stood, pickaxe in hand, returning the stare. Morris didn't think Ingoldsby could see the expression on his face. He'd never let Ingoldsby outstare him. Stare down a vicious dog.

A woman with red hair, wearing a long white dress, rested a hand on Ingoldsby's shoulder and turned her back to the shore. No one could tell that Morris had been punched in the solar plexus. He did not flinch, although the shock of seeing Nancy on the barge left him gasping for air. The pickaxe was heavy. Ingoldsby kissed Nancy. Morris wondered where Annick was. Would she object? Other people started jostling on board, dancing perhaps, then the boat began a slow glide forward through the filthy brown water. Morris dropped the pickaxe and stared at the barge (yacht was too elevated a description) down the river out of sight, hearing his breathing. Professor Ruskow appeared on the edge of the grave.

"Mr. Bunter."

"Oh, hello, sir. How are you?"

"It's not how I am, Mr. Bunter. It's how my trees are. Two of them look decidedly unhappy."

"It takes time for saplings to adjust to their new environment, sir. A bit of transplant shock is to be expected. But they're healthy trees, and I guarantee they'll survive the winter."

"I shall hold you to your guarantee, Mr. Bunter."

Dressed in a grey lamb's-wool overcoat, wearing a brown fedora, and carrying a walking stick with the head of a silver lion, Ruskow had the kind of voice that made him sound taller than he was.

"The residence needs new windows or a coat of paint more than it needs flowers, if you ask me."

Fortunately, Morris did not ask as he smiled, wishing Ruskow would continue his daily constitutional through town and let a fellow catch his breath. Jesus! Nancy on the boat with Ingoldsby!

"I see our friend is amusing himself on the river."

"Sir?"

"Don't tell me you don't recognize Ingoldsby, Mr. Bunter."

"I do."

"Well, what do you think of his pleasure craft?"

"A man has the right to sail a river, Mr. Ruskow. Not much I can do about it, is there?"

"No, I suppose there isn't. As to rights, we certainly don't wish to violate the rights of poor, misunderstood Ingoldsby, do we?"

"Shame, isn't it, Professor Ruskow—I mean, how he doesn't think about anyone else's rights, to my way of thinking."

Although he was taller than Ruskow, Morris's position in the garden trench allowed Ruskow to look him directly in the eye. There was some strange flicker of subtle recognition, like the rapid blur of a hummingbird's wings as it whizzed from blossom to blossom, in Ruskow's gaze. Not superstitious, at least he didn't think so, Morris listened to the old professor's comments about Ingoldsby, hearing undertones, indefinable meanings he could not fully grasp, as though both men knew each other's most secret and—Morris blushed—most criminal thoughts. Ruskow, who hadn't hesitated to offer instruction during the planting of the trees, hesitated on the edge of the perennial bed, his ironical smile inviting a confidence in return for direction, if need be. Morris's worries about Nancy might have been more evident than he supposed. Ruskow clearly disliked Ingoldsby. He shook off the odd sensation of being examined under the professor's penetrating eye, attributing his desire to look away to the sense of inferiority he often felt in the presence of professors.

"As for Ingoldsby's rights, I do believe we are in agreement on that subject, Mr. Bunter. By the way, I'm very sorry to learn from an associate at the university that Kate has decided to withdraw. A regrettable decision but, under the circumstances, not entirely a surprising one. After a semester's absence or two, she'll think better of it, clever girl. Marvellous season, the fall—nothing as sharp and clear as the October light. We shall have a full moon next week, and if it's cloud-free, you'll be able to see your shadow. Well, good day to you, Mr. Bunter. I shall keep my eye on those birch saplings, mark my word."

He flicked the walking stick over the embankment railing, as if to ward off a sudden assault by invisible agents. Ingoldsby's boat left a trail of ever-diminishing rock music as it floated toward the city. The once gentle sunlight on a cool October day hardened, pierced. Morris squinted, raised a hand to shade his eyes. He had forgotten his sunglasses. Despite his jacket, he was cold. Ruskow was right about the sharp and delineating light of October. Under a full moon, a man could walk the woods and find his way without a flashlight. He could see where he was going in the dark.

The workers perched on a fender of the truck, smoking. Kate had quit university? Couldn't be. Ruskow could be wrong, but Morris doubted it. Why hadn't she told him? In the distance, the stern of Ingoldsby's boat caught the sun and flashed in his eyes. The glare hurt. He could no longer see Nancy, now blurred out of recognition by the fierce light. Kate had quit? What the hell? He stepped out of the bed and leaned against the railing, wishing that he smoked. He watched the comings and goings of traffic in the gas station on the corner across the road. She had such plans for graduate work—get her degree in fine arts and then go to another university, possibly teach art in public school. Why would she quit? The last strain of a Beatles' song reached Morris from Ingoldsby's barge. Would Nancy ever marry him? He answered his own question.

No end to the damage Ingoldsby had done. Like verticillium wilt that invaded tomatoes. The plants had to be destroyed and the soil itself practically quarantined from nearby still-healthy plants. Once it infected the ground, the disease could remain for years. Or botrytis rotting chrysanthemums and cyclamens, or stem rot affecting carnations, necessitating cutting and spraying or destroying the diseased plant entirely. It seemed to take the police forever to apprehend so much as a suspect in the killing of the women. Secretive and pernicious, the murderer attacked when they least expected it, except everyone now seemed to be warier, Old Town practically paralyzed with fear. Yesterday, patrolling police stopped Morris twice on the road and asked for identification. One of his clients in Old Town installed a sensor alarm that hurled ear-splitting, continual hoots like a sonic foghorn when anybody set foot on the property until someone shut it off. Another client let vicious guard dogs roam free, supposedly trained not to rush and attack off their property. It was only a matter of time before some child had her face ripped open by an overprotective, improperly controlled Rottweiler. Morris refused to garden there unless the dogs were visibly chained or kept inside.

Kate was a strong, vigorous kind of plant. She could have told him her plans, though—why not? How did she think it made him feel to find out something like that from a stranger? Well, Ruskow wasn't really a stranger. With his retired fingers in the university pies, he probably knew more about what was going on there than anyone else. Look at the unspeakable damage bulb nematodes could do to the healthiest hyacinths, tulips, and narcissi, which his plan called for hundreds of in the new beds. If infested, the garden beds themselves could not be used for bulbs for three years. No end to the secondary problems caused by the first attack. Something must be done. The student workers, finished their smoke, walked toward him. Across the street, he saw a man in a truck who looked familiar. Parked in the No Parking zone in front of a row of townhouses facing the river, the man was staring at him out of a truck the same colour as Morris's. Or was he staring at the river? Or the sailboats drifting in the wake of Ingoldsby's barge? Was that a hat, its flaps covering both ears, or the man's hair parted in the middle and hanging thick and flat like felt against the sides of his head?

What was that creep staring at? Morris surveyed the river again—nothing unusual.

The truck pulled away from the No Parking zone and entered the traffic on the main street. So Kate had quit the university. Professor Ruskow knew more than Morris. All her dreams and plans—and Nancy sailed on the polluted river with Ingoldsby. Wait till he got home this afternoon, he'd have a serious heart-to-heart with Kate, maybe persuade her to change her mind. Maybe ask Nancy to talk to his daughter. No, that would hardly be a wise thing to do now. He was beginning to feel awkward and invasive around his daughter, afraid of trespassing over unfamiliar terrain, wary of breaking some hitherto unknown exclusively female rule about attitude and behaviour. But Nancy and Kate got along fine. How could Nancy have anything to do with Ingoldsby? Having learned from experience, he'd propose again, this time take Nancy out to dinner in the city, buy her a brooch or something, not a ring, that would be too pushy, not until she said yes, then he'd bust the bank for a ring, if she wanted one. Take her out to a restaurant serving real Szechuan food in Montreal's Chinatown, which she loved, propose over hot-and-sour soup, and not once mention murder.

"What's next, boss?"

He liked the students, good workers if you told them exactly what and how to do something and didn't rely on their limited ingenuity. Szerkasy, wearing a brown suit, sauntered toward them. Had he been standing still too long? Was the director coming out to check on the progress of their work? Morris was charging by the job, not by the hour, but Szerkasy still mentioned the expense.

Ignoring Szerkasy on the edge, Morris directed his attention to the young workers. He didn't want the manager to think the guys were layabouts, sucking up the resources of the old folks' home.

"We need the sand before we place the stones."

"You mean today, Morris?"

"It's been ordered. Delivered tomorrow. Tell me something," he asked Louis, a science major at the university who, despite the chill, worked with his shirt off. His torso was covered with a layer of dust from all the digging. "If you quit university, will they let you back in?"

"Sure, they give you credit for whatever courses you've completed, but I think you need to take a minimum number, though, or they won't let you register. Why?"

"So you can always go back, even if you quit, is that right?"

"Sure thing. Why?"

"Just wondering. Listen, what we need to begin next is cut and roll about twenty feet of sod down the way—I'll show you—and shape the grounds into a half-circle."

"You mean now?"

"No, next year would be fine, if it fits your schedule."

"Mr. Bunter, a word with you, please?"

Morris was startled by the manager's voice. Over Szerkasy's shoulder, Ingoldsby's barge floated into view again, the music so loud that Szerkasy turned. From the stern Ingoldsby waved to the shore. Nancy's red hair shimmered like a cap of embers. He tried not to imagine Ingoldsby's skull split open, one blade of the pickaxe lodged in the middle of his soft, spilling brains. Something had to be done to get that man out of his mind.

"I'm sorry to say that one of our clients passed away last night in her sleep. We're planning an outdoor memorial service, weather permitting, next Tuesday. I wonder if you would arrange not to work on the gardens then."

"No problem, understand perfectly. There's something else I can do."

"Fine. Thank you."

He glanced at the trenches, the piles of dirt, the wire on the path, and the two students. Given the state of the grounds, Morris wondered where a service could be conveniently held outside without people stepping in newly dug beds or crowding around mounds of soil.

"Well, it seems you have everything under control."

Morris did not reply that he knew what he was doing. Somewhere on the river in the distance Nancy floated away in Ingoldsby's embrace. Morris examined the work accomplished thus far. The garden beds did indeed look like shallow graves. He reached for the tools at hand, their touch gratifying and soothing. With a tool a man knew what to do. A full moon. How lovely it would have been to ask her for a stroll on the boardwalk under the moonlight. So much work lay ahead; he would have to take advantage of the evening, when the sky was clear and all there was to see were the moon, the stars, and shadows among the trees.

EPILOGUE

• • •

A man of words and not of deeds
Is like a garden full of weeds.

—ANONYMOUS NURSERY RHYME

A SLEEPING HOUSE in the dead of night is alive with its own unique sounds. Like the steady, muffled marching of a distant army out of sight beyond the horizon, the refrigerator motor hums. I do not hear a furnace. Perhaps Ingoldsby has not switched it on yet, despite the cool October nights. The snaky vines against the wall, yes, even they create the sound of imperceptible pressure against the brick, a pressure like the unwavering water drop kissing a bony forehead hour after hour, day after day, year after year. I can almost hear the bricks softening, the walls beginning to attenuate under the ceaseless clinging of the vines. One step and a floorboard creaks. I smell the gas I carry in the can brushing against my leg.

The parlour is high and cold, furniture old and uninviting, ornate or stiff, Empire stuff and Louis Quatorze, filigree trim and soiled brocades bleached and worn-looking even in the night. So many family portraits. Framed by filigreed silver, their austere, grey images dead behind glass, Ingoldsby's parents, he a surgeon, she a public school teacher. I had forgotten what they looked like. Out of their pre-eminently ordinary lives emerges an artist of unsurpassed gifts. Ah, but what violations, what unspeakable violations. A corner glass cabinet with his mother's tea and choco-late cup and saucer collection, dozens, unstained, probably never used, each an eighteenth-century porcelain jewel. And one of his large canvases on the wall, an abstract landscape, slashed, ripped wide open, a breach in the sky.

Pruning shears in hand, Morris Bunter turns and, good man, looks like death warmed over, his face pale as moonlight, his body trembling. He sees what I carry. I put my fingers to my lips. The understanding runs wordlessly between us. He doesn't move, his breathing loud enough to wake the sleeping, unearthly, paralyzed by his own action or by my discovery of him in Ingoldsby's house. He has cause, he has just cause, too. Although his lips seem to shape my name, Ruskow, he is not speaking. I could stop now, go no farther, assuage the gardener. What Morris Bunter has done emboldens me to do more, to continue. How far he would have gone, I shall never ask. His body shakes and he doesn't know where to look, his fear so palpable that it disturbs the quietness of the room. I motion for him to leave. We are together, his action protected by mine. On his behalf I intercede. There is no necessity for explanation. Collusion bonds us man to man, soul to soul. Morris, shears pointed downward, approaches. I touch his shoulder. Great deeds sometimes require consolation. I believe he knows that we can trust each other, and he says nothing. Glittering and gold, his moist eyes follow the direction of my arm pointing to the back door. He understands that what he has begun I shall finish. The room is almost whitened by the moon.

Listen: the house is breathing the soft steady breathing of the heavy sleeper. I hear waves lapping toward the shore, the rippling of moonlight on the water as if a boat has slipped by the beach, the slide of Morris's feet over the evening dew. The chandelier in the dining room, a cone-shaped configuration of whorled and spun crystals hangs from the ceiling like fossilized candy floss. To eat off Limoges dinnerware on display in the hutch, drink wine from Venetian stemware: why would he not be content with the beauties bequeathed to him? Some questions are beyond answers.

The first step and not a sound, the pile of the stair's runner worn so flat that the flower pattern has all but disappeared, the suggestion of a lush garden barely visible in its threads. The second step and a slight sound like a man exhaling his last breath. The third step soundless, the fourth squeaks, a mouse caught in a trap. The fume of gas rises from the gallon can knocking against my leg as I climb the stairs. The fifth and sixth steps also squeaky, but the eighth where I pause makes no noise. I tread on faded roses and pale peonies, leaves and branches imperceptible. On the wall of the second floor landing, one of Ingoldsby's paintings flares out, the colours so vibrant that they shed light into the dark. His genius hurts my eyes and I cringe as I take two, three, four more steps. I will not study the art. I quail before the masterpiece. Down the corridor the bedroom where Ingoldsby sleeps, I know, in a canopied, four-poster bed, the canopy sagging with age and rot. The house smells of dust undisturbed, of dirt congealed in corners, of cobwebs clouding light fixtures.

Indifferent to the goods of the world, he would have us all believe, the typical view of the artist, never more so than one born into privilege. His parents' wealth accommodated his fantasies. How easy to rise above the bourgeoisie when your roots sink deep into their privilege and property. Sleeping naked. Predictable. A relief he is alone. Would not have the death of the innocent on my conscience. Will the fumes disturb his dreams? Will the smell of gas spreading on and sinking into the Oriental carpet wake him? He stirs. His still-youthful legs bend and he shifts position. His face is untroubled, puffy with sleep but smooth as wax, like the embalmed face of dear Mrs. Grant in her coffin. She did not deserve to die so horribly. None of them did. My head, dizzy, the gas fumes seeping into my brain, headache. I see a window blackened by vines. They will burst and writhe like serpents in flames. Step out, the gas soaking the felt boots. They'll burn the brighter at sunrise. So many paintings on the bedroom walls, their light searing. How can he sleep in the midst of brilliant creation?

Down the stairs, not so concerned about squeaks, dribbling gas behind me down the corridor to the back door until the gallon has emptied at the threshold. I step outside, leaving the container in the hall, and, now, need only light the match. The moon so bright and round, now lower in the sky; it's almost day. Why am I not seen? Why would anyone think to look here, the home of an artist, no longer a suspect, next door to the empty home of the murderer's first victim? This is a finished story. Attention has turned elsewhere. The burst of flame—the sound of air sucked into a vacuum. Loud enough to wake the dead. I feel the first heat shooting out the door. The hall erupts into fire, impassable, fire races up the stairs like a wild dog, hurls itself into the bedroom where it swirls, madly chasing its tail. Ingoldsby wakens, aghast, his pale face bright and blue and orange, his paintings melt on the wall, the canopy a burning heaven dropping charred bits, his blankets puffing up in flame.

What's that? Sounds like a bomb? Jesus, the sky lighting up like fireworks somewhere. Over the trees. So cold that my hands are blue. What the hell's happening over there? Sirens? Cops? I'm outta here. Looks like a fire. Engines, fucking fire engines. Good thing. Cops racing to the fire, everyone looking the other way and I'm free. Orange, even the moon looks like it's caught fire, the fire eating up the sky like the world's gone to hell.

I do not look back like the wife of Lot. Following the path I imagine Morris must have taken, I do not see the house explode through the trees. The noise is unearthly, nothing I have ever heard before, and it shakes the ground beneath my feet. Gas in my nostril mingles with the rank odours of the woods. Ingoldsby's spirit rises above the flames. He now joins the pantheon of dead artists whose work I have admired; he is harmless now, imprisoned in the history of art. Behind me a conflagration roars and sirens tear through the night. I choose not to see. Justice is blind.

ACKNOWLEDGMENTS

MANY THANKS to Denise Bukowski for her confidence and to Andrea Crozier for editorial guidance.

A special thanks to Alison Reid for the meticulous copy editing.